D0801999

CASSIE EDWARDS,
AUTHOR OF THE *SAVAGE* SERIES

Winner of the *Romantic Times* Lifetime Achievement Award for Best Indian Series!

"Cassie Edwards writes action-packed, sexy reads! Romance fans will be more than satisfied!"

—*Romantic Times*

THE STRENGTH OF THUNDER...

Suddenly Thunder Horse stopped and turned to Jessie. He swept her up into his arms and carried her onward to the camp. He kissed her as he leaned low and placed her atop the blankets.

"*Techila*—in my language that means, 'I love you,'" he whispered against her lips. "I have wanted you from the moment I first saw you. I want you for my *mitawin,* my woman, for always."

"I want you as much," Jessie murmured, overwhelmed by the feelings and emotions exploding within her.

As he kissed her he slowly removed her clothes, until she lay splendidly nude beneath him. He quickly tore off his own clothes so that nothing remained between them….

Other *Leisure* and *Love Spell* books by Cassie Edwards:
TOUCH THE WILD WIND
ROSES AFTER RAIN
WHEN PASSION CALLS
EDEN'S PROMISE
ISLAND RAPTURE
SECRETS OF MY HEART

The *Savage* Series:
SAVAGE VISION
SAVAGE COURAGE
SAVAGE HOPE
SAVAGE TRUST
SAVAGE HERO
SAVAGE DESTINY
SAVAGE LOVE
SAVAGE MOON
SAVAGE HONOR
SAVAGE THUNDER
SAVAGE DEVOTION
SAVAGE GRACE
SAVAGE FIRES
SAVAGE JOY
SAVAGE WONDER
SAVAGE HEAT
SAVAGE DANCE
SAVAGE TEARS
SAVAGE LONGINGS
SAVAGE DREAM
SAVAGE BLISS
SAVAGE WHISPERS
SAVAGE SHADOWS
SAVAGE SPLENDOR
SAVAGE EDEN
SAVAGE SURRENDER
SAVAGE PASSIONS
SAVAGE SECRETS
SAVAGE PRIDE
SAVAGE SPIRIT
SAVAGE EMBERS
SAVAGE ILLUSION
SAVAGE SUNRISE
SAVAGE MISTS
SAVAGE PROMISE
SAVAGE PERSUASION

CASSIE EDWARDS

SAVAGE ARROW

LEISURE BOOKS NEW YORK CITY

A LEISURE BOOK®

February 2006

Published by

Dorchester Publishing Co., Inc.
200 Madison Avenue
New York, NY 10016

ISBN 0-8439-5272-5

Printed in the United States of America.

Visit us on the web at www.dorchesterpub.com.

In the deepest of friendship I dedicate Savage Arrow *to Tammy Russotto (my fan club president! Thank you, Tammy!), and also Jai Clark, who does so much to support America's fighting heroes! (Thank you, Jai!) I also dedicate* Savage Arrow *to my special friends Paul and Carol Welton.*

Love,
Cassie

Rain beats down on our bodies tonight;
as if blessed by the Great One, our two souls unite.
To never again be alone, we love as one,
and as each day dawns, we will rise with the sun.
Take me to where the ravens fly,
so high in your hands—don't ask why.
The souls that wander the great plains
will be forever true.
When the night comes, they will smile,
as our love shines through.
So tell me, warrior, that you forever need me
as the moon does the sky.
Then we shall become as one, as the ravens fly high.

—Angela Dawn Reinhardt,
a poet and sweet, dear friend

Chapter One

Arizona, 1880
Moon When Cherries Turn Black—August

The sky was a turquoise blue overhead, with only a few puffy white clouds breaking its vastness. The air was hot and dry; an occasional breeze stirred the dust on the ground into small swirls.

Weak from fasting, Chief Thunder Horse rode across a high hillside on the way home to his village. He had been praying for the strength he needed to protect what remained of his Fox band of Sioux.

Because of one *wasichu*, one white man, Thunder Horse's small band was out of tune with their universe. He had fasted to regain harmony with all things encompassed by the Great Powers.

As it had been from the beginning of time, it was incumbent upon the leader of his people to purify himself of the demands of the flesh by fasting on a high place. And so Thunder Horse had done, hoping for guidance through dreams, for sometimes dreams were wiser than waking thoughts.

It had been three days and nights since Thunder Horse's fasting had begun. As always, he had prepared himself spiritually through song. It was well known that songs shut off twisted thoughts and emotions.

The fasting was now behind him, for he had received the answers he had sought in his dreams. He felt assured now that the course of action he planned was right.

Suddenly his thoughts were interrupted by activity down below him. He heard the thunder of horses' hooves, and the screams of a *mitawin*, a woman.

He drew rein, stopped his steed, then wheeled his sorrel around.

His eyes widened when he saw a stagecoach down below, pulled by a team of six horses running totally out of control.

But what surprised him the most was that there was no stagecoach driver. The reins were flopping here and there while the horses raced onward as though they were crazed.

Hearing frantic screams for help, Thunder Horse spotted a woman leaning out one of the stagecoach windows. Not one to interfere in white people's troubles, he hesitated to help the woman in distress.

But when he saw the horses suddenly veering to the right, now galloping hard toward a cliff, he knew that he could not just sit there and watch the horses and the woman plunge to their deaths.

Although weak from lack of food these past three

days and nights, Thunder Horse sank his moccasined heels into the flanks of his steed. He scrambled down the hillside, then urged his horse into a hard gallop toward the stagecoach.

When he drew alongside the team of horses, their hoofbeats sounding like thunder in his ears, he steadied himself, then leaped onto one of the lead horses.

He reached out and finally was able to grab the reins. Pulling hard on them, he finally managed to get the horses under control.

Once the animals had come to a halt, he spoke soothingly to them until they had quieted. Thunder Horse then leaped from them to the ground and ran to the stagecoach door.

The woman's eyes watched him fearfully through the window as Thunder Horse opened the door.

As she came fully into view, Thunder Horse found himself gazing onto a face of pale pink perfection. It was complemented by hair the color of a setting sun, which flowed across her tiny shoulders and down her back.

She was young, surely no more than nineteen winters of age, and petite in every way. Her tear-swollen green eyes were filled with fear as she looked upon him.

Needing to make her understand that he was a man of peace, a man of honor, who had never harmed any white woman in his lifetime, who especially would not harm someone as tiny and helpless as this woman, Thunder Horse released his hold on the door and stepped back. He spoke to her in good English, which he had learned long ago in order to be able to parlay with whites.

"I am a friend," he said slowly. "I saw your trouble. I came to save you from harm. The horses were running straight toward a steep cliff."

When she still didn't say anything, but only sat there trembling and staring at him, he again spoke to her.

"You have nothing to fear from me," he said softly, marveling at her loveliness. She was like no other woman he'd ever seen, with her hair the color of fire hanging long past her shoulders from beneath a fancy bonnet.

He looked back in the direction from which the stagecoach had come, then gazed at the woman again. "Where is the driver?" he asked, imploring her trust with his midnight dark eyes.

He could not help her any further if she would not communicate with him. Yet he did not want to leave her alone out here in the desert.

"How is it that the horses got so spooked, they came close to carrying you to your death?" Thunder Horse asked, frustrated that the woman still did not trust him enough to answer his questions.

Truly mesmerized by the Indian, Jessie Pilson stared back at him in utter fascination. She was held silent not so much by fear as by surprise. Never had she imagined being so close to an Indian. And this Indian, with his bronze and noble face, his flowing black and glossy hair, was perhaps the most handsome man she had ever encountered in her life!

He was a man of regular, yet striking features. His cheekbones were high.

His midnight-dark eyes spoke of a free and open life on the plains and in the mountains.

Although he was dressed in fringed buckskin that covered most of his body, she could tell that he had a powerful build; that he was a physically perfect man.

Afraid that the Indian's patience might be wearing thin, and feeling more at ease as she saw the concern in his eyes and heard the kindness in his voice, Jessie finally found the courage to speak.

"I was on my way to Tombstone. The stagecoach was ambushed a short while ago by outlaws," she blurted out. "The outlaws shot and killed the driver and threw him from the stagecoach. They . . . they . . . took my bag from the top of the stagecoach and ransacked it. They became angry when they only found my personal things, which were of no value to them."

Seeing that she still had more to say, and glad that she did not seem afraid of him any longer, Thunder Horse said nothing, but instead listened.

"For a moment I was afraid that the outlaws would kill me," Jessie said, her voice breaking as she recalled the vile, filthy men, whose features were hidden behind neckerchiefs tied around their faces.

"Go on," Thunder Horse softly urged when he saw that it was hard for her to continue telling him all that had happened. "Tell me. Then the fear will be lifted from your heart and you can live better with it."

Stunned that this Indian could be so gentle with her, so patient and caring, Jessie gazed more intently into his dark eyes.

She was shaken by how his eyes affected her. There seemed so much in their depths, unspoken words that might show her a world so different from any she had known before.

Jessie made herself focus on what she should be saying, instead of what she had been thinking. Today's meeting with this Indian was just a chance encounter, and would soon be relegated to the past, like so many other things that had brought a moment of sunshine into her life.

"When the outlaws found nothing of value in my bag, or in the stagecoach, they grew so angry, they purposely spooked the horses," she said, her voice breaking again. "I was left stranded inside the stagecoach."

She looked to her right, toward the window at the other side of the coach, and saw the steep drop-off.

She shivered at the realization of how close she had come to dying there.

Feeling truly blessed that the Indian had come when he did, and had cared enough to save her, she glanced up again at him and smiled. "Thank you for rescuing me," she murmured.

Then without even thinking about the fact that he was an Indian, not a white man, she said, "What . . . am . . . I to do now?"

Thunder Horse was so taken aback by the question, for a moment he could not respond. Instead, he searched her eyes, shaken to the core by what he saw.

Was it possible this woman had been brought to this place, at this moment in time, just for him to meet her? Had destiny brought them together?

Up until now, his life's purpose had been to keep his people safe. Unwilling to allow anything to distract him from that purpose, Thunder Horse straightened his spine.

"I cannot take you into town on the stagecoach," he said tightly. "The white eyes in Tombstone would not understand my reason for being with you, a white woman, on a white man's stagecoach. They would shoot first, ask questions second."

Jessie nodded. "I understand," she murmured. "I am skilled with horses. I'll drive the stagecoach into town myself."

Quickly forgetting that only moments ago he had decided to ignore his feelings for this woman, Thunder Horse marveled at her strength and courage.

"Your name . . ." he asked, gazing into her green eyes.

"Jessie. Jessie Pilson," she murmured. "And yours?" she blurted out. "Would you mind telling me your name?"

Thunder Horse's shoulders squared proudly. His chin lifted. "Chief Thunder Horse," he said. He noticed a new look of respect in her eyes as she realized that he was no mere warrior, but a chief.

"I am Chief Thunder Horse of the Fox band of Sioux," he added.

Jessie was speechless again for a moment. She was in the presence of a powerful chief, someone whose main purpose in life was to protect his people. Yet he had gone out of his way to save her.

"*Hiyu-wo*, come, and I will help you up to the driver's seat," Thunder Horse said, reaching a hand out for Jessie and helping her as she stepped from the stagecoach to the ground.

"Thank you," Jessie said, her heart pounding when she found herself standing close to him. She was so close she could smell the fresh mountain scent that seemed to come from his skin.

She gazed up into his eyes from where she stood a head shorter than he, and found him gazing just as intently back at her. Her knees felt strangely weak.

She smiled somewhat bashfully, then stepped away from him and hurried toward the front of the stagecoach.

Suddenly she felt strong hands at her waist, lifting her, and a moment later she found herself sitting on the driver's seat. Thunder Horse placed the reins in her hands.

She tried not to see the blood on the seat that had been left there by the horrible murder of the driver.

She made herself focus on getting into Tombstone.

"Are you certain you can do this?" Thunder Horse asked, bringing her eyes back to his. "Will you be alright?"

Jessie still could not believe the gentleness of this chief.

But it was clear he was concerned about her. She could tell by the softness and the careful way he had lifted her onto the seat.

Actually, she hated to leave him, for she doubted that she would ever see him again. It was obvious he normally avoided white people.

"Yes, I'll be alright," she finally replied. "But . . ."

The pleading in her eyes as she gazed into his made

Thunder Horse feel there was a real connection between them, yet he knew that he must avoid these feelings.

He must remember that she had come to this territory for her own reasons. Reasons that had nothing to do with him.

Someone must be waiting for her in Tombstone, where many evil men lived. He could not even imagine that sort of man touching this beautiful, sweet, and gentle lady.

"You were about to say?" Thunder Horse prompted, eager to know what else she might need from him.

In truth, he hated letting her go, for more than likely, he would never see her again.

"I would feel better if you could stay close enough to watch me get safely to Tombstone," Jessie blurted out.

Then she said, "But I wouldn't want you to be close enough so you would be seen. I . . . wouldn't . . . want you to get into trouble over me."

She wondered at herself for asking help of an Indian, when it would make more sense to be afraid of him. She had read horror stories about what some Indians did to white women. But she just couldn't see this man committing such crimes as rape or murder.

"I will ride far enough behind you not to be seen, yet close enough to make certain you are not accosted again before you reach the town of Tombstone," Thunder Horse promised.

He was curious to know why she was going to a place like Tombstone by herself. But he didn't ask. Such a question would surely make her uneasy.

Instead, he would see her safely to the outskirts of Tombstone, then hurry on his way. He was anxious to get back home to his ailing father.

His father did not have much time left on this earth, and it was his father's health that had kept Thunder Horse from taking his people to the reservation assigned to all Sioux.

"Thank you again for what you did for me," Jessie said, hating to say good-bye.

These moments would stay with her forever. When she was sad and lonely, she would think of Thunder Horse.

"Go with care," Thunder Horse said, nodding at her.

"I shall," she murmured, then took one last lingering look into his eyes before forcing herself to turn away from him.

She snapped the reins, and the team of horses responded to her command, taking off in the direction of Tombstone.

Thunder Horse waited for a moment, then followed a good distance behind her. As he watched her riding ahead of him, his thoughts went again to his people's situation.

Ho, yes, the white chief in Washington had given permission for some of Thunder Horse's band of Sioux to stay at their village until his father passed on to the other side. His father would then be placed with the other chiefs in the sacred burial cave of those who had gone on before him.

Afterward, Thunder Horse would lead what was left of his Fox band on to the reservation.

The white chief had met personally with Thunder Horse's father in Washington, to discuss peace between them. A final agreement had been made that Thunder Horse's people would join other Sioux bands on the reservation. But on the way home from Washington, his father had become desperately ill.

When the white chief learned of his father's illness, he had sympathized with Thunder Horse's dilemma and had given his permission for some of Thunder Horse's people to remain at the village, while others had gone on to the reservation. Everyone would come together again after his father's interment in the burial cave.

When Thunder Horse saw Jessie reach the outskirts of Tombstone, his thoughts returned to her again.

He dismounted, tied his horse in a clump of scrubby bushes, and made his way stealthily to the shadows of an outbuilding at the edge of town. He had decided he would not return to his village until he saw who met her . . . whom she had come to Tombstone to be with.

He hoped that she hadn't come to live in prostitution as so many of the women in town did.

He watched her stop at the stagecoach station. He kept watching as several men came out and began talking to her.

The longer he watched her, the more he was taken by her loveliness, and by her courage!

Chapter Two

Jessie tried to remain calm as several men ran up to her as soon as she drew the team of horses to a halt in front of the stagecoach station.

The men all seemed to talk at once, making Jessie's head spin as she looked from one to the other.

"What happened?"

"Where's Tom, the driver?"

"Why are you driving the stagecoach?"

"Where is your luggage?"

"Please . . . please . . . !" she cried, waving a hand in the air toward them. "Please stop all these questions. Just . . . just give me a chance to get off this horrid stagecoach and then . . . then . . . I'll tell you everything."

One of the men stepped forward and raised a hand to help her, which she readily accepted.

Once she was on solid ground, with her beaded purse, which she had rescued from inside the stagecoach, gripped in her hand, she inhaled a nervous breath. Before she spoke, she looked past them in the direction where she had last seen Chief Thunder Horse. There was no sign of him.

"Well? Where's Tom?" one of the men said, bringing Jessie out of her thoughts to the morbid task at hand, for she had the terrible chore of telling these men that Tom had died at the hands of outlaws.

"I'm so sorry," Jessie said, her voice catching as she looked slowly from man to man. "Tom is dead. We were ambushed—"

"Dead?" they all seemed to say at once.

"Yes," Jessie said solemnly. "The masked men seemed to come out of nowhere. They killed Tom, stopped the stagecoach, and—"

"How did you live through it?" a man shouted.

"I truly don't know," Jessie said, visibly shuddering. "Once they had the stagecoach stopped, all they seemed interested in was my trunk. They took it down, but when they opened it and saw that it held no valuables, they cursed, then . . ."

She stopped before telling the truth of what had happened next, for to tell them that the outlaws had fired their guns into the air and spooked the horses would be to tell them Thunder Horse's role in rescuing her.

She knew it was not best to tell them that, although what he had done was valorous. He had saved her life.

Still, she knew that Thunder Horse would not want to be mentioned. He would not want these men to know that a powerful chief was so close to their town.

"I've never seen anything like it," one of the men

said, staring incredulously at Jessie. "A mere woman managed to get out of that fracas alive, and then drove a team of horses on into Tombstone."

Several others commented favorably about what she had done, while others quietly studied her, as though they suspected that she had left an important ingredient out of this tale.

"And so they just rode away without another thought of you?" one of the men said, raising an eyebrow.

"Seems so," Jessie murmured. "When they saw that only my clothes were in the trunk, they were furious, but fortunately they didn't shoot me. They were masked. I could never identify them."

"Yep, all masked men look alike," one of the men said, kneading his whiskered chin.

"Poor Tom," another one said, then tightened his jaw. "We've got to go and get him."

"And I'll send out a search party for the hooligans that did this to Tom," the sheriff said, edging his way through the crowd until he reached Jessie's side. "Ma'am, I'm sorry your trip to Tombstone was marred by the likes of these outlaws." He removed his wide-brimmed cowboy hat and half bowed toward her. "My regrets are real, ma'am." He straightened his back and plopped the hat back on his head. "While the men are getting Tom, some will retrieve your luggage. I'll have it back to you before nightfall."

Then he idly scratched his brow. "Might I ask what brings you to our lovely town of Tombstone?" he asked, staring directly into her eyes. "Where can we deliver your luggage once we rescue it?"

Jessie looked slowly around her at the men. Their attitude had changed at this question and their eyes seemed to glisten suddenly.

She recognized their prurient interest in her. Did they actually believe that she was there to work in a saloon, dance hall, or worse . . . ?

"I've come to Tombstone to live with my cousin Reginald Vineyard," Jessie said, noting disappointment in some of the men's eyes. Others seemed taken aback by the mention of her cousin's name.

"I've arrived on an earlier stagecoach than Reginald had expected," she murmured. "Could someone among you direct me to his house?"

"You won't find Preach at his house right now," the sheriff said, looking past her, down the long road, at the white church that sat at the far end. He turned slow eyes back to Jessie. "It's Sunday. Preach is always at the house of the Lord on Sunday."

The men's way of calling her cousin "Preach," made Jessie's eyebrows rise. She never would have guessed that Reginald would become a preacher. Although as children he had been good and kind, he had not been one to go to Sunday school or church services with his family and Jessie's, who always attended together.

As an only child, Reginald had been spoiled rotten, always getting his way with his parents. His mother and father had said that he would only have to go to Sunday services when he wanted to.

And Reginald had never wanted to.

Jessie thought it odd that the boy she remembered

should have dedicated himself to the church. But perhaps he'd had a change of heart after his great silver find. Perhaps becoming so rich so quickly had brought him close to the Lord. Maybe he felt blessed for having been led into a life of luxury.

Jessie hadn't set eyes on Reginald for many years, but she recalled that the last time she had seen him, he had turned into a mousy little man.

She had actually dreaded coming to live with him, but she, too, was an only child, and all of her family was dead.

As far as she knew, Reginald was her only living relative, as was she his.

As children, they had ridden horses and played and fussed.

He'd hated it when she got the best of him in everything they did, because of his tiny size.

She was also petite and had never regretted it, but for Reginald, being small had become a curse.

He had to look up at most men from his four-feet-eight-inches height. Even Jessie was taller than he.

And he wore spectacles with such thick lenses, they made his eyes look twice their size. His eyeglasses had often frightened the girls away, while the boys mocked him and called him "four-eyes."

She was suddenly aware of singing. She turned and looked down the long street. At the far end was a lovely church with a tall bell tower.

The windows were open. The people were singing hymns that Jessie recognized at once, and not just from her childhood churchgoing.

Her dear departed husband had been a preacher.

Living in the wild and woolly city of Kansas City, her husband had died on the streets of the city, shot down by lawless gunmen.

She had had no choice but to come and live with her only living relative in Tombstone, but she had been afraid that this town would not be any tamer than Kansas City. The name itself had sent chills up and down her spine, but she had no place else to go, no one else to turn to.

She knew she ought to be grateful to Reginald, who had invited her to come and live with him. In his telegram, he had bragged about his house, saying it was the finest in town, which was only right since he was the richest person there.

She could not help being proud of her cousin, for he had shown them all that size wasn't all. He was a small man with a huge fortune!

But even wealth had not gained him everything. He had not remarried since the death of his wife, Sara. Maybe there was only one woman on this earth for a man who was smaller than most.

"Is that the church where Reginald is the preacher?" she asked, turning to gaze questioningly at the men.

That brought low chuckles from them.

The sheriff leaned down into her face. "He ain't no preacher," he said smugly. "He just has that nickname since he pretends to be holier than anyone else in this town."

"Oh?" Jessie said, confused.

"But yonder is the church where you'll find him," the man quickly added, pointing to it.

"Thank you for your help," Jessie said softly. "I appreciate it." She looked up at the sheriff. "Will you please see that my trunk is taken to Reginald's house when it is found?"

"I certainly will, ma'am," the sheriff said, again taking his hat from his head and giving her a half bow. He watched her as she turned and began walking down the long main street of his town, her purse clutched in her hand.

Jessie quickly discovered that she had to watch where she stepped, for the road showed signs of recent rain; wagon wheels had made deep ruts in the dirt.

She lifted the hem of her skirt and walked onward, her eyes misting with tears as she remembered the last time she had been inside a church . . . to attend the funeral services for her husband.

It had been his church, for he had been a Methodist minister in Kansas City, admired by everyone. One stray bullet had claimed his life.

That bullet had left Jessie totally alone. Both her father and mother had been gunned down on the streets of Kansas City a few years earlier.

Before Jessie was born, her father had been a notorious outlaw, called Two Guns Pete. When his wife had announced that she was pregnant, he had hung his holstered pistols on a peg on the wall and had not taken them down again.

The law had never caught up with him. No one recognized Two Guns Pete in that peace-loving man who came to Kansas City with a pregnant wife.

But all that changed one fateful day when his daughter Jessie had been seventeen. He was spotted by Bulldog Jones, an outlaw he'd double-crossed when they rode together in the same outlaw gang.

This man had apparently searched high and low and finally found his old rival buddy. It had taken only two bullets to take him and Jessie's mother away from her, leaving her orphaned and penniless.

Although her father had been a loving and doting father, as well as a devoted husband, he had squandered his money away, gambling.

The young Reverend Steven Pilson had taken Jessie under his wing. Eventually he had married her.

She had learned to adore this soft-spoken man, but had never loved him with passion. It was an easy, sweet love.

As she continued walking down the middle of the street, still clutching her beaded purse to her side, Jessie noticed the false-fronted buildings on each side, among them saloons, gambling halls, and whorehouses.

Through the doors of the saloons she could hear the rumble of voices, poker chips rattling, and dealers calling the cards while presiding over games of poker, faro, and monte.

She could smell the strong, offensive odor of whiskey.

It was obvious to her that this was a wicked city, one that did not close down even for God's special day.

Suddenly Jessie saw a crowd of men in front of a row

of small square buildings. In each one, sparsely clothed young women were standing in the front window.

Among them was a very pretty Chinese girl who seemed no older than fifteen. Her eyes met Jessie's with a mixture of emotions in them—shame, pleading, sadness . . . fear!

Jessie was stunned to see such a young girl there, for she knew very well what went on inside. Jessie had seen the same shameful buildings in Kansas City.

They were called "cribs," where prostitutes practiced their trade.

But none had ever been on the main street of the city like these were, in Tombstone. She was beginning to believe that this town was far more wicked than Kansas City had ever been.

She made herself look away from the pretty Chinese girl and focus on what lay ahead of her. Surely her life here would be a decent, comfortable one. Her cousin had found a mountain of silver, as he had described it. He must have all the comforts anyone would ever want.

Finally reaching the lovely church, she slowly climbed the steps, then went inside.

The pews were filled with people.

She smiled as two women scooted over, giving her a place to sit. After getting settled in among the people in the back row, Jessie stared straight ahead, at the man who stood behind the pulpit, then softly gasped.

She couldn't believe her eyes.

Her cousin was at the pulpit. He was reading verses from the Bible as the Methodist minister stood aside.

Reginald's reddish brown hair, which at one time had

been so thick, was now thin, yet hung long to his white collar. He wore a black suit, white shirt, and narrow tie.

He seemed even tinier than Jessie remembered. In fact, he seemed almost shrunken, his shoulders slouching, as though they carried a heavy weight.

When Reginald was finished, the minister thanked him. "Reginald, every town should be as lucky as Tombstone to have such a fine citizen as you," he said, placing a gentle hand on Reginald's thin shoulder. "You know the Bible well and practice its teachings in your daily life."

Everyone said, "Amen."

Jessie watched Reginald go to his seat among the congregation.

She could tell that he was still a man very much caught up in himself. He was obviously pleased by what the preacher had said about him.

She was puzzled that he had shown no sign of recognition as she came in the door. He couldn't have helped seeing her as he had glanced up from the Bible when she'd entered.

Had she changed that much since they had last seen one another?

She didn't think she looked so different. The only real change in her was not yet apparent: she was pregnant.

She placed a hand on her stomach. She had only realized that she was with child during the long, tedious journey from Kansas City.

But it wasn't at all obvious to anyone else. She would not be showing for a while.

Finally the church service was over.

Jessie slipped out of the building before everyone else and stood back. She watched Reginald again as everyone came up and shook his hand; he stood beside the preacher as though he belonged there.

She saw how he peered through his thick eyeglasses as though he had difficulty seeing. Surely that was why he hadn't recognized her. His eyes must have weakened since the last time they were together.

And he had other signs of physical decay. She could hear him wheezing and wondered if he had some sort of chronic lung problem.

She began to pity him and decided that it would be her job to make this man happy. She would care for him when he was ill. She would make him glad that he had taken pity on his widowed cousin.

When everyone else had gone past Reginald and the preacher, and even the preacher had left the church, Jessie shyly went up to Reginald. She reached out a gloved hand toward him.

"Hi, Cousin," she murmured, watching for his reaction.

Reginald gazed intently at her through his thick glasses, even adjusted them on his long, thin nose, then smiled and reached his arms out for Jessie. "Jessie," he said between wheezes. "I'm so glad you made it safely to Tombstone."

He stepped away from her, still peering at her through his glasses. "I thought you were to be on a later stagecoach," he said questioningly.

She started to tell him about the ambush, then stopped. She didn't want to get into it again.

And she still didn't want to tell anyone about Chief Thunder Horse. Not even her cousin, whom she should trust with anything.

But . . . there was something about Reginald, a strange sort of demeanor, that made her hesitate to tell him much of anything. It was a cold aloofness, which was vastly different from the way he had treated the people of the congregation. He had welcomed them heartily as they walked past him and the preacher for handshakes and embraces.

She wondered now if he truly wanted her there with him. Was she going to interfere in his life?

She would soon find out, for he had walked her to a horse and buggy as fancy and fine as those owned by the wealthiest families in Kansas City.

"Let me help you," Reginald said, placing a hand at Jessie's elbow and struggling as he tried to help her board the buggy, when she needed no help at all.

She could tell that he was trying to make a good impression on her. She had always bested him in everything . . . until now.

He was the rich one.

She was as poor as a church mouse.

As Reginald drove them back down the rutted street, Jessie found it hard to make conversation with him. He hadn't even inquired about her trunk, which was obviously absent.

He didn't inquire about her journey either, didn't ask whether it had been comfortable, or safe.

They sat in a strained silence until they arrived at his ranch on the outskirts of town. It was then that Jessie truly understood the wealth of this man. He lived in a beautiful, sprawling ranch house. His spread reached out across a wide, beautiful valley. A flowing stream bisected it.

Indeed, it was an impressive sight.

She now also saw a corral full of beautiful horses. She could hardly wait to choose one for her personal use.

Out there, in the great open spaces, she could ride and ride and ride.

She might even happen upon Chief Thunder Horse's village!

That thought was wrenched from her mind when the buggy pulled up in front of the long, low, rambling ranch house of hewn logs. It had shaded galleries and a comfortable-looking veranda running across the front.

The house was connected by an open walkway to a building that she assumed contained the kitchen and dining room, which was so often separated from the main house to minimize the danger of fire.

A garden of flowers stretched out luxuriant in front of the house.

"Jessie, welcome to my humble abode," Reginald said as he stepped down and came to her side. He reached a hand toward her, helping her down from the buggy.

Reginald gently held her by an elbow as they went up the front steps. Inside, his wealth was even more evident to Jessie.

"My parlor," Reginald said, leading her into a huge room dominated by a large stone fireplace.

The place was lavishly decorated. Jessie saw carved furniture, red velvet drapes, fine paintings on the walls, and deep, soft rugs covering the floors.

"May I introduce you to my maid, who is also my cook," Reginald said as a short and plump yet lovely Chinese woman came into the room. She was dressed in clothes other than Chinese—a black dress with a white collar—and her black hair was coiled in a tight bun atop her head. But in her eyes Jessie thought she read some kind of warning.

"Her name is Jade," Reginald quickly said, without bothering to introduce Jessie to the woman.

Jade bowed gracefully to Jessie.

Jessie returned the bow. "It's so nice to meet you. I'm Jessie," she murmured as the woman straightened her back and looked uneasily at Reginald.

"Go on with you now," Reginald said to the servant, shooing her away with a flick of a hand.

Jessie watched the woman walk away in short, quick steps; then she turned her eyes back to her cousin, even as her mind turned to someone else. Jade reminded Jessie of the beautiful Chinese girl in the crib. She could not forget the shame on her face as men watched her and said filthy things to her.

She was uncomfortable with her thoughts, so she tried to center her attention on her cousin, who *had* been kind to invite her to live with him.

"Jessie, you must be so tired," Reginald said, turning and walking toward his liquor cabinet. He looked at her over his shoulder. "I would like a glass of port. Will you join me?"

"Yes, that sounds nice," Jessie said, truly liking the idea of having something to soothe her nerves.

He brought a crystal glass of wine to Jessie and gave it to her, then nodded toward an antique sofa.

"Let's sit here," he said, with his free hand taking Jessie's elbow and guiding her down. "I had it shipped from New York. It's comfortable, don't you think?"

"Yes, quite," Jessie said, sitting down beside him.

She laid her purse beside her, then took a sip of the wine.

She looked around her again, and smiled at Reginald. "You have such a lovely home, Reginald," she murmured. "I'm happy for you, Cousin."

"Nothing comes easy," Reginald said, taking a sip of wine, then setting the glass on a table beside him. "As you know, all of this came as a result of my having discovered silver."

"Please tell me about it," Jessie said. "It must have been so exciting."

"Well, yes, quite," Reginald said, stopping to wheeze several times, then coughing into his hand. "I don't confide in just anyone about my find. But you are my cousin. I know you won't divulge any information that I tell you."

"No, I won't," Jessie said, her eyes wide. "Reggie, oh, Reggie, when we were small children, would you have ever thought you'd have such wealth?"

"*Reginald*, Jessie," he said tightly. "No one calls me Reggie. It seems so . . . so . . ."

"I won't call you Reggie again," Jessie said, interrupting him.

"To continue with my tale," Reginald said, taking his glass and gazing into its depths. "I had discovered several pieces of horn silver in a creek, and then found an outcropping of high-grade silver ore. All along the wash I found scattered pieces of silver floating. Then the stream disappeared into a cave. I lit a torch and went inside. I found a red and black ledge of silver ore. I ran my hands over its rough surface, then sank my pick into it, prying out several pieces. They were dark and heavy with pure silver. It was a real strike. I'd found a bonanza!"

"How exciting!" Jessie said, her eyes wide. "Tell me the rest."

"Only if you promise not to repeat my story to anyone," Reginald said, leaning forward so that he could look directly into her eyes. "I haven't told anyone else. You're the only one."

"I promise not to tell," Jessie said, glad that he trusted her enough to confide this secret.

"After all those years of wandering through lonely, desolate mountains, starved and blistered and frozen, I finally had myself some silver," he said. He chuckled. "Not only some silver. Tons! The vein I'd exposed was pure and soft. A coin pressed into it left a clear imprint. I had always heard that all I'd find out there would be my tombstone. But I showed them."

"You said no one knows about where your silver was found," Jessie said guardedly. "How could you keep it a secret?"

"There are ways," Reginald said tightly. "No one knows but me . . . and a band of Sioux."

"Indians know?" Jessie said, her eyes widening. "And . . . they are Sioux?" Her mind went back to Thunder Horse. He had said that he was Sioux!

"Yes, the Sioux," Reginald said through clenched teeth.

"Aren't you tempted to go and get more silver?" Jessie asked.

He grew pale at her question.

"No, never!" he gulped out. "And I'm tired of talking about it."

"Come with me," he said, rising quickly from the sofa. He set his glass aside, took hers, and placed it on the table as well.

He nodded toward her. "I'll show you to your room," he said, his voice drawn.

Then he stopped and stared at her. "Your luggage," he gasped. "You have no luggage."

It was then that she knew she must tell him about the ambush, and that her trunk would soon be delivered by the sheriff. As quickly as possible, she told the tale, managing to leave out any mention of Chief Thunder Horse.

"My word," he gasped, paling at the thought of what she had gone through. "Are you alright? Truly alright?"

"I'm fine, just tired," Jessie murmured.

"Then let's get you to your room," he said, walking down the long, narrow corridor, with her following him.

Just as she started to enter the room he had assigned her, she stopped abruptly. She had caught a glimpse of something in the room at her left side that was so beautiful it took her breath away.

"A grand piano," she gasped, her eyes taking in its beauty. The piano sat at one end of what she knew had to be Reginald's music room.

She hadn't had the opportunity to play a piano since her husband's death. Even then, the only piano she had ever had access to was the one in her husband's church.

She hurried into the room and started to run her fingers over the keys. Playing the piano had been part of her life ever since she was a child, when her mother had paid for her lessons.

Suddenly Reginald was there. He grabbed her wrist and led her away from the piano.

"Never play this piano," he said gruffly. "Never play it. Never!"

Jessie was stunned by his behavior, and by the hard grip he had on her wrist.

She wanted to ask him why he was treating her in such a strange way, but his coldness made her yank her wrist free and recoil from him, silent.

She rubbed her raw wrist and stared at Reginald. As he closed the lid over the keys of the piano, she realized he was someone she no longer knew.

And although the townsfolk seemed so admiring of him, she believed Reginald was cold and indifferent. He was like a stranger to her.

His cold aloofness made her decide not to tell him about the child she was carrying just yet. Perhaps he wouldn't want a child to bother him amid his expensive things!

And if not, oh, where on earth could she go next as she tried to make sense of her life?

Chapter Three

Blue threads of smoke trailed off into the early evening above the shadowy river valley.

Thunder Horse was sitting in his tepee on a pallet of blankets and plush furs before his lodge fire, watching the flames caressing the logs. His mind was deep in thought.

Upon first arriving at his village, he had checked on his ailing *ahte*. His father was a man whose face revealed the many trails he had walked in his long life, and whose body was now frail and thin, instead of muscled and strong as it had once been. Still, Thunder Horse had been relieved to see that his father was no worse than when he had left to fast.

After visiting his father, Thunder Horse had bathed in the nearby river, then pulled on a breechclout and returned to his lodge.

His hair glistened in the fire's glow, sleek and thick, as it flowed down his bare, muscled back.

His sister, Sweet Willow, who supplied both Thunder Horse and his father with daily nourishment, had only moments ago brought him a meal before he retired for the evening. He would sleep well tonight, now that his fasting was behind him.

He had quickly eaten the baked grouse and mushrooms his sister had gathered this morning. He had eagerly eaten the fried bread and stewed gooseberries that accompanied the meal. His belly was now comfortably full after these past days without food.

Although his belly was full, and his eyelids lay heavy on his eyes with the need of sleep, Thunder Horse's mind was not yet ready to rest.

His father was lingering much longer than the white chief in Washington had expected him to. Thunder Horse was afraid that one day soon the great white chief might change his mind and force Thunder Horse's Fox band on to the reservation, after all.

If his father died on the reservation, he would have to be placed in the ground there. The reservation was far from the sacred burial cave.

Thunder Horse thought of his widowed older sister, Sweet Willow, and her son, Lone Wing. Both were among those who remained at the village. Both were now Thunder Horse's responsibility since Sweet Willow's husband had died two moons ago at the hands of vicious renegades.

Although they were his responsibility, they lived in a lodge separate from his, as did his father, White Horse, who still resided in the tepee that he had lived in when he was a powerful chief. White Horse lived alone, for his wife had died some time ago, and he had not taken another wife. His memory of his first wife was too strong inside his heart.

But Thunder Horse's family and his responsibility to them were not the only things on his mind this early evening.

The flame-haired woman he had saved today often came into his mind's eye.

He had watched her until she had safely arrived in Tombstone. But instead of wheeling his horse around and riding away, he had waited and watched as the woman named Jessie walked to the worship house.

He had wanted to see who she had came to Tombstone to meet. He had been mesmerized by not only her loveliness, but also her strength.

When he had seen her leave the worship house in a buggy, his mouth had filled with bitterness. For the man driving the buggy was Thunder Horse's most hated enemy, a man he loathed.

This man had defiled . . . had desecrated . . . the sacred burial cave of his people's departed chiefs.

And the *wakan*, or evil man, had done this before Thunder Horse and his people were aware of it. He had gone inside and taken white gold—silver—enough to make him the wealthiest man in the area.

No one but Thunder Horse and his people knew where he'd found the silver, and thus far no other white men had entered the cave. It was known far and wide that this was a sacred place, where the bodies of many chiefs were interred, and where drawings on the walls told of the history of the Fox band.

Only one man had dared to desecrate this sacred

place, and he had taken more than silver from the cave. He had taken some of its sacredness away. He had disturbed the remains of those interred there.

After discovering who had gone into the sacred cave and disturbed the spirits, Thunder Horse had warned Reginald Vineyard that if he ever entered the cave again, he would die a slow, unmerciful death.

He had also told Reginald that he would be haunted from then on by the spirits of those he had disturbed. The evil man would never know another night's rest as long as he had breath in his lungs!

Now that Thunder Horse knew who the woman had come to be with, he was full of questions.

What was her connection to this terrible man?

Had she come to Tombstone to marry him?

Or was she his wife already?

In another time, when vengeance had been keen on the mind of every Sioux warrior, Thunder Horse would have thought of a way to use this woman to right the wrongs this man had done his people.

But today things were different. If Thunder Horse tried to avenge himself against Reginald Vineyard, the white government would step in. Thunder Horse's people would be in danger, and what remained of his band in Arizona would immediately be ordered to the reservation in the Dakotas. If there was ever trouble between whites and red men, it was always the whites the soldiers protected, even if those whites were the ones who wronged the red man.

No. He would not use this woman for vengeance. He would put her from his mind. He would do nothing now to cause his people to suffer any more than they already had at the hands of whites. The blood of his Sioux people had already turned too many rivers red.

Suddenly he was brought from his deep thoughts by the sound of a voice outside his lodge. He turned his head to the closed entrance flap. It was his nephew Lone Wing.

"Enter," Thunder Horse said, smiling at the youth as he came inside the tepee. He looked questioningly at the boy when he saw that Lone Wing was nestling something in his hands.

Lone Wing approached Thunder Horse and knelt beside him. He smiled as he held his hands out for his uncle to see.

"A baby bird," Thunder Horse said softly, then gave his nephew a questioning gaze.

"I saved the bird after older boys killed its mother and several of her babies," Lone Wing explained as he gazed down at the tiny thing, whose feathers had not yet thickened on its frail body. "The braves left this one baby to die in the hot sun outside its nest. After they left to practice shooting their arrows, I rescued the bird. I will feed and care for it, then watch it fly away."

"You are a kind young brave," Thunder Horse said, reaching a hand to Lone Wing's shoulders, which were beginning to show signs of muscles now that he had fifteen winters of age.

Thunder Horse enjoyed seeing his nephew's kind heart, but worried that his kindness might lead him into trusting too easily. Too often the red man had trusted in the promises of whites and had died because of it.

But this was not the time to remind his nephew again of these things. There were right times for teaching the young, and wrong.

This was a wrong time.

"Let me help you make a nest for the bird," Thunder Horse said. He rose and got a small piece of doeskin that he used to bathe himself in the river. He took this to Lone Wing and showed him how to make a nest from it, then watched as his nephew placed the tiny bird comfortably in it.

"He will sleep now," Lone Wing said, setting the nest aside. "His belly is full. Before I came to talk with you, I fed it tiny insects."

He laughed as he pointed to the bird's bulging belly. "You can see his filled belly," he said, then sat down beside Thunder Horse and gazed thoughtfully at him. "Tell me, my chieftain uncle, did you complete your fasting and praying?"

"I did," Thunder Horse said, sitting now with his knees drawn up to his chest, his arms wrapped around them.

"Did you dream?" Lone Wing asked anxiously.

"*Ho*, I dreamed often while I was alone beneath the stars," Thunder Horse said thickly. "And in those dreams came answers."

"Would you tell me those answers, or are they only for you to know?" Lone Wing asked, searching Thunder Horse's eyes as his uncle turned and gazed at him.

"In time you will know all because of how things

will be," Thunder Horse said. He then smiled and again placed a hand on his nephew's bare shoulder. "And you? While I was gone, did you study? You know that it takes much time and thought to become the Historian of our band. To record the events of our people by painting pictures on skins, you must be alert and knowledgeable of all things pertaining to our people."

"*Ho*, as you told me, watching and observing is studying, and I did that well while you were fasting, my chieftain uncle," Lone Wing said, proudly squaring his shoulders. "I feel that I am ready even now to become our people's Historian."

"We have one now who is our Historian, who is called 'Old One.' He is very skilled at what he does, but he is eager to teach you things that you cannot teach yourself by observation," Thunder Horse said. He lifted his hand from his nephew's shoulder and rested it again on his knee.

"My chieftain uncle, I not only want to be our people's Historian, I want to be like you," Lone Wing blurted out. "I want to be a man of strict honor, a man of undoubted truthfulness and unbounded generosity."

"You will be all of those things," Thunder Horse said, smiling at Lone Wing. "Give yourself time and you will become the man your heart is leading you to be."

"If I could, I would be you," Lone Wing said, then giggled as he saw his uncle's eyes twinkle at that comment.

He watched as Thunder Horse looked away from him to gaze into the flames of the fire. His uncle's eyes seem to fill with shadow and thought, and Lone Wing wondered what had taken him away so quickly.

He sat there quietly as he waited for Thunder Horse to remember that he still sat there with him.

As Thunder Horse gazed into the fire, the orange of the flames reminded him of flowing, flame-colored hair, catapulting him again back in time to the moment when he had seen the white woman up close and realized just how mesmerizingly beautiful she was.

Something deep inside him warned against thinking about the lady.

Whites had taken much from his people. She was white, and worse still, she was somehow connected to the man all of Thunder Horse's people despised.

Yet no matter how wrong it was to think about her, or how hard he tried not to, Thunder Horse could not let go of his memory of her. Like no other woman before her, she had put fire in his heart!

He suddenly rose and went to where he stored his clothes. Hurriedly he pulled on a fringed buckskin outfit.

Suddenly he was not as bone-weary as he had been earlier. Thinking of the woman had revived him.

He would no longer just speculate about her. He would go and observe her.

"Chieftain uncle, are you going somewhere?" Lone Wing asked as he gathered his nest and bird into his hands and rose to his feet just as Thunder Horse placed a sheathed knife at the left side of his waist.

"*Ho*, but I will not be long," Thunder Horse said. He gently placed a hand on Lone Wing's shoulder and escorted him outside, where the sky was now black and filled with sequined stars and a tiny sliver of moon.

Lone Wing nodded and watched his uncle prepare his steed, then ride away into the night.

"Perhaps he needs another night of fasting after all," he whispered, then shrugged his shoulders and hurried toward his own tepee, where he would show his mother the sweetness of the baby bird.

Chapter Four

A string quartet played music as people danced on the highly polished oak floor of Reginald's music room. A crystal chandelier in the center of the ceiling cast sparkling droplets of light onto the crowd.

Jessie stood back from everyone. She was alone for the moment, taking in the party Reginald had thrown to introduce her to the community.

Sometimes laughing, sometimes wheezing, he mingled now with the crowd. For the moment he seemed to have forgotten Jessie, which made her feel tremendously relieved.

She felt so out of place among Reginald's friends. As yet, only a few had come up to her and introduced themselves.

Although the party was for her, Reginald was truly the center of attention. Everyone praised his house, his paintings in the other rooms, and his beautiful grand piano, which no one had been asked to play.

Jessie was dressed in a lovely pale green satin ball gown that Reginald had had waiting in her room for her. Lace fell down the front of the bodice in billows of white, and her tiny waist was accentuated by a green velvet ribbon that wrapped around to the front and was tied in a bow so the ends trailed down the full skirt.

Jade had fussed endlessly with Jessie's hair, bringing it up in long curls to her crown, where it was fastened by diamond-encrusted combs. She had left the ends of the curls free to fall loosely down to the nape of her neck.

As Jade had stood behind Jessie, combing and twining her auburn hair into those huge curls, Jessie had watched her in the mirror. The lovely Chinese woman had hidden the bruises on her face tonight with powder the same color as her skin, and Jessie knew that Reginald was responsible for the beating. No one but Jessie and Reginald had been in the house prior to the arrival of his guests.

Jessie had wanted so badly to ask Jade about the bruises but knew that the woman would say nothing. No doubt she feared Reginald's reaction should he discover that she'd confided in anyone that she was physically abused by a man whom everyone saw as pure and holy. Jessie was quickly discovering that he was anything but that.

She dreaded being a part of his household now and wished that she had somewhere else to go, someone else to help her in her time of trouble. Being with child, she was even more vulnerable now than ever.

She had to do everything she could to protect this child, for in truth, her baby was all she now had on this earth!

Jessie watched Jade as she walked around, offering drinks to the guests. Jade walked with humbled, lowered eyes, as she tried not to allow anyone else to see her injuries.

Jessie once again thought of the lovely Chinese girl she'd seen in the window of the crib this morning. She could still feel the girl's shame inside her heart.

Trying to force her thoughts to more pleasant things, since she knew that at any moment someone could come up to speak to her, Jessie straightened her back and squared her shoulders.

She could tell that Reginald was a man who enjoyed giving grand parties and showing off his magnificent house. He moved from person to person, talking and laughing despite his constant wheezing.

The music room had been cleared of all furniture but the grand piano and a wide oak table on the opposite side of the room.

On that table his guests could choose from such delicacies as capers, plover's eggs, green olives, truffles, mushrooms, and meringues. There were also platters heaped with roasted prairie chicken, broiled antelope steaks, and smoked elk meat.

The drinks offered were sherry, burgundy, champagne, and Reginald's favorite wine—Château Lagrange.

Jessie's attention was drawn to several women who had gone to the piano and were now standing around it, admiring it. They looked over at Jessie and beckoned her nearer, smiling.

"Can you play?" asked one of the smaller women, who was dressed in a low-necked, floor-length, blue velvet dress.

"Yes, I can play," Jessie said, then stiffened when she saw Reginald give her a sour glance as he heard her reply.

She still didn't know why he had warned her away from the piano, but she knew she must not play it. He had made that perfectly clear!

"Will you play for us?" one of the ladies asked.

"I haven't practiced for some time, so I would feel more comfortable not playing the piano tonight," Jessie said, again feeling Reginald's eyes on her.

"My, my, how disappointing," one of the women said in a strange sort of squawking voice.

"Very," another woman said stiffly. Then all of them turned with a whirl of skirts and left Jessie standing alone again.

Feeling uncomfortable since Reginald had gone back to ignoring her, Jessie lifted the hem of her skirt and hurried from the room through French doors that led outside to a veranda.

She stepped up to the rail and placed her hands there, sighing at how out of place she felt. Again she wished that she was anywhere but there.

When Reginald had first written to her, he'd made her feel as though she was truly wanted. She had thought coming to live with him would be the answer to her problems. She had envisioned them going horseback riding together often as they had as young children.

Jessie felt anything but welcome now, even though she was supposed to be the guest of honor at this party. Reginald had not taken the time to introduce her to anyone, and the guests ignored her. She felt so uncomfortable that more than once she had wanted to flee to the privacy of her bedroom.

But standing out there in the night air, where the slight sliver of moon hung in the sky and the stars were sparkling against the black backdrop of the heavens, was much better than being cooped up in a bedroom. Although it was furnished lavishly and should please any woman, she did not feel comfortable there. From the very first moment she had entered Reginald's house, she knew that this was not going to be a place where she would feel loved, wanted, or needed.

Coyote calls echoed off the distant butte, startling her. She had noticed earlier that coyotes howled here even in broad daylight.

She shivered and placed a hand on her belly.

When should she tell Reginald about the child? He certainly didn't seem the sort who would want children around.

It would be a while before she began showing, so she would wait and hope that she could find the right moment to tell him. If she was lucky, he would not go into a rage when he discovered that he had not only taken in a lonely woman, but also a child.

"Here you are," Reginald said, stepping out into the night air on the veranda next to Jessie. "Why are you out here all alone? Cousin, this party is being held in your honor. You should be a part of it."

"I just got so tired suddenly," Jessie murmured, looking past his thick-lensed glasses into his beady eyes. Her heart turned cold when she saw their unfriendly gaze.

"Well, let's see what we can do about that," Reginald said, taking her by an elbow. "Let's get some food in you. Did you see the various local dishes that Jade cooked up for us? She is a marvel, that one. I don't know what I'd do without her."

Recalling Jade's hidden bruises, and guessing just how unhappy and afraid Jade must be with her situation, Jessie stiffened. She had to wonder if she, herself, would ever be a recipient of blows that could cause such bruises.

That possibility made her almost sick to her stomach.

"Here's our guest of honor," Reginald announced as he took Jessie to the center of the floor, where everyone gathered around them. "Isn't my cousin a beauty?" He laughed. "As you see, it runs in the family."

The music had stopped. All eyes were on Jessie. At this moment she felt like a fixture someone might buy from a general store.

Now she understood the reason she'd been asked to live with him in the first place. He enjoyed having her there to show off to everyone as if she were a trophy.

Oh, how she was beginning to loathe this man! Anyone who would beat a woman was not a man at all. He was a weasel.

She forced herself to smile as Reginald continued to

fuss over her, telling everyone about how they had been so close as children.

"My cousin Jessie is bringing a lot of life and love back into my home," Reginald said solemnly. "Since my Sara's death, you all know how hard it has been for me."

Everyone seemed to nod at once as looks of sympathy were given to Reginald.

But when Jessie looked at him, all she saw was smugness. She knew right then and there that this man had everyone fooled.

Everyone!

She could not help but suddenly feel trapped.

Chapter Five

Truly curious about the *wasichu mitawin*, the white woman, Thunder Horse hid in the shadows of the veranda wall at Reginald Vineyard's house. Nearby, double doors led into a room filled with music and laughter.

Thunder Horse had been watching the people through the sheer curtains of the closed doors, and had jumped out of sight just as the woman named Jessie walked through the doors to step out on the veranda.

He had scarcely breathed as she stood there alone for a while, as though she were contemplating life as she gazed up into the heavens, as he so often did.

He was tempted to join her there, to witness her reaction when she learned that he had come to see her again. But he knew if he did that, he might frighten her.

He was almost relieved when Reginald came and got her, removing the temptation to reveal himself to her. He knew that was best. He would have to find another way to speak to her again, to understand his fascination with her.

Seeing that no one was near, he stepped back to the doors again, where gauzy white curtains kept him from being seen.

He could see through them well enough, for the room within was well lit. Candles glowed from above, placed in a fancy contraption that hung from the ceiling in the center of the room.

He searched the gathering until he found Jessie and Reginald.

He could tell that the man was proud to show off the beautiful *wasichu mitawin,* but Thunder Horse could read expressions very well and could tell that Jessie was uneasy.

He wondered why.

Had she not come to Reginald Vineyard's house because she wanted to?

Or . . . had she been coerced somehow?

His gaze was drawn elsewhere, for there was much to wonder at.

He had never seen white people dance. It was much different from the red man's dances. This dancing was the dizziest thing he had ever seen.

His eyes focused next on four people at the far end of the room, who sat in chairs beside one another. They sawed away at stringed boards that made music. These instruments were nothing like what his people used to make music.

Again he gazed at the people who were dancing in time with the music. It puzzled him to see men dancing with women. And they actually touched while dancing. That was something his people never did.

Suddenly the dancing and music changed.

One of the musicians stood up and began shouting while another sawed away at his stringed board as men began swinging the women around on the shining wood floor.

This sort of dancing, and the loud shouting, looked and sounded very rude to him.

Then a young man and woman faced each other and danced in the middle of the floor as others watched and clapped their hands. Soon those people left and others took their place in the middle of the floor and began doing the same strange thing.

Voices close by outside in the dark came to Thunder Horse, and his heart skipped a beat.

He stepped quickly away from the doors and the candlelight that shone through them. He placed his back against the wall of the house once again, hoping that he was hidden well enough, for there were men outside. They were not far away, standing and smoking what Thunder Horse knew were white men's cigars.

He could tell that the men hadn't seen him yet.

He hunkered low and moved stealthily away from the veranda, blending in with the darkness as he ran to safety in the close-by trees. He hurried onward to where he had left his sorrel picketed.

But before mounting, he glanced again toward the bright candlelight spilling from the windows and doors and listened again to the stringed boards making their noises while people laughed and danced.

In his mind's eye, he saw Jessie. He had not gotten any answers tonight as to why she was living with Reginald Vineyard.

Was she planning to marry him?

Or was she married to him already?

Surely it was one or the other!

One thing was certain. The woman had suddenly complicated his plans, for he truly didn't want harm to come to her. He feared it might if she stayed with the evil man.

Thunder Horse could tell that she was a sweet, soft-spoken person . . . and obviously uneasy with the tiny weasel of a man.

But, again . . . why? Why would she come to Tombstone if she disliked him so much?

Thunder Horse swung himself into his saddle and rode away into the night, away from the woman who intrigued him so. But putting distance between himself and Jessie did not erase her from his mind, or his heart.

Ho, there was something about her that would not allow him to forget her. That first moment they had made eye contact, he'd known she would not be someone he could easily forget.

He had saved her life then.

Would she need to be saved again . . . saved from a rat such as Reginald Vineyard?

From the way she had looked at the man, with a contempt she had tried so hard to hide, Thunder Horse knew that she had no good feelings for the tiny white man.

So what did that mean?

Why *was* she with him?

Thunder Horse's heart would not rest until he had the answers to those questions.

He rode onward, glad that the music and laughter were far behind him now, for the silence all around allowed him to think more clearly. The main focus in his life at this moment must be his ailing father and his duty to his people, both those here in Arizona as well as the ones already living on the reservation.

In time, he would see the latter again and embrace them. But until then, he had those who remained at his village to see to and keep safe.

And he must protect his father's interests. White Horse deserved to be interred with the other great, noble chiefs of their Fox band.

"It will be so, *ahte*, my Father," he said into the wind as the glow of his people's lodge fires appeared ahead of him in the darkness.

But suddenly a woman's voice came to him in the night, causing him to flinch in the saddle. He knew that voice.

It was the flame-haired woman! He knew that she wasn't anywhere near him, yet he could hear her call to him inside his heart.

He brought his horse to a sudden halt and turned in the saddle, staring back in the direction he had last seen the woman called Jessie.

Although she was still at the white man's house, she had managed to come to him in the night inside his heart. It seemed to Thunder Horse that she was crying out to him not to forget her.

"What does this mean?" he whispered to the heavens as he sought answers from the Great Spirit high above.

Suddenly things were still again except for the soft wind whispering through the trees, and the occasional yelp of a coyote off in the distance.

A chill raced up and down Thunder Horse's spine as he turned his steed back in the direction of his village once again . . . a chill caused by the unknown. . . .

Chapter Six

Relieved that the party was finally over and she was secluded in her bedroom, Jessie sat in her soft lacy nightgown at a mirrored vanity while Jade stood behind her, brushing Jessie's long auburn hair.

As Jessie looked into the mirror, she could see the reflection of the room behind her.

Although she had found Reginald vastly different from the person she had known years ago, he had remembered her fondness for pretty, delicate things. Before her arrival he had decorated her room thusly.

The four-poster bed projected a luxurious ambiance of elegance. It was a stunning, tall, hand-painted bed of black chinoiserie, its canopy draped in rose-colored French silk damask, trimmed with handmade fringes and a cream-colored silk lining.

She had loved the bed the first moment she set eyes on it. The canopy gave her a sense of sanctuary; this would be a place where she could get away from the day's woes and discomforts, and no one could disturb her.

Everything else about the room was pretty, too. The matching draperies at the window were of velvet and decorated with ribbons and lace.

"Jessie, I have a daughter," Jade suddenly blurted out.

"You do?" Jessie said, now gazing at Jade's reflection in the mirror instead of the grandeur of the bedroom. "Where is she? Is she still in China?"

"No, she isn't in China. She is in Tombstone," Jade murmured, pausing in the brushing of Jessie's hair.

Instead, she nervously turned the brush in her hands, her eyes revealing her worry as she told Jessie about her daughter.

"She is . . . in . . . one of those awful cribs?" Jessie gasped when Jade had finished. She turned on the bench and faced Jade, who now sat on a chair beside her.

"*Ah hao*, yes, she is there," Jade said, resting the brush on her lap. "Her name is Lee-Lee. She is tiny and so very afraid of what has been forced upon her. I'm helpless to do anything for her except . . . except . . . to take food to her, and that only once a week."

"Once a week?" Jessie gasped. "What does she do on the other days?"

"She is fed, but it is her mother's food that she craves," Jade murmured, casting her slanted eyes downward.

Then she looked in desperation at Jessie again. "Crib women don't live long," she blurted out, tears shining in her eyes. "They die from disease passed on by the men who frequent the cribs, or . . . from . . . suicide."

"Suicide?" Jessie said, her eyes widening. "Do you think your daughter will—"

Jade interrupted her. "I have seen the hopelessness in my daughter's eyes the last few times I have gone to her," she said tightly. "She won't last much longer. She can't stand the humiliation. She can't stand the men's callous treatment, or being locked up all day."

"How horrible," Jessie murmured, truly horrified by what Jade was telling her. She placed a gentle hand on Jade's cheek, then drew it away again. "Who is responsible for your daughter's misfortune?"

Jade looked quickly and nervously toward the closed door, then leaned closer to Jessie. "Your cousin," she said in a whisper.

"Reginald?" Jessie said, searching Jade's eyes. "He—?"

"Yes, Reginald Vineyard," Jade said tightly, her eyes filled with rage. "My daughter is a prisoner of your cousin. He owns several cribs in Tombstone. He has forced not only my daughter into prostitution, but many other unfortunate women who have no family or anyone to care for them."

Jessie was totally stunned and sickened by what Jade had told her, not only about her daughter's troubles, but also about Reginald being such a demonic sort of man. She slid her feet into soft slippers and went to stand at the window, gazing out into the pitch-blackness of night.

"I don't understand," she said. She then whirled

around to face Jade again. "He . . . he . . . is loved by the people of the church. How can that be if he—?"

Again Jade interrupted her. "The decent townsfolk who go to church with him have no idea he does this," she said flatly. "He has threatened anyone who tells. And . . . he has threatened to kill any woman who tries to escape. He has told them that he will hunt them down and kill them. I am afraid to try to flee his clutches, myself. Where could I even go? Reginald would send out word to everyone not to hire me. I would be homeless. I would die of starvation."

Almost speechless now at what she was learning about her cousin, Jessie realized he was anything but religious. Religion was just a front for him, to keep people from discovering his illicit activities.

"Should you be telling me all of this?" Jessie asked, placing gentle hands on Jade's thick shoulders. "If Reginald finds out—"

"I felt that I could trust you not to tell," Jade murmured. "You won't, will you?"

"Heavens, no!" Jessie said. "I would never tell him what you have confided in me tonight."

"Jessie, can you find a way to help Lee-Lee?" Jade asked, her eyes pleading. "You are free to come and go as you please, aren't you?"

"So far," Jessie gulped out.

She stepped away from Jade and began slowly pacing the floor; the rug was thick and cushiony beneath her slippered feet.

After hearing all of this, and realizing just how uncomfortable she was with Reginald, who was a stranger to her now, Jessie wondered about her own future. How could she stay with Reginald now that she knew what a monster he was?

Yet where would she go?

Of course, Kansas City had been her home, yet those she loved . . . her family . . . were no longer there.

But she did have friends there.

She had much to decide now, but most of all she must keep in mind the best interests of her unborn child.

"Jessie, can you help my daughter?" Jade asked again as she came up beside Jessie, causing her to stop pacing. "She is the only tiny, pretty Chinese girl there in that particular set of cribs. The other Chinese cribs are far back from the main street in a portion of Tombstone called Chink Town."

Suddenly she grabbed Jessie desperately by the arm. "Please, oh, please say that you will help my daughter escape that terrible place," she begged, her eyes wild with fear.

"Even if I did, where could she go?" Jessie asked. "Reginald would surely hunt her down, as well as the one who helped her escape."

Suddenly Jessie heard screams of horror . . . of fright, out in the corridor.

Eyes wide, she looked at Jade. "What in the world . . ." she gasped.

"This is becoming a nightly ritual," Jade said, a slow smile curving her lips.

"What?" Jessie asked, shaken when another terrible scream of horror came through the closed door. "Who . . . ?"

"Reginald," Jade said nonchalantly.

"Reginald?" Jessie gasped out.

"For some time now Reginald has been having terrifying nightmares," Jade said, her voice revealing a glad smugness. "Each night his screams of torment get worse than the last."

Again his screams came through the door.

Now Jessie could even hear him running down the corridor!

"Why is this happening?" Jessie asked. Part of her wanted to go to Reginald, to comfort the boy with whom she had shared such a precious childhood. But now that she knew the sort of man he had become, the rest of her wanted to leave him to his torment, because he did seem to have brought it on himself by his evil deeds.

"Why?" Jade repeated, staring at the closed door, then turning back toward Jessie. "Because he's done so much meanness in his lifetime," she said tightly.

Stunned by how terrified Reginald sounded, Jessie wondered what could be the seed of such fear. Allowing herself to remember the good times they'd shared, she pulled on a robe and hurried out into the corridor.

She stopped abruptly when she found Reginald crumpled to the floor, breathing hard, his face in his hands.

Jessie stood there a moment, staring down at the pitiful sight, then knelt down beside him.

"Reggie?" she murmured, starting to reach out for him.

Reginald's head jerked up.

The fear in his eyes changed quickly to anger when he saw Jessie kneeling there.

He scrambled to his feet, fists at his sides. "Didn't I tell you never to call me Reggie again?" he shouted. He pointed toward her room. "And get back to your room. Mind your own business!"

Horrified by his reaction to her kindly meant gesture, Jessie stared dumbfoundedly at him for a moment. Then she hurried to her room and closed the door between herself and her cousin.

Seeing how distraught Jessie was, Jade took her into her arms. "Now you know the true ugliness of this man," she murmured, gently embracing her. "Jessie, be careful. Be . . . very . . . careful about what you do or say around him."

Jessie eased from Jade's arms.

Pale, her heart thumping wildly inside her chest, she laid a hand on her belly. She was truly afraid now for her child. One blow from this man and she could lose her baby!

Tomorrow she would start her plan of escape.

She would explore the countryside on the horse Reginald had given her. He had remembered how she had always enjoyed horseback riding.

But he had told her not to go far from the ranch; that it was dangerous. She now realized he was afraid she might meet people who could eventually help her!

But the main thing she knew now was that she would have to find a way to flee, the sooner, the better.

But how?

She had no money. And now she had not only herself and her unborn child to think about, but also Jade and her daughter Lee-Lee. They were in danger as long as they were under the thumb of her cousin Reginald.

"What are you going to do?" Jade asked, sensing Jessie's tumultuous thoughts.

"I'm not sure yet," Jessie said. She took Jade's hands in hers. "But there must be a way for us to get away from this man. He might be my cousin, but I'm beginning to believe he is a madman!"

Jade flung herself into Jessie's arms. "Then you'll help us? Thank you, oh thank you," she sobbed. "Still, I can't help being afraid."

"Yes, I know," Jessie said, returning Jade's hug. "I am afraid, too."

They both stiffened when they heard Reginald rant and rave in the corridor as he walked back toward his own bedroom.

"I wonder what caused him to change," Jessie said, her voice drawn. "There isn't anything about him that is the same as he once was."

"I hear the Indians put a curse on him," Jade said, leaning away from Jessie to peer intently into her eyes.

"A curse?" Jessie gasped, paling. "Why?"

Jade shrugged. "He must have wronged them, too, somehow," she said. She lifted the hairbrush. "Come, and I will finish brushing your hair so that you can go to bed. You look tired, Jessie. Very, very tired."

Jessie took the robe off, laid it across the back of a chair, then sat back down before the mirror.

As Jade resumed brushing her hair, Jessie's thoughts went over all that the lovely Chinese woman had told her.

That part about the Indians intrigued her. She wondered if it might be true. If so, might it have anything to do with Thunder Horse's Sioux people?

Yes! She recalled now that Reginald had said the Sioux knew about where he had found the silver, but no one else did!

Had the Sioux put a curse on him? Did Thunder Horse have a role in this?

Thunder Horse.

Ah, just the thought of that handsome chief made everything bad leave Jessie's mind.

She hoped that tomorrow, when she was out horseback riding, she might possibly see him, or even find his village.

Might she eventually seek help from the Sioux, and especially Thunder Horse?

He had already helped her once. Were she to ask, would he save her a second time?

Chapter Seven

The day was bright and filled with a soft wind as Thunder Horse rode on his sorrel horse beside his nephew Lone Wing. He was constantly impressed by the boy's growth; he seemed to have the spirit and skills of someone twice his age.

There was no true purpose for their excursion today except for Lone Wing to develop his skills on his palomino pony. One day, when he was a warrior full grown, he would ride a horse as powerful as Thunder Horse's muscled steed.

As they rode onward, and turned past a thick stand of tall ponderosa pines, Thunder Horse's eyes were drawn ahead to someone kneeling beside a granite stone that his people worshiped with prayers and offerings.

It was a woman!

One of her gloved hands was clutching the reins of a brilliantly white horse, which stood behind her, lazily munching oat grass.

When Thunder Horse realized who this person was,

his heart skipped a beat. Her hair was flame-red beneath the rays of the early afternoon sun, and her tininess was even more pronounced in what appeared to be riding clothes—a white blouse, a leather skirt, and leather boots.

Ho, it was the same woman who had unknowingly lured him to Reginald Vineyard's ranch house last night, to observe her as she mingled with the crowd of white people.

While horseback riding today, she had discovered the stone that was sacred to Thunder Horse's people.

Lone Wing saw Thunder Horse slow his steed to a trot and followed his uncle's lead. Then he noticed the path his uncle's eyes had taken and saw what . . . who . . . Thunder Horse was looking at so intently.

A *mitawin*, a white woman!

Lone Wing's eyebrows rose in surprise.

"You are looking at this woman as though you know her," Lone Wing said, edging his pony closer to Thunder's Horse's steed. "Who is she? Why is she kneeling beside the sacred stone of our people? Do whites worship it, too? Do some whites have the same beliefs as we Sioux have? And . . . why are you looking at this *mitawin* with such . . . such . . ."

Lone Wing didn't finish his question, for he was not certain that he should.

Yet his curiosity remained. His uncle had chosen not to allow a woman into his life while he had so many troubles on his mind about his people and his ailing father.

Thunder Horse glanced quickly at Lone Wing. As they drew rein, Thunder Horse felt a little unnerved that his nephew had caught him gazing with such fascination at this woman.

Since Thunder Horse wasn't certain why he could not let go of Jessie in his mind, or his heart, he knew that it would be hard for him to explain this attraction to anyone else. So he chose to ignore part of his nephew's question.

"No, Lone Wing, no whites have the same beliefs as we Sioux," he said. "This woman has surely been drawn here out of curiosity."

"What are you going to do about her?" Lone Wing asked. "Are you going to order her away, or let her remain here?"

Thunder Horse didn't respond right away. He still gazed at Jessie, aware that she had not heard their approach.

She seemed caught up in studying what lay at the foot of the stone. He understood that to a white woman, the objects lying there would be curious.

He was glad that she had not reached out to touch anything that had been placed there by his people. He found her respect for his people's beliefs commendable.

"What will you do about her being here, where she does not belong?" Lone Wing asked again, surprised when his uncle's only response was to sink his heels into the flanks of his steed and ride onward toward the woman.

Lone Wing caught up with him. "Will you allow her to remain, or order her away?" he prodded.

"Neither," Thunder Horse finally said, looking over

at Lone Wing. "We will go and speak with her, then allow her to do as she pleases. Stay or go. It is apparent that she means no harm."

Jessie's insides tightened when she became aware of approaching horses. She had been so caught up in studying what lay around the stone, and the stone itself, that she had not heard the horses earlier.

She knew they were very close now, and she could not help being suddenly afraid. She was alone and someplace she obviously shouldn't be, especially if these were Sioux warriors riding toward her.

She rushed to her feet.

When she turned and saw who was approaching, her pulse raced. Thunder Horse was riding toward her on a lovely steed with a teenage boy on a pony close beside him.

She no longer felt threatened, but quite the opposite. She had hoped to see Chief Thunder Horse again, and here he was, his eyes looking squarely into hers. Her insides melted when he smiled at her.

But no words were exchanged.

He drew rein a few feet from her, and she knew that any other white woman would be afraid to be discovered by Indians so far from home.

But she wasn't afraid.

She would never forget Thunder Horse's kindness toward her, how he had saved her life!

Thunder Horse raised his left hand in greeting, palm out, in his people's gesture of friendship . . . the left hand because it was nearer the heart and had shed no blood.

"I remember you," he said in a deep, masculine tone as he lowered his hand and again took up his horse's reins. "We became friends on that day when I stopped the runaway stagecoach. I remember your name, too. It is Jessie."

Pleased that he had remembered not only her, but also her name, Jessie nodded. "Yes, I remember you, too," she said, nervously twining and untwining the reins around her left hand. She occupied her hands in the hope of keeping him from noticing that they were trembling.

If he saw them trembling, he might think it was from fear, when actually it was because she was so taken by him.

"It . . . is . . . nice to see you again," Jessie blurted out.

"I am pleased also," Thunder Horse said. Then he motioned with a hand toward Lone Wing. "This is my nephew. He goes by the name Lone Wing. Lone Wing, this woman's name is Jessie."

"It is good to know you, Jessie," Lone Wing said, beginning to understand why his uncle seemed so fascinated by this woman. Even Lone Wing could see how beautiful she was. And she seemed sweet, as his own mother was.

"It's nice to know you, too, Lone Wing," Jessie said, reaching a hand out toward the boy, which he didn't take. It was obvious he did not understand that her way of greeting someone was with a handshake.

She again toyed with the reins.

"Why have you stopped at the sacred rock of my people?" Thunder Horse blurted out.

His abrupt question made Jessie's smile fade. He wished now that he had not been so quick to demand an answer.

"I was horseback riding and was drawn to this huge stone," Jessie explained. Only now did she realize that she might have done something wrong in examining the stone. Obviously, it was something sacred to Thunder Horse's people. "First I noticed, from a distance, that the stone was painted red, then when I grew closer, I became even more curious when I saw the many things on the ground around it."

"What you see are votive offerings," Thunder Horse said, nodding toward small bags of tobacco, pieces of cloth, hatchets, knives, and a lone arrow. "There are certain stones such as this that are worshiped with prayers and offerings by my people."

"I apologize for coming here," Jessie murmured. "I didn't know about the meaning behind the red stone, or the gifts, or I wouldn't have come close. I will not do so again."

"You can come often, if you so choose," Thunder Horse said thickly. "The stone is there for everyone, not only us Sioux." He reached his hands heavenward and motioned all around him. "In these things, the stone, the clouds, the trees, the buffalo, all things are one."

He ended with the sign for "all," moving his right hand, palm side down, in a horizontal circle at the height of his heart.

He had noticed that all the while he sat on his horse so close to Jessie, she kept placing her hand on her stomach.

He had seen this before, when a woman with child felt that the child inside her might be threatened by something or someone. The thought of this woman possibly carrying Reginald Vineyard's child was repulsive to him, for it surely meant that she was his wife . . . and absolutely forbidden to Thunder Horse.

But besides that, he didn't like to think that this woman felt threatened in his presence. He had told her more than once that he was a friend.

And hadn't he proved it to her? Had he not saved her life?

The sound of an approaching horse and buggy, seen now in the distance, interrupted his thoughts. Thunder Horse recognized the deranged Reginald Vineyard by his tiny size. Could he truly be the husband of this woman who might haunt Thunder Horse with her sweet loveliness forever and ever?

Thunder Horse wheeled his horse quickly around.

"*Hiyu-wo*, come, nephew!" he said, giving Lone Wing a nod. "It is time to go. Quickly!"

As he rode into a stand of trees with Lone Wing beside him, Thunder Horse could not stop thinking about how Jessie had placed her hand on her stomach. Surely she *was* with child.

"Why did we flee so quickly?" Lone Wing asked. "I like the lady. You seemed to, also."

"Why did I decide to leave?" Thunder Horse said, continuing farther and farther away from where he felt he had left his heart. "Because the man who is approaching in that buggy is our *toka*, our enemy, Reginald Vineyard. I do not wish today to see him face to face."

"Is the woman then a *toka*, as well?" Lone Wing asked. "For surely she belongs to the man. He seems to be coming for her."

"I am not quite certain yet what to make of her," Thunder Horse said, his voice tight. "Or what her true relationship is with that man. But in time I will find out, and then I will know how to act."

Lone Wing gazed silently at his uncle. He had seen in his eyes that he did care for this *mitawin*, whether or not she had skin the color of his enemies, and even if she belonged to the Fox band's worst enemy of all: Reginald Vineyard!

He could not help wondering how his chieftain uncle was going to act on *that?*

Chapter Eight

Jessie felt uneasy as Reginald rode up in his horse and buggy and drew rein close to her. His eyes seemed even more beady than ever as he glared down at her.

When he glanced at the beautiful horse he had been generous enough to give her, then looked hard at her again, she could guess what he must be thinking. She knew he had seen Thunder Horse with her only moments ago.

Reginald was probably thinking that she was taking advantage of his generosity to ride her horse to meet with another man. His next words confirmed her guess.

"When did you first meet him?"

That question, asked so suddenly and with such venom, made Jessie's spine stiffen.

She didn't want to tell Reginald the truth of how she and Thunder Horse had first met. That was something she wanted to keep inside her heart like a wonderful secret . . . a secret that only she and Thunder Horse shared.

That might be the only thing they could ever have between them.

"Today," Jessie said quickly, hating to lie.

"Today?" Reginald scoffed, now glowering at her. "And I am to believe that? You must know it is not a normal thing for a white woman and a powerful Indian chief to come together as friends. It is forbidden in all respects."

"He just happened along and found me studying his people's sacred stone," Jessie said, refusing to back down. "I was horseback riding. I saw this strange stone painted red, and then when I got closer I saw all those things lying around it. I stopped and took a better look, and that was when Chief Thunder Horse and his nephew found me here."

"You say that name—Chief Thunder Horse—so easily, as though you have no fear of that Sioux warrior," Reginald said, his eyes holding a strange twinkle, as though he had guessed Jessie's feelings for Thunder Horse.

"Why are you here?" Jessie blurted out, angrily placing her hands on her hips. "Are you going to watch everything I do . . . everyone I happen to speak with?"

Reginald shifted nervously on the buggy seat. "I'm tired of this conversation," he said stiffly. "But listen well to what I have to say, Jessie. That Sioux chief is someone you must stay away from."

"Why?" Jessie asked, slowly dropping her arms to

her sides. "What on earth did it hurt to have a short conversation with him? He seemed kind enough. I did not feel at all threatened by him. And if you are going to preach to me about it being forbidden for a white woman to talk with an Indian, I call that hogwash."

"Hogwash?" Reginald said. His eyes narrowed even more angrily than before. "Jessie, the reason I am warning you to stay away from that chief is because we are bitter enemies," he said tightly.

"Enemies?" Jessie said. Then suddenly she recalled something that Jade had told her last night about Reginald's nightmares having to do with an Indian's curse.

Could that Indian be Thunder Horse?

"Why are you . . . enemies?" Jessie asked cautiously.

"Never mind," Reginald said flatly. "Like I said, I'm tired of this conversation. Get on your horse. I'm taking you into town."

"You're taking me into town?" Jessie asked, mounting the beautiful white steed. "What is the occasion?"

"I'm going to buy you a bonnet, that's all," Reginald said, idly shrugging. "Come on. I want to take you by horse and buggy. We must first go home before going to town. I want you to leave your horse in the stable."

"A bonnet?" Jessie said, questioning him with her eyes.

He ignored her question, turning the buggy around without waiting to see if she was following. He now seemed intent on returning the horse home.

As she rode next to the buggy, she glanced over at Reginald. He was neatly dressed in his usual black suit and white shirt, with a thin black tie at his collar. His thinning reddish-brown hair, worn to his collar, was blowing in the breeze, revealing more scalp than she knew he wanted anyone to see.

She would have thought that he was the one needing something to wear on his head, not her! But she had never seen him wear a hat.

Why should he care whether she had a bonnet or not? She knew he wanted her to make a good impression among the townsfolk. But up to now he had bought things without her being with him. He had had several pretty dresses and hats already waiting for her when she'd arrived at Tombstone.

She wished that she could feel better about him as a person, for she did enjoy being treated to new things. For so long she had not had the money to buy trinkets or pretty dresses.

A preacher's salary had not gone very far, and usually her husband had spent most of the money helping others who were less fortunate than him and his wife.

Jessie and Reginald rode in silence the rest of the way. After they reached the ranch, Jessie left the horse in the stable and quickly returned to the buggy. She noticed that Reginald was gazing at her attire, and as she sat down on the seat beside him, he began his scolding again.

"You should change into something more appropriate, but too much time has already been wasted by my having to search for you," Reginald said, snapping the reins and sending the horse and buggy down the long, white gravel road toward town.

"Why the rush?" Jessie murmured.

She could not help feeling uneasy, for she didn't trust this little weasel of a man any farther than she could throw him. Everything about him seemed loathsome to her now.

Yet she knew there were many who admired him. How could she feel one thing for him, when so many others felt the opposite?

Perhaps she was wrong to have judged him so quickly. He might be a genuinely nice person. . . .

She shook her head when she recalled Lee-Lee and Jade. Nothing about how he treated them was kind. No genuinely nice person made women live in cribs, forced to sell their bodies to filthy, drunken men.

And no decent man struck a woman!

She felt Reginald's eyes on her.

"Why the rush to get into town?" he mocked. "Jessie, be quiet. Just always do as I say and we'll be able to get along fine."

She looked quickly at him, stunned that he would say such a thing to her!

Jerking her head so that she no longer looked at Reginald but instead at the false-fronted buildings that came into view as they approached the main part of the town, Jessie forced her thoughts away from her cousin. The more she tried to understand him, the more confused she became.

But for now, she did as he asked. She sat quiet.

Her mind was now on something far more pleasant: Thunder Horse and how genuinely kind and soft-spoken he was, and handsome.

She wondered why she got such a tender feeling

when she thought about him. He should not matter at all to her.

Yet she couldn't help being intrigued by him. As strange as it seemed, he was all that made her feel sane *or* safe since her arrival in Tombstone. Her cousin only made her feel confused, even threatened.

If it weren't for Thunder Horse, she would truly feel threatened and trapped, for she had no money to go anywhere else. She had no one to go to.

She was at the mercy of a man she now saw as a total stranger . . . even a madman!

She gave Reginald a slow glance, wondering if she had ever known him at all.

As they entered Tombstone's main street, the first things Jessie saw were the tiny, horrible houses . . . cribs . . . used by prostitutes.

It was unbelievable that some were actually owned by Reginald, who pretended to be so holy and proper. If the townsfolk knew the truth, how would they treat him then?

Like the devil, she was sure!

Her insides grew cold when she saw Lee-Lee standing in her assigned window, sparsely dressed again, as men stared at her, thrusting hands filled with coins toward her.

Jessie flinched when she saw one of them go into the tiny window space from the back side and get Lee-Lee. Both then disappeared into the room behind the window.

It made Jessie sick to her stomach to imagine what was about to happen to the poor girl!

Her thoughts and eyes were drawn back to Reginald when he stopped his buggy and laughed throatily.

"I lied," he said, his voice filled with a strange glee. "I didn't bring you into town for a new bonnet, but for you to watch the Indians coming into Tombstone today to beg. Because of the trouble I've had with the likes of Chief Thunder Horse, it gives me pure joy to see what is happening to these Indians."

He leaned closer to Jessie's face. "Chief Thunder Horse's days are numbered," he said between clenched teeth. "Then, like these savages you'll see today, he'll be lowered to begging, too."

Jessie gazed through the thick-lensed glasses into what she felt was pure evil.

She tried to hide the shudder that engulfed her. She didn't want Reginald to know the depths of her loathing for him, not until she found a way to escape his madness.

"Which Indians are these?" she asked as calmly as she could when she saw a number of Indian warriors walking down the middle of the street.

"Cheyenne," Reginald said, looking away from Jessie and focusing on the Indians. "These Cheyenne live on a reservation a few miles outside of Tombstone."

"A reservation?" Jessie said, swallowing hard. She had heard of the harsh lives the Indians lived on reservations, where they were no longer free as they had been since the beginning of time.

She had never seen a reservation, and had never desired to. She didn't want to look upon the faces of those who had lost everything to the white man, even their pride.

She wanted to ask Reginald if Thunder Horse lived on a reservation, too, but knew better than to mention his name.

But hadn't Thunder Horse said he lived in a village? Surely if he lived on a reservation, he would call it that, and would have spoken the name with much venom. She had heard that Indians hated to be rounded up like cattle to live on land that was no longer theirs but instead, the United States Government's.

"Just watch what happens here today," Reginald said, drawing his horse and buggy to the side of the road, yet remaining inside it. "Jessie, this is 'beef issue' day for this band of Cheyenne. Deprived of the hunt as they had always known it, the Indian warriors gather at that cattle pen over yonder to 'hunt' their quarry."

Reginald pointed to a pen, filled with cows. She felt sick to her stomach as she turned toward the warriors again and saw them painting their faces as though they were going to war. When they were finished, they secured quivers of arrows to their backs, then walked toward the penned-up cows, carrying long, huge bows.

"Jessie, let me explain this to you so that you'll know the true meaning of what's about to happen," Reginald said, gazing at the warriors as they took positions around the outside of the fence, their eyes narrowing in eagerness. "The government agents buy the cattle necessary for this hunt from local ranchers, who are glad to have a handy market for their stock. The Indians have claimed the right to kill and butcher their cattle today."

"But I still don't understand," Jessie murmured, not sure if she even wanted to.

"The warriors are going to pursue the white man's buffalo—in other words, these cows," Reginald said throatily, obviously anticipating what was about to happen. "They feel this is their last chance to play out their ritual hunt and also ensure themselves of fresh meat."

"It seems so . . . so . . . indecent of the government to put the Indians in this position," Jessie said, looking around at the Indian women and children who were gathering to watch and encourage their husbands, fathers, brothers, and cousins. For whoever killed the most cows today would be the ones who would have full bellies for the long winter ahead of them.

"What's indecent is Indians themselves," Reginald snarled, his eyes narrowing angrily. "They're nothing but a bunch of filthy savages. I'd hate to get near any of them. I'm sure I'd have fleas all over me from their long, filthy hair."

"Reginald!" Jessie gasped, paling at the depths of his hatred.

But her thoughts returned to the hunt at hand when the warriors began whooping and hollering as they slaughtered one cow after another. Arrows protruded from the cows that now lay on the ground, dead.

But still several remained that were not yet slain. And those that were still alive were frantic to escape as they clamored and fought to get away from the massacre.

"Lord!" Jessie cried as one of the bulls broke down a section of the fence and began running wildly down the street.

The bull was running straight toward the spot where several Indian children were playing, completely unaware of the approaching danger. Suddenly all but one of the children scattered, screaming.

Jessie saw that the one remaining child, a young brave, stood stone still, his eyes wide with fear, as the bull ran closer and closer to him.

Unable to stay there and merely watch the inevitable, Jessie jumped down from the buggy.

She lifted the hem of her skirt and raced toward the child although Reginald was screaming at her to stop. She grabbed the boy out of the way just in time to save him.

Jessie knelt down and hugged the boy, feeling his fear. He was panting in terror and clinging desperately to her.

When he said something in Cheyenne to her, she guessed that he must be saying "Thank you."

A young woman she assumed was his mother came crying and took him into her arms. Her tear-filled eyes showed Jessie just how much she appreciated what Jessie had done.

"Thank you," she finally managed to say in surprisingly good English. "Thank you for saving my son Little Sky."

"I'm so glad that I was in time," Jessie said, pushing herself to her feet.

"Jessie!" Reginald screamed, obviously embarrassed by what she had done.

He grabbed her by an arm and whisked her quickly away. Before she could say anything to him, he had rushed her into the buggy, hurrying to climb aboard beside her. They were soon on their way back down the main street, toward his home.

"Jessie, listen to what I say now," Reginald snarled. "Never do anything this foolish again. I have my name to protect."

"But I just saved a child," Jessie said, stunned by Reginald's reaction. "He . . . would have died if I had not done something to help him."

"The town was filled with people. Did you see anyone else go to help the little savage?" Reginald snapped back at her, giving her a look that turned her cold inside. "Listen to me, Jessie. Never do anything like that again to embarrass me."

"Reginald, no man of God would ever forbid someone to save a child," Jessie replied angrily, but her response seemed to infuriate him even more.

Suddenly she had to fight hard to keep herself from vomiting.

She knew this sudden urge to vomit was not only because of how she felt about Reginald and his behavior, but also . . . because she was with child.

She prayed that she wouldn't be ill. She didn't want to be forced to tell him about her child.

It was obvious that he hated children; why else would he have objected to her saving one?

But of course the child was *Indian*. She supposed that was the main reason for his anger.

"You are suddenly so pale," Reginald said, his eyebrows lifting. "You look like you might puke. Jessie—damn it, Jessie, don't puke in my buggy. Do you want me to stop?"

"No, I'm fine," she murmured, and just as they began to ride past the cribs, she saw Lee-Lee stumble back into view again in her assigned window, her hair mussed, her lipstick smeared.

Suddenly Jessie was aware of Lee-Lee looking back at her.

Their eyes met.

Now more than ever, Jessie knew she had someone else to save besides the Indian child.

She had to find a way to help Lee-Lee and at the same time save herself and Jade from this madman. She now knew beyond the shadow of a doubt that Reginald was nothing at all as he had been when they were young.

Something in his life had caused him to become deranged.

Thunder Horse was in the village council house with his warriors, discussing the upcoming hunt, when Two Stones, one of Thunder Horse's favored scouts, came in to report to him.

"Today I saw something I thought you might be interested in knowing," Two Stones said. He wore only a breechclout and moccasins. His hair hung in one long braid down his muscled back.

"And that was?" Thunder Horse asked.

"The white woman who has came to live with Reginald Vineyard showed today that she is a woman of good heart," Two Stones said.

"What did she do?" Thunder Horse asked, his heart suddenly pounding.

"She saved the Cheyenne child Little Sky from being trampled by a bull during the slaughter today," Two Stones said. "One crazed bull escaped the kill. It was headed directly toward Little Sky when the woman ran and pulled the child aside just in time to keep him from being trampled and killed."

Thunder Horse took a deep breath. Once again Jessie had proved herself to be a woman of heart . . . of courage.

Yet how could such a woman care for such a man as Reginald Vineyard? She was not only courageous, she was beautiful!

He again thought about how she had held her hands over her stomach.

Was she really pregnant? She had only recently arrived to live with Reginald. Had he met her somewhere else and married her?

Yet if she was truly with child, would she have risked losing her own baby to save the red-skinned son of another?

He was drawn from his thoughts when another warrior spoke his name.

Thunder Horse hurried into a discussion about the upcoming hunt. It was of great concern to his people. Their meat supply was low. He had allowed it to dwindle since he'd thought they would be traveling by now to the Dakotas, to join the others of their Fox band at the reservation.

But still his father lived. And while he did, life at the village must continue.

After hearing of this mock hunt today in Tombstone, Thunder Horse firmed his jaw and made a promise to himself that none of his people would ever lower themselves to such a degrading act.

But he doubted they would be put in that position, for the white chief in Washington had told him that *their* reservation was far from where the Cheyenne were imprisoned. He'd been told that the people who were already there were being treated fairly.

They even had normal hunts and normal times of merriment among themselves.

Thunder Horse hoped that the white chief in Washington was not speaking with a forked tongue!

Chapter Nine

"Come with me and I'll show you my library," Reginald said as Jessie pushed her chair back from the huge dining table. "You can content yourself with reading tonight while I go into town to attend a meeting."

Hardly able to eat her supper because she was still haunted by all that she had seen today, Jessie was glad to leave the dining room and to have something else to fill her mind.

A book would be wonderful.

Always while she read, she forgot herself and everything else as she entered another world, another time; fantasies provided a wonderful escape from the real world.

Her real world was anything but wonderful. Jessie couldn't get Lee-Lee off her mind, nor those Indians who had pretended to hunt while being laughed at by white men.

And then there was that child. If Jessie had not gotten to him in time, he would have been trampled to death.

She had been the only white person who seemed to care.

Jessie couldn't help wondering about Chief Thunder Horse and his people.

Were they also forced into such mock hunts? Did they live on a reservation like the Cheyenne?

Would she ever know? Would she ever see Thunder Horse again?

All that Jessie did know was that she was in no position to help anyone. How could she help get the young Chinese woman free when she felt more and more like a prisoner herself?

"Here it is," Reginald said as they stepped into a room where the walls were lined with shelves of expensively bound books. "Jessie, do you remember how much I loved to read when we were children?"

"Yes, I remember the times I wanted to go horseback riding and all you wanted to do was keep your nose stuck in a book," Jessie said, walking into the library with her cousin.

She was very aware of the wealth necessary to purchase all the books that lined the shelves.

Small windows at the top of the room let in some moonlight, which cast its white sheen onto a huge oak desk that sat back from the center of the room. Two rich leather sofas sat on opposite walls, and two luxurious-looking leather chairs sat before a blazing fire in the huge stone fireplace on the far wall.

"Yes, many of the boys called me a bookworm," Reginald grumbled. "Even the girls." He shrugged. "But I don't care what they said. Look at me. Look at how I live. I bet your bottom dollar I'm the wealthiest of all those we knew as children."

"No doubt you are," Jessie said, walking along one row of books and running her hands across the leather bindings.

"Choose which one you want and I'll leave you to your evening of reading," Reginald said, standing with his hands clasped behind him. "I can assure you, all are good reads."

Jessie turned to him, her eyes wide. "You've read them all?" she gasped.

"Sometimes twice," Reginald said, his eyes gleaming.

"My word," Jessie said, turning again and staring at the many volumes of books.

Reginald took it upon himself to choose a book for her. He lovingly eased it from between two others, then handed it to Jessie. "This is my favorite," he murmured. "I'm sure you'll enjoy it. It's a classic."

She took it and gazed at the title. "*Wraths Decided,*" she said, then gave him a questioning look. "What is this about?"

He chuckled. "Read it and then you will know," he said, turning and walking toward the door. "Enjoy, Cousin. Enjoy."

When he was gone from the room, Jessie sat down before the fire, stretching her legs out and resting her feet on a footstool. If she could only forget the ugliness of the things she'd discovered since her arrival in Tombstone, this could be a relaxing evening before the fire, for she did love to read.

But even after opening the book to the first page, she couldn't concentrate on reading. Too many images kept flashing before her eyes: Thunder Horse; the child she had saved; Lee-Lee. . . .

"Jessie?"

A soft, cautious voice drew Jessie quickly from her thoughts.

She looked over her shoulder as Jade came into the room, her hands clasped humbly before her.

"Jessie, did you see Lee-Lee today?" Jade asked as she went and stood before Jessie.

"Yes," Jessie murmured. "Yes, I saw her."

"Was . . . she . . . alright?" Jade asked, tears filling her eyes.

Jessie tried to blink away the memory of Lee-Lee having been chosen by a man and taken quickly from the window. She tried not to imagine what Lee-Lee had had to endure while alone with that man.

She knew better than to tell Jade about it.

"Yes, she's fine," Jessie murmured, and saw relief enter Jade's eyes.

"That's all I needed to know," Jade said, wiping the tears from her cheeks.

She looked guardedly over her shoulder, then at Jessie again. "I must go now," she said softly. "I can never allow Reginald to find us talking about Lee-Lee."

"He's gone, and I'm sure for some time," Jessie tried to reassure her.

"One never knows about him," Jade said, reaching a soft hand to Jessie's face, smiling, then hurrying from the room.

Jarred somewhat by this newest confrontation with the lovely woman, feeling so helpless to know that she couldn't help Jade or Lee-Lee when she couldn't even help herself, Jessie opened the book in the hope of being able to lose herself in the story. But no matter how hard she tried, she couldn't concentrate.

She couldn't forget everything that had happened today. She couldn't get Jade's worried look off her mind, or how her voice revealed her terrible fear for her daughter.

"This isn't working," Jessie murmured, closing the book and laying it aside on a table.

She rose and slowly paced the room, then looked toward the door as she thought of something that might distract her. She was remembering how she had always calmed herself when she was sad or troubled.

A piano.

While she was playing the piano, her soul became peaceful.

Her heart pounded now as she remembered Reginald's warning about playing his grand piano. For some reason, he absolutely forbade it.

"But he's gone," she whispered.

Her eyes brightened at the realization that he would never know she had played his piano.

Surely that would be all it would take to bring some peace to her troubled heart. And then she would go to bed.

"No, he'll never know," she whispered as she walked quickly from the library, her heart pounding with the thought of finally being able to sit at a piano again.

After her parents had died, she had found solace in the piano until the debtors came and took not only her piano, but everything else that had mattered to her.

And then when her husband had died, she had found solace in the piano at the church until the new minister took over and she felt awkward using it.

When she came to the music room, she stopped just outside the door, for she knew she was about to enter a place that was absolutely forbidden to her unless Reginald was giving a party.

And even then, the piano was forbidden to everyone there—especially, it seemed, Jessie. She would never forget his scolding look when some of the women asked her to play.

But he wasn't there now to stop her, or forbid her anything! Yet she still went cautiously into the room.

She stopped and listened for any sound of a horse approaching, just in case Reginald had returned sooner than she had thought.

He had not been gone for long, yet one could never guess what he might do next.

Yes, he was a most unpredictable man!

Hearing nothing but an occasional whinny from the corralled horses, Jessie slowly circled the grand piano, running her hands over its smooth surface, and then reverently touching the keys.

Surely if Reginald did happen to return and heard her, he would do nothing drastic.

It was only a piano, for heaven's sake—not a precious stack of silver coins like the ones she had seen him playing with more than once when she had gone past his study.

Determined to play, and casting all doubts and fears aside, Jessie sat down on the bench and placed her fingers on the keys. A feeling of peace came over her as she began playing.

The room . . . the entire house . . . was filled with the passion of the music.

She soon lost track of time, or concern about what she was doing. She didn't even hear Reginald enter the room.

She didn't know he was there until he came and slammed the lid over the piano keys, capturing her hands between the lid and the keys. She screamed in pain as he raised the lid and allowed her to pull her fingers free.

"I warned you never to play this instrument!" he screamed. "You were warned never to play my wife Sara's piano! Never! No one but Sara ever played it!"

Her fingers throbbing unmercifully, Jessie rose from the bench.

She glared at Reginald through her tears. "I've never truly known you!" she cried. "You're . . . you're . . . a monster!"

Sobbing, she ran from the house into the moonlit night and didn't stop until she reached the creek at the back of Reginald's property.

She fell to her knees and sank her hands into the cold water, momentarily numbing the pain.

"You get back here!" Reginald shouted as he came stamping toward her.

He began wheezing, almost uncontrollably.

"You get back inside that house," he gasped out. "Go to your room!"

When he came and stood over her, like some crazed animal in the night, Jessie stumbled to her feet. She gazed at him with a loathing she had never known she could feel for anyone . . . except the outlaw who had claimed her mother's and father's lives.

She knew now that she must flee this man. Somehow, she would.

She winced, then cried out with pain when he grabbed her by the wrist and half dragged her to the house. He marched her to her room and shoved her inside, slamming the door as he left.

Her hands were swollen now, the fingers throbbing even worse than before.

After a while, once Reginald was in bed, Jade came into Jessie's bedroom, carrying a bag, and closed the door behind her.

"I saw and heard it all," Jade murmured, setting the bag aside. "I've brought something to help you."

"I doubt anything can," Jessie sobbed out as Jade urged her down onto her bed.

"Let me try, Jessie," Jade softly encouraged. "Please let me try to help you."

Jessie nodded and held her hands out for Jade as the Chinese woman took several things from her bag.

"What is that?" Jessie asked.

"It's something I put together," Jade murmured. "It's

a concoction of oatmeal and glycerine. Let me place this on your hands. I'll be gentle."

Jessie nodded and watched as Jade gently applied the medicine. Jessie soon discovered that it did ease her pain somewhat.

"And now slide these soft gloves onto your hands," Jade said, handing them to Jessie. "They will make sure the medicine stays on better. I have also brought medicine that will make you sleep better tonight."

Jessie winced as she slowly pulled the gloves on. But when Jade handed a pill toward her, she shook her head. "No, I don't want anything to make me sleep," she said, her voice breaking. "I want to be aware of things around me at all times. I . . . I . . . have lost all trust in my cousin."

Then she made a quick decision. "And . . . and . . . I don't want to sleep because . . . because . . . I am leaving tonight," she blurted out. "As soon as I'm confident that Reginald is fast asleep . . . I'm . . . leaving."

"You're leaving?" Jade gasped, her eyes wide as she gazed into Jessie's.

"Yes. Tonight proved that I must not wait any longer," Jessie said, swallowing hard. "I only wish that you could go with me and that I knew how to help Lee-Lee escape from her terrible situation."

"Tonight think only of yourself," Jade said, trying to fight back tears.

Then she smiled almost wickedly as she placed her things back inside her bag. "I put a sleeping potion in Reginald's glass of milk," she said. "He drinks a glass of warm milk every night before he goes to bed."

She paused, then said, "But you must give it time to work."

"You drugged him?" Jessie said, glad to see that Jade was beginning to fight back against Reginald.

"*Ai*, yes, and you can soon leave," Jade said, picking up the bag.

"I wish you could go with me," Jessie said, searching Jade's beautiful, slanted eyes.

"If I did, my daughter would pay for it," Jade said, her voice drawn. "Nay. I cannot leave. Until my daughter is set free, I am also Reginald's prisoner."

"I'm not sure how, Jade, but I will find a way to get Lee-Lee out of that damnable crib," Jessie said firmly. "And then I'll come for you. Somehow I'll find help for you both."

"You had just better think of yourself," Jade replied. "If you can manage to get free of Reginald Vineyard, count yourself blessed. You see, I'm working on plans, myself, to get my daughter free. It'll happen one day soon. You'll see. I believe that if you can get away from this horrid place, someone will take you in and have mercy on you."

"But everyone knows Reginald," Jessie said. "No one who knows him will help me."

"I must go now to my room, but you'll find a way, Jessie," Jade said, creeping toward the door and slowly opening it. She stuck her head out and looked from side to side down the corridor, then gave Jessie a smile and hurried away.

After Jessie closed the door, she began pacing as she

waited for the right moment to leave. She truly had no idea where she would go.

Then someone came to her mind!

Thunder Horse! He was kind. He was caring.

Perhaps he could hide her until she figured a way out of her mess.

And, ah, wasn't he so handsome . . . ?

She felt she should confide her plan to Jade. She even wanted Jade to consider going with her to seek help from Thunder Horse, too.

But she knew that Jade was scared to death of Reginald and what he might do to Lee-Lee if Jade ran away. Perhaps the first step was for Jessie to escape.

She went to Jade and explained about where she was going, and from whom she would be seeking help.

Jade hugged her. "I so wish you well," she murmured. "If Thunder Horse agrees to help you, perhaps Lee-Lee and I will soon join you."

"I'm sure Thunder Horse would welcome you, too," Jessie said, then gave Jade another hug and went back to her bedroom to wait for an opportune moment to flee. She would be setting out in the darkness of night, alone, and afraid, and hoping for help from Thunder Horse.

"Will he take me in, or will he be too afraid to get involved?" she whispered as she gazed out her window, only now realizing that she had no idea where Thunder Horse's village was located.

She no longer felt as sure of her plan as before.

Chapter Ten

Thunder Horse's *ahte's* tepee was lit by the burning embers of the lodge fire. Concerned about how his father had seemed to worsen today, Thunder Horse had decided to sit with him for a while longer than usual tonight. White Horse was sleeping now on his bed of blankets and furs, a warm pelt covering him to his armpits.

Earlier, when Thunder Horse had came to see how his *ahte* was faring, he had become concerned when he heard just how labored his father's breathing was.

Thunder Horse knew that his father had these spells often now. Thus far, he had come out of them in a matter of hours. But each time he was left even weaker.

Thunder Horse knew that one of these times, his father would slip away from him to begin his long journey to the hereafter to join his ancestors in the sky.

White Horse would become one of the stars in the heavens. Thunder Horse would gaze upon them each night and know that his father would be looking down at him.

His eyes never leaving his *ahte* as he sat beside him on a blanket on the warm rush mats covering the earthen floor, Thunder Horse drew his knees up against his chest. He held them in that position by wrapping his sleeping robe tightly around his loins and knees.

In this fashion he had made of himself a rocking chair, and even now he slowly rocked back and forth, his troubled thoughts on his father. He knew that his father's time to leave this earth was near, but would it be days or weeks?

White Horse had proved to have a strong constitution and an even stronger will to live.

When Lone Wing said Thunder Horse's name outside the lodge, Thunder Horse rose and held the entrance flap aside.

"Chieftain uncle, may I sit with you?" Lone Wing asked, looking into Thunder Horse's eyes, then gazing past him, at how still White Horse lay.

"*Ho*, *hiyu-wo*, come in," Thunder Horse said thickly, stepping aside so that Lone Wing could move past him.

"He seems so still tonight," Lone Wing said as he went and stood over White Horse. "Is my grandfather worse?"

He watched Thunder Horse as he sat down by his father. He took the same position as before, again slowly rocking.

"It is hard to say," Thunder Horse said, then patted the blanket next to him. "Sit. I welcome your company."

"Should we talk? Will our voices disturb your father?" Lone Wing asked, settling down beside Thunder Horse, his own sleeping robe wrapped about his knees as he tried to imitate the way Thunder Horse was sitting and rocking.

"If we talk and my *ahte* hears us, that will be good, not bad," Thunder Horse said, gently touching his father's cheek, then drawing his hand slowly away again. "His flesh is warm enough. He is still with us for a while longer."

"He was a good chief before you," Lone Wing said softly. "But he is now . . . so . . . much smaller than I remember him being."

"Age shrinks a person sometimes," Thunder Horse said, sighing heavily. "But all who knew my *ahte* remember vividly how muscular and able he was before age took him in its iron grip. It is sad to see how much has been taken from him by aging."

"*Ho*, very sad," Lone Wing said softly.

To change the subject, Thunder Horse urged Lone Wing to talk about his own life for a while. To Thunder Horse's surprise, Lone Wing brought the white woman with the flame-colored hair into the conversation.

"I do not understand how the pretty white woman that we saw kneeling at our worship stone today could belong to such an evil-hearted man as Reginald Vineyard," Lone Wing blurted out. "Do you think she is his wife?"

Stunned that his nephew had thought of Jessie at all, much less be puzzled about who she might be married to, Thunder Horse looked quickly at him. His jaw tightened.

"I do not want to talk about another man's woman," Thunder Horse said. He gave his nephew a frowning glance. "If you want to sit with me and discuss anything further tonight, it is best that we talk about how you aspire to be our people's Historian, how you will record our people's history as we have lived it in these troubled times."

"*Ho*, that is more important than . . . than . . . a mere woman who means nothing to either of us," Lone Wing said, seeing that those words made his uncle's jaw tighten even more.

Deep down he knew that this woman did mean something special to his uncle. It was clear in Thunder Horse's eyes and voice that he felt something for her, yet apparently he denied those feelings.

The fact that she was associated with the evil white man seemed to trouble his uncle. If that white man had not appeared with his horse and buggy, Lone Wing had to wonder just where that conversation between his uncle and the flame-haired woman would have gone.

"I look forward to the time when I will be the one to record our everyday deeds," Lone Wing said, trying to change the subject. "I am learning quickly, my uncle. I want to please you."

Realizing that he had become too gruff upon the mention of the white woman, and knowing that Lone Wing did not deserve such gruffness, Thunder Horse reached a comforting hand to his nephew's shoulder. "You always please me," he said, smiling. "Always."

Lone Wing smiled broadly, but they both jumped when White Horse awakened and started coughing uncontrollably.

White Horse's eyes were wild, and he seemed to be strangling as he coughed.

"Lone Wing! Go for our shaman!" Thunder Horse cried as he bent to his knees beside his father and wrapped his arms around him, trying to comfort him as he continued to cough.

As he felt his father's body quiver and quake violently with each cough, Thunder Horse was afraid that these might be his final moments with his *ahte*.

Hawk Dreamer, their people's shaman, came hurriedly into the lodge. He carried his parfleche bag of healing materials.

"Leave him to me," Hawk Dreamer said, placing a gentle hand on Thunder Horse's shoulder. "Step aside. I will make him better."

Thunder Horse gave his father over to Hawk Dreamer's care.

He stood back with Lone Wing and watched as Hawk Dreamer ministered to White Horse until finally his coughing was under control and he was lying back down on his bed of blankets and pelts, his breathing shallow.

"He will be alright now," Hawk Dreamer said, lifting his bag into his arms. "He will sleep again and rest."

"Thank you, my shaman," Thunder Horse said, embracing him.

"But do not leave him alone," Hawk Dreamer said.

"When you leave, make certain someone else sits with your father."

"My sister takes my place when I am gone," Thunder Horse said.

Hawk Dreamer nodded, then left the tepee.

"He is going to be alright?" Lone Wing asked, coming to stand beside Thunder Horse as he stood and gazed down at his father, who was already asleep again.

"For now," Thunder Horse murmured. "Will you send your *ina* to me? I want to go and seek comfort and answers in prayer."

Lone Wing quickly embraced Thunder Horse, gazed down at White Horse, then left the tepee at a run.

Thunder Horse knelt down beside his father again. He gently touched his ashen cheek. "*Ahte*, oh, *ahte*, why must you leave me?" he said, a sob catching in his throat. "As I miss my *ina*, my sweet mother, I will sorely miss you."

His father did not respond, only continued to sleep.

When Sweet Willow came into the lodge, Thunder Horse rose to his feet and embraced her. Then he stepped away from her and gazed down at their father. "For a while tonight I thought he was leaving us," he said, his voice breaking. "But he is still with us."

He gazed into her eyes. "I must go now and pray," he said thickly.

"I will stay with him," Sweet Willow murmured. "Should anything change, I will send Lone Wing for you. You will go to your usual hillside, will you not?"

"*Ho*, I will be there," Thunder Horse said, again embracing her.

Then he stepped away from her and left his father's lodge.

He went to his own tepee and changed into breeches and shirt, putting warm moccasins on his feet.

He then ran to the hillside that was so familiar to him. His *ina* and *ahte* had brought him there when he was a child and taught him many prayers as they gazed up into the starry heavens or a brightly moonlit sky.

Tonight there were many stars but only a sliver of moon. He felt the spirits all around him as he knelt and began the prayers that always brought such peace and enlightenment to him.

Tonight, his prayers were not only for his father.

He found himself including a woman. He prayed to understand why he could not get Jessie off his mind.

After kneeling there for many hours, he came out of his prayers with a determined mind. He felt more able to accept his father's death, and he'd also come to the conclusion that he must ignore the white woman at all cost. He was on this earth to lead his people, to keep them safe, to guide them once they were all reunited on the reservation.

That last thought was a bitter one. He knew he had no choice but to take the remainder of his people to the reservation after his father died. He had given his word to the white chief in Washington.

His mind drifted to the woman again; to the woman called Jessie.

His jaw tightened as he vowed to himself never to think of her again!

Chapter Eleven

Jessie was torn by many conflicting feelings as she sat before the fireplace in her bedroom. She knew that she must leave this hellhole of a prison, yet she still could not quite believe the predicament she was in. She never would have thought that her cousin, with whom she had shared such fun and camaraderie as children, could have changed so much.

She thought about the curse that Jade said had been placed upon Reginald by Indians. Had that curse changed him?

But no. That curse must have been placed on him because of his behavior. She wondered what he might have done to cause the Indians to hate him so much.

All she knew for certain was that she did have to leave, and soon. She had her child to consider if not her own self. She would do nothing to endanger this precious being growing inside her.

Yet she had done that today, hadn't she, when she

had risked her life by saving the Indian boy? It had not even occurred to her not to save him. All she knew was that she must do what no one else had done.

And she would never forget the young brave's smile of gratitude. Yes, she had done the right thing, and as far as she knew, it had not harmed her own child.

But now?

What would her leaving do to her child? If she didn't find a place to live, where she had good nourishment while she was pregnant, wouldn't that be almost as harmful as staying with Reginald, at least until after the baby was born?

Oh, what *should* she do?

Did she truly dare leave Reginald's house? Would he come looking for her? Or would he be glad to be done with her, especially once he heard that she was with child?

He did not seem the sort who would want a child in his home.

Her thoughts went to Chief Thunder Horse. She wondered how he might react to her being with child if he did, in fact, offer her shelter in his village.

Yes, if she did go to him, what could she truly expect from him? What if he didn't want to be involved?

She was white, wasn't she? And . . . hadn't whites been inhumane in their treatment of most Indians?

"All I need is for someone to let me stay long enough so I can get my bearings," she whispered to herself.

And then there were Jade and Lee-Lee. How could

she forget their plight? They were in danger as long as they were at the mercy of her cousin.

But she had to put her child ahead of everyone. She must do what was best for her baby!

"I have no money," she whispered, rising from the chair to pace the room. With no money, she could not even travel back to Kansas City, where she did have friends who might help her in her time of trouble.

She didn't dare steal from Reginald. He would be out for blood if she dared to take anything of his.

"I have no choice but to try to find Thunder Horse's village," she said aloud, stopping.

She looked with a start toward her closed door when she heard Reginald screaming and running down the corridor. He must have had another nightmare.

But Jade had said that she'd given Reginald a potion to make him sleep more soundly than usual.

Had it, instead, intensified his nightmares?

Cold shivers raced up and down her spine when she heard Reginald screeching and hollering, "Get that snake away from me! Please, oh, Lord, save me!"

Then suddenly everything was quiet again.

Jessie wondered whether he had returned to his room, and if so, would he go to sleep again tonight?

Had her opportunity to leave passed her by? Would she have to wait another long day before finally gaining her freedom?

She hurried to the door.

She winced with pain when she placed her sore hand on the knob, then opened it very slowly and carefully just in case Reginald might still be in the corridor.

Just as she opened it, she gasped, for Reginald was on his knees only a few feet away.

His pajamas and face were wet with sweat. His eyes were glassy and wild as he looked over his shoulder and saw her standing there, her eyes wide as she stared back at him.

Jessie jumped when Reginald leaped to his feet and stepped directly in front of her.

"What are you staring at?" he stormed at her.

He grabbed her painfully by the shoulders and shook her. "Quit staring at me!" he shouted, spittle running from the corners of his mouth as he looked hysterically into her frightened eyes.

Afraid now of what he might do, for he seemed totally out of his mind, Jessie felt nauseousness sweep through her. Her shoulders hurt from his fingers digging into them as he held her in a tight grip.

"Oh, no," she cried, knowing that there was no way to hold back the vomit. It spewed out, most of it landing on Reginald's pajamas and his bare feet.

He yanked his hands away from her as he stared down at the mess all over the front of his pajamas. He shivered with disgust when he saw the vomit on his bare feet and felt the heat of it creeping between his toes.

He looked wildly at Jessie, then slapped her.

Jessie recoiled from the blow, and when Reginald seemed ready to hit her again, she took a shaky step away from him.

"Please don't," she cried as she wiped her mouth

clean of vomit with the back of her sleeve. She put her hand to her cheek. It was hot from the blow he had inflicted on her.

"I . . . I . . . am with child, Reginald," she sobbed. "Please! You might harm my baby! Reggie, oh, please remember how close we were as children. Remember how we cared for one another when either of us fell, or got stung by a bee. Reggie, please, oh, please."

He looked taken aback by her announcement. He stared at her, his gaze moving down to where her hands lay protectively over her belly.

Footsteps could be heard coming down the corridor, but he ignored Jade, even when she stopped only a few feet from him, her eyes wide, her whole body trembling. All his attention was focused on his cousin.

"Jessie, I don't want a whining brat around my house," he shouted. "Nor my expensive things. You are enough to deal with. I'll take you to Doc Storm tomorrow. He'll get rid of the baby. The baby's father is dead anyway, so why have the child?"

Jessie felt the color leaving her face and an iciness she had never known before circling her heart.

Had she heard him say those terrible things?

Did he actually think she would allow anyone to abort this child?

"How could you say such things to me?" she asked, her voice quivering with emotion. "How could you think I would agree to such a thing as that? Reginald, what has happened to you? I . . . don't . . . know you at all. You aren't anything like the boy you were those years ago."

"Just you shut up," Reginald yelled, flailing his arms in the air. "You've come here and disrupted my life by telling me you're with child, and you think I'll allow it? No, Jessie. I won't. You'll go with me to the doctor tomorrow and do as I tell you."

He shrugged. "Anyway, no one will believe you about having been married," he snarled. "They'll say that you've come this far to live with me only to hide from those you knew back where you came from . . . that you'd sinned and got pregnant out of wedlock and fled to hide the sin."

Jessie's mouth opened in a gasp; then she swallowed hard and fought back tears as she took another step away from her cousin. "Do you believe this, yourself?" she asked, a sob catching in her throat. "Don't you really believe that I was married?"

"I'd not put anything past you, for you are nothing but a stranger to me now," he said, shivering as he became suddenly aware again of the vomit on his pajamas and feet.

Then he looked up at Jessie again. "Those times when we were children are far in the past now," he said coldly. "And, anyhow, you don't know just how jealous I was of you then, because you were always healthy even though you were petite, and I was always sickly. I was poked fun at all the time because I had to wear thick-lensed glasses. I was called four-eyes. You were called beautiful."

He snickered and stared down at her stomach. "I should let you get big in your pregnancy," he said.

"You'd no longer be the belle of the ball . . . someone so pretty no other woman compared to you."

He kneaded his chin as he looked her slowly up and down, then gazed again into her eyes. "But, no, that isn't what's best for me," he said, dropping his hand to his side. "I need you to be tiny and beautiful. That brings attention to me. Yes, tomorrow I'll take you and have you fixed. You'll not be allowed to get big with child, not while you're in my house, and probably never, for I've heard that once a woman has an abortion, it messes her up forever inside."

He laughed. "That's just fine with me."

Unwilling to listen to another word, Jessie turned and rushed into her room. She closed the door between herself and Reginald as Jade stood and watched, horrified.

Again Jessie rubbed her lips, trying to erase the vile taste of vomit, then felt the heat of her face where Reginald's hand had surely left an imprint from hitting her.

"Reggie, oh, Reggie," she sobbed. "Why? Oh, why?"

Then she flinched when she heard someone being slapped out in the corridor.

She knew that Jade had just been struck.

Reginald was shouting at Jade, telling her to mind her own business and get back to her room or he'd make her wish she'd never been born.

Jessie hung her head and cried as she heard Jade's sobs and the sound of running feet as she returned to her room.

Jessie knew that she must flee, and now, before daybreak, or her future would be altered forever.

She eyed the window. Yes, she would leave as soon as she thought Reginald was asleep.

If only she could take Jade with her. But Jessie had to consider Lee-Lee's welfare. If Jade was missing, Reginald would take it out on Lee-Lee, and there was no way to help her escape the crib tonight.

Jessie's own future was in question now, and her unborn child's life lay in balance.

Everything she would do from this day forth would be for the welfare of her baby!

Chapter Twelve

Jessie couldn't believe it. She had actually been brave enough to leave Reginald's house and was now on the lovely white horse that he had given to her for her riding pleasure, never guessing that she would eventually use it to escape his madness.

With only the clothes on her back, she had fled as soon as Jade told her that Reginald was asleep again.

They had embraced, shed a few tears, and then Jade watched from the front porch as Jessie rode into the darkness of night.

Jessie was concerned at how much her hands still hurt as she took control of the horse's reins. She was glad that Jade had applied one last bit of ointment to them before she left and had slid the soft gloves onto her hands. She hoped that in a few days the hands would finally stop hurting.

But she had more on her mind than worry about her hands. She wasn't sure now what her future held for her.

As she rode beneath the stars and the sliver of moon, she had no idea where to go to find Thunder Horse's village. Finally she decided she would just ride in the direction of the sacred rock and pray that she'd find him.

And then a new thought came to her like a bolt of lightning. Even if she did find where Thunder Horse and his people lived, it would not be wise to arrive there in the middle of the night. Sentries might be posted and take her for an enemy.

She wished the moonlight were brighter, for if it were, the sentries would see that she was a woman. But the moon wasn't bright.

She had to find somewhere to stay until morning.

She glanced over her shoulder in the direction of Tombstone.

If only she could have gone there, things would have been much simpler for her.

But as it was, Reginald had the townsfolk eating out of the palm of his hand. She could not reveal to any of them that she had left him. They probably wouldn't even believe her when she told them the reason why.

Somehow he had them blinded to the sort of man he was. If they were to learn about his "cribs," ah, then they would know the devil that he truly was.

"Where can I go until morning?" she whispered as she clutched the reins, trying not to think about how painful it was to do so.

She looked to both sides of her as she rode onward, the white steed like a ghost in the night. And then she saw something that made her slow the horse to a trot as she rode toward what appeared to be an abandoned shack.

It was all but falling down, precariously leaning to one side, where several boards had rotted away, leaving sharp edges protruding from the ground. There was no smoke at the chimney, or lamplight at the windows.

As she rode up to it, she drew rein and gazed questioning at the front door, which stood agape. She knew that no one lived there except for perhaps some wild animal. She shivered at the thought that some creature might be sleeping inside.

But at least it would be a roof over her head for the night. When dawn broke, she would travel on.

With luck, she would find Thunder Horse's home.

But even if she did, would he welcome her, or turn her away?

Chapter Thirteen

The sun pouring through cobwebs at the two windows of the shack and the pain in her hands awakened Jessie.

She ached from having slept on the cold floor. Her flesh was cold and clammy beneath her clothes.

She was thankful that she had had the horse's blanket to wrap up in during the night. But the horse and the blanket were all that she had taken from her cousin's ranch.

Other than that, she was a woman without any possessions or means to fend for herself. She didn't even have a weapon.

She was so hungry her stomach ached unmercifully, but she had nothing to eat. Jessie pushed herself slowly up from the floor and folded the blanket as she looked around her.

Someone had lived in the shack, but surely a long time ago. There were cobwebs on everything, even the cooking utensils that sat on shelves over a table.

A wood-burning stove stood at one end of the room, but there was no wood, or she could have had at least some heat during the night.

She saw empty tin cans where food had once been.

She saw a dead rat, twisted and mangled in a thick cobweb at one corner of the room. She felt nauseous at the sight.

She rushed outside to where she had left the beautiful stallion secured beneath a tree. At least it could eat the thick oat grass, by its feet.

"Seems you're much luckier than I," Jessie said, slinging the blanket over the horse and then adding the saddle.

The steed gazed at Jessie with large brown eyes, then resumed munching grass.

Jessie took the time to run her fingers through her long, thick, auburn hair to get the witch's tangles out of it, then untied the reins that she had secured to a low tree limb.

She swung herself into the saddle and was on her way again. She still had no idea where to find Thunder Horse, but hoped she was heading in the right direction. She soon passed the sacred rock and continued onward.

As she rode, her hunger pangs became even more distracting than the pain in her fingers. Once again she began to wonder what she would do if she didn't find Thunder Horse.

Then her heart skipped a beat when she spotted smoke spiraling up from above the treetops. She smelled the very identifiable scent of food cooking!

Had she found the village, or some white person's ranch?

She reined the horse to a trot and rode slowly toward the smoke. As she passed through a thick stand of aspen trees, the smell of food was almost an assault on her senses, she was so painfully hungry.

Suddenly she saw something that made her heart sing. Ahead were many tepees; the smoke she had spotted was coming from the smoke holes of the Indian lodges.

She also saw several women and men coming and going, and a circle of children playing what appeared to be a game of tag. Their laughter came to her like a joyous song, for children always gave her a sense of peace.

Tears came to her eyes. She had found a safe haven from her tyrant of a cousin.

But the next moment she gasped as several warriors on horseback appeared on all sides of her. They had come so stealthily and quietly, she had not heard them until they were there, their arrows notched on their bowstrings, their eyes showing mistrust.

She drew rein and watched as one of the warriors came up to her. He slowly circled her, then stopped right beside her.

"Why are you here?" he asked in English, his voice filled with a coldness that frightened Jessie. Had she been foolish to hope that she would be welcomed here? Was this even Thunder Horse's village?

"I am looking for Chief Thunder Horse," Jessie said, her throat dry, not only from thirst and hunger, but also fear.

"And why are you looking for my chief?" the warrior Two Stones asked, his eyes filled with suspicion.

A relief that Jessie had never felt before washed through her when she learned that she had found Thunder Horse's village. Surely once he knew that she had come, all would be well. She would be greeted in a friendly way, and allowed to stay until she got her life sorted out.

"He knows me," Jessie said. "I believe he might welcome me into his lodge. Will you please take me to him?"

Two Stones looked over his shoulder at the others, who still sat on their steeds, studying her even more closely.

When they all nodded, indicating it was alright to take Jessie to their chief, the warrior closest to her turned back and nodded.

"Come," he said to Jessie, as the others lowered their weapons and removed the arrows from their bowstrings.

Finally Jessie felt safe. She hoped she would soon be welcomed by Thunder Horse. There had been an instantaneous connection between them the two times they had spoken. She wasn't sure what it meant, but only hoped that he had felt it, too.

She rode with the warriors into the village. They stopped in front of a tepee that was larger than all the others, and she knew it must belong to Thunder Horse.

Her pulse raced as she dismounted, then she smiled in pleasure as Thunder Horse emerged from his lodge.

She felt a rush of heat to her cheeks when she saw

his attire, a brief breechclout. His chest was bare, revealing his muscular body, and his hair was long and loose down his powerful back.

"Why have you come?" Thunder Horse asked, folding his arms across his chest.

He forced himself to remember what he had vowed to himself only last night. He had vowed never to think about the woman again, to forget any feelings he had for her.

Yet here she was today!

How could he forget her if she came to him, looking so pretty and sweet, her beautiful, fiery red hair as glorious as a sunset?

Yet there was something about her hair, her attire, that troubled him. Her clothes were wrinkled, her hair seemed somewhat tangled, and her eyes looked weary.

He could not help feeling concerned about her, although duty warned him away from her.

"I . . . I . . . became frightened of Reginald," Jessie said, her voice breaking. "He is a madman. I . . . left his house. I have come to you to seek shelter until . . . until . . . I can figure out what to do or where to go."

Thunder Horse saw tears in her eyes, and his heart was moved by what she had said. Still, he could not allow himself to trust any white that easily, not even a lovely woman who only yesterday had saved a Cheyenne child from being trampled.

After all, she was probably the wife of Reginald Vineyard. Reginald could have sent her as a way to trick him.

Reginald could then come to the village and claim

that Thunder Horse had abducted her to achieve vengeance against his enemy. If so, it would be the end of Thunder Horse's people.

No. He could not allow himself to trust her.

"There is no place for you here," Thunder Horse said stiffly, everything within him crying out against speaking such harsh words to this woman he would never forget. "Leave. Return to this man. I know he is using you to trick me. I will allow no harm to come to my people."

"What?" Jessie gasped. "What do you mean—a trick?"

When Thunder Horse didn't say anything else but instead stood stiffly glaring at her, his arms folded in a stern way across his massive chest, Jessie was stunned. Having believed he was a man of kindness, of courage, of integrity, she was stunned that he would turn her away, a woman in trouble.

Yes, she was white. But she had thought he would look past the color of her skin and see a woman in need . . . a woman alone.

And what on earth was this about a trick? How could Thunder Horse believe that?

She felt beaten now by two men.

She wasn't about to tell this one that he was wrong, that she was not there to trick him, that she truly was alone in the world with a baby on the way.

He wouldn't believe her.

Not sure now whom she could turn to, yet too proud to cry in front of Thunder Horse, Jessie gave him a defiant stare. Then with her chin held high, she wheeled her horse around and rode away from the young chief and his village.

Oh, where could she go? she wondered desperately.

And her fingers. They ached so much. Jade's medicine had worked, but for only a short time.

First she must find water to soak her hands in, and then she would decide what her next move would be.

She felt, oh, so very, very alone!

Chapter Fourteen

Thunder Horse watched Jessie ride away on her white horse until he could no longer see her, then dispiritedly turned and went back inside his lodge. Uneasy about what he had just done, he sat down before his fire and went over again in his mind what had just transpired between himself and the beautiful woman.

Deep down he felt he was wrong to have turned her away. The more he thought about the look in Jessie's eyes, and the pleading in her voice, the more he thought she might truly be in trouble. If not, she was quite an actress.

He hated to think that he might have sent away a woman in distress.

"Uncle?"

The voice of his nephew Lone Wing broke into Thunder Horse's thoughts. He looked quickly toward the closed entrance flap.

"*Ho*, nephew," he said. "What do you want with your uncle?"

"I wish to speak with you," Lone Wing said. "May I come in and sit with you? May I speak my mind about something?"

Thunder Horse rose to his feet and held the flap aside.

"Enter, nephew," he said. "You are always welcome in my lodge."

"*Pila-maye*, thank you," Lone Wing said, his manner a little awkward.

Thunder Horse saw much in his nephew's eyes and could guess what he wished to speak about.

The woman.

His nephew had seen the woman's plight, and believed her words.

"Sit," Thunder Horse said, gesturing toward the blankets beside the fire.

Lone Wing nodded and sat down with Thunder Horse.

"Speak your mind, nephew," Thunder Horse said, folding his legs and resting his hands on his knees as he gazed at Lone Wing.

"I heard what transpired between you and the woman," Lone Wing said, searching his uncle's black eyes. "I saw much between you, yet even more in the woman's behavior. My uncle, I listened well to what the woman said. I watched your reaction to it. I believe you said to her what you do not truly feel. You saw, as I did, how frightened she is of Reginald Vineyard."

"I have thought about all of this, too, yet still fear that she may have come because she is a part of a scheme . . . a trap . . . formed by our enemy to get back at the Sioux for having caused him many sleepless nights," Thunder Horse said tightly. "If this is so, and if I took her into our village, all would be lost for our people. That man would come and say crazy things, and he would not come alone. He would bring white authorities to witness it all. And which of us do you think the white authorities would believe? The man whose skin is white."

"I understand your fear, yet what if it is not so?" Lone Wing said softly. "What if the woman did leave because of her fear of that man, and she is alone now with nowhere to go, or no one to look after her? She is such a frail thing, more frail than any of our women."

There was a strained silence; then Lone Wing moved to his knees and faced Thunder Horse. "There is more I want to tell you," he blurted out. "Chieftain uncle, there is another woman, a woman-girl, who is entrapped by that same man. She is his slave and is forced to sell her body to evil men. I have watched her. I have seen her misery and shame. One day I waited outside her back door, and when she came out to throw water from the door, I spoke to her. She was not afraid of me. She talked. She told me things that made my heart turn cold."

"You say this woman-girl belongs to Reginald Vineyard?" Thunder Horse said. "And . . . how would you know this? Where did you see her? Which house? Why did you chance talking with her?"

"You are aware of the houses in Tombstone that men call cribs, are you not?" Lone Wing said guardedly, afraid that his uncle would scold him once he heard the entire story.

But he felt he had no choice but to tell the whole

truth. It was a way to prove that Jessie was not lying.

"*Ho*, all are aware of those evil places," Thunder Horse said, taken aback that his young nephew should know of such things.

"The girl-woman lives in one of those houses," Lone Wing said. He saw his uncle's eyes narrowing, which meant that he was fighting back anger.

But Lone Wing had begun this. He had to finish it.

"And she is not white, chieftain uncle," he said. "She is Chinese."

"Lone Wing, I know of those women. They *are* owned by whites. Are you saying that this Chinese girl-woman is owned by Reginald Vineyard?"

Lone Wing nodded, then said, "She and other women are owned by that evil man, and forced to display themselves in those windows of the cribs. Men watch and choose which one they wish to be with, then pay for some time alone with the woman. This man, who pretends with whites to be godly, is a man who owns women in order to make money with them."

Thunder Horse was not really surprised to discover that Reginald Vineyard was involved in such immoral practices. He had already proved to be a man who was evil through and through.

But it stunned him to know that his young nephew had mingled with whites and gazed at the women who stood in the windows of the cribs begging for men's money.

"Why did this girl-woman trust you so much that she told you things that could get her in trouble?" Thunder Horse asked.

"She felt safe confiding in me because I am Indian,

a people who are also mistreated by *wasichus*," Lone Wing said softly. "I could tell that she was happy to have me to talk with . . . to confide in."

He swallowed hard and lowered his eyes, then met Thunder Horse's gaze again. "And who could not look at Lee-Lee? She is so pretty. She is a sweet, soft-spoken person," he said, his voice breaking. "I . . . I . . . explained to her my own feelings about Reginald Vineyard and how that man had wronged our Sioux people. A sudden bond was made between me and Lee-Lee that day. I hope that somehow we can release her from that place she hates."

He paused, then said, "Surely Lee-Lee's need to escape is the true reason she confided in me. But now it has gone much farther than that. I care. She cares. And she is being terribly wronged by that man, as I am certain Jessie was also wronged."

"And now I have wronged Jessie, too," Thunder Horse said thickly.

He kneaded his brow as he gazed into the fire. Then he looked over at Lone Wing.

"Nephew, you risked much by talking to the girl-woman called Lee-Lee," he said sternly. "If Reginald Vineyard had come and seen you with Lee-Lee, it could only have brought trouble to our people."

"I will be more careful, but please, for now, reconsider your decision to send the white woman away," Lone Wing pleaded. "Surely Reginald will find her wandering alone and place her in a crib, for he is the sort who would impose terrible punishments on those who cross him. Chieftain uncle, I truly believe that

Jessie was telling you the truth about fleeing that man's house, and why."

"My nephew, you speak with the voice of a man today. Yes, I will go for Jessie," Thunder Horse said, rising to his feet. "I will bring her back, but much care must be made to keep Reginald Vineyard from finding out. Also, we must make certain that no white eyes learn she is here. I have promised the white chief in Washington that there will be peace between our people and the white community in exchange for allowing our Fox band to remain in this village until the day of my father's interment. I do not go back on my promises."

"What about beautiful, sweet Lee-Lee?" Lone Wing blurted out as he stood beside his uncle.

Thunder Horse placed a gentle hand on his nephew's bare shoulder. "I do not know what to think about your insistence on saving this Chinese girl-woman, nor your recklessness in meeting and speaking with her. You have a planned future among our people," he said sternly. "Your future is mapped out for you. There is no place for this girl-woman in it."

Yet even as Thunder Horse spoke, he wondered if it was truly recklessness on his nephew's part. Was not pure kindness behind everything Lone Wing did? Was not that the sort of young brave that Thunder Horse had trained him to be?

"Nephew, we must work out one problem at a time," Thunder Horse said, lowering his hand to his side. "For now, the white woman is in more peril than the Chinese. Hopefully, in time, we can find a way to help Lee-Lee, too."

Lone Wing gave Thunder Horse a hard embrace, then stepped away from him and gazed up into his eyes. "Chieftain uncle, may I go with you today as you go for the woman?" he asked, his eyes pleading.

"Lone Wing, you have much to study today in order to prepare yourself to be our people's Historian," he said. He nodded toward the entrance flap. "Go. Do your duties. I shall do mine."

Lone Wing nodded, then walked from the tepee with his uncle. He went with Thunder Horse to his corral as he led his horse from it, then watched Thunder Horse ride away at a hard gallop.

He smiled, for he knew that he had accomplished much today. Someday, Lee-Lee would be a part of his people's lives, for he would not give up on finding a way to bring her to his people's village.

Although he was a young brave, he had the ideals and thoughts of a warrior . . . of a man.

He also had the feelings of a man for beautiful, sweet Lee-Lee!

Chapter Fifteen

Crying and shivering from the shock of what she had just gone through, and feeling so alone in the world now, Jessie wasn't sure what to do, or where to go.

And her fingers! They were hurting so much! She could hardly bear to hold the horse's reins, but she had no other choice.

She had been ordered from the Sioux village by a man she had thought could never be cruel. But he had been, and to her!

He seemed a different man today, someone far removed from the man who had saved her from the runaway stagecoach.

She had no idea where to go but back to the abandoned shack. Perhaps she could make a home out of it. She could clean it up. She could gather dry wood for the stove.

But even if she did make the place livable, where would she get food? She had no weapon to kill anything.

And she had no money, even if she was brave

enough to ride into town, where almost everyone knew her now as Reginald's cousin. The scalawag had probably already sent word to everyone in Tombstone to keep an eye out for her. No doubt anyone who saw her would promptly return her to his home.

She wiped the tears from her eyes with her glove, then made her way toward the shack. But when she saw the shine of a stream up ahead, she impetuously went in that direction instead. She needed to soak her hands in the cool water again. That seemed to be the only thing that gave her some respite from the pain, if only for a moment or two.

She would soak her hands, and then go on to the shack and start cleaning away the cobwebs. She dreaded the thought of removing the dead rat. By nightfall she might at least have the cobwebs and dirt removed and a fire going in the stove.

She could only hope and pray that Reginald would not happen along and find her. Even if he did, though, she wouldn't return with him, and she doubted that he would force her at gunpoint. He surely would not go that far.

When she reached the stream, she dismounted and sank down to her knees beside the water. She slowly removed the gloves and cringed when she saw how red and swollen her fingers were. She shuddered at the thought that her hands might have actually been broken by what Reginald had done.

She sank her hands into the water, sighing at the relief she felt.

But she couldn't hold back the tears any longer. Her body shook as she sobbed.

She closed her eyes and sat there crying as she slowly swished her hands back and forth in the cool stream.

Thunder Horse had searched until he saw Jessie in the distance. As he approached, he was able to make out that she was kneeling beside a stream, her hands held in the water.

He realized that she had not gone toward Reginald's ranch, but in the opposite direction. That could prove that Lone Wing was right.

His jaw tight, he dismounted and tethered his horse to a tree. He continued on foot, his footsteps so quiet she didn't hear him.

When he had almost reached her, he stood a few feet away and watched as she drew her hands from the water. He was stunned to see how red and swollen they were. Carefully she slid them back into her gloves, and he realized that was why he hadn't noticed their condition earlier.

Jessie rose and turned, gasping with surprise when she found Thunder Horse standing only a few feet away from her.

"I was wrong to send you away," he said thickly. "Your hands. How were they injured?"

She hesitated, then told him about how Reginald had forbidden her to play the piano, how she had done it anyway, then how he had injured her hands in his fury.

Touched by her story, and now certain that she was

in need of his help, he stepped closer and gazed apologetically into her eyes.

"Come home with me," he said huskily. "I have a shaman who knows all the skills of healing. And . . . Jessie . . . you can stay with my people as long as you need . . . to feel safe."

Overjoyed by his change of heart, and his gentleness, Jessie could not help herself. She ran to him and flung herself into his strong arms.

"Thank you, thank you," she sobbed. "Oh, Thunder Horse, thank you so much."

He felt the sweetness of her embrace and smelled the wildflower freshness of her hair as his nose was pressed into it. He was stunned to find her in his arms.

Realizing the boldness of what she had done, Jessie stepped away from him.

Their eyes met and held.

"Reginald is my cousin," she blurted out, then told Thunder Horse how she had come to live with him, but left out several of the reasons why.

She didn't tell him about her husband's death, nor her parents', which had left her alone in the world except for Reginald. And also she did not reveal that she was with child. She thought it would be better to explain those matters later.

She felt something beautiful flower in her heart as she looked again into Thunder Horse's eyes. It was something she had never felt before.

Her husband had been more friend than lover. Their relationship had never been passionate.

For the first time in her life, she felt sexual attraction for a man. But she knew that she must fight these feelings.

He was an Indian. He was a powerful chief with much more on his mind than the welfare of a mere woman.

Thunder Horse was vastly relieved to know that Jessie didn't belong in any way to Reginald Vineyard, that she wasn't his wife, but a cousin.

He knew now that she was free to be loved, yet he reminded himself again that his first duty was to his people, especially his ailing father.

It was wrong to become romantically involved with any woman at this time, especially one with white skin.

But he did feel many things for Jessie; feelings he found hard to fight.

For now, the first thing he must do was to get her to safety at his village. All else would come later.

Strange how knowing that she wasn't married made him feel giddy—a new feeling for him!

He walked her to her horse and helped her into the saddle, then went to his sorrel and swung himself onto its back. They rode off together toward his village.

Jessie prayed to herself that Reginald would never find her, or it could bring trouble not only to herself, but also to Thunder Horse and his people. She knew the history of the Indians in this area, and realized that none of them needed any more trouble from whites. Whites had already taken almost everything from them, including their freedom.

But what did remain was pride.

She saw it in Thunder Horse's every movement, and heard it in everything he said.

He was more of a man than most white men ever could be!

Chapter Sixteen

Lone Wing stood just outside Thunder Horse's tepee as his chieftain uncle rode toward it, the flame-haired woman called Jessie riding beside him on a magnificent white steed.

Lone Wing smiled proudly at Thunder Horse as their eyes met. He was so proud that his uncle had done as he'd asked.

The woman, ah, she was so beautiful, and so vulnerable, but now no longer alone.

He looked around, noticing how all activity in the village had stopped as everyone watched the arrival of their chief with a white woman. Lone Wing saw a mixture of emotions in the people's eyes.

Some showed contempt for the woman because she was white. Some showed wonder that their chief had gone to get a woman they had all heard him order away only a short while before.

Lone Wing smiled at that, certain they would all know in time why their chief had changed his mind.

"Lone Wing, go for Hawk Dreamer," Thunder Horse said as he drew rein before his lodge. He nodded at a young brave who stood nearby. "Little Wolf, come and take my horse and the woman's. See that they are put safely in my corral."

Thunder Horse dismounted and handed both reins to the brave, then went and helped Jessie from her steed and motioned toward his entrance flap with the wave of a hand.

"Come with me," he said. "My nephew has gone for our village shaman. He will look at your hands and place medicine on them that should make them feel better soon."

Touched deeply by Thunder Horse's change of heart, Jessie could not say thank you enough times to prove her gratitude, but she said it again anyway.

"You are so kind," she murmured. "Thank you so much, Chief Thunder Horse."

When he took one of her hands, Jessie felt her knees grow suddenly weak from the passion his touch invoked within her, for he was not only holding her hand, but also gazing into her eyes with a look that melted her heart.

"You do not need to address me as chief ever again," Thunder Horse said, searching her eyes with his. "I am Thunder Horse to you and my closest friends."

"Thank you, Thun—" she began, but was interrupted by him.

"And you need not thank me for every kindness I give you," he said, his eyes dancing with quiet amusement. He nodded toward the entrance flap. "Let us go inside and make ourselves comfortable beside the fire.

My shaman should be on his way here. He always comes quickly when I summon him."

Feeling as though she were in a dream, afraid that she might wake up at any moment and find herself back at that shack, or worse yet, in her bedroom at her cousin's house, with Reginald only a few footsteps away in the corridor, Jessie entered the lodge with Thunder Horse. She caught her breath at what she saw inside.

It was obviously a chief's lodge, for everything she saw was of exceptionally fine workmanship. She gazed at a long, eagle-feathered staff, as well as a lance that was also adorned with eagle feathers. She saw magnificent bows and a quiver of arrows hanging from one of the support poles of the lodge. And there was a buffalo-hide shield with colorful drawings on it, which she thought were surely the symbols of a great warrior's life.

But her eyes were taken from all this when Thunder Horse led her to a soft pallet of blankets beside a warm fire that was built into the ground and encircled by large stones.

One thing was certain: This was the lodge of a man. No woman's belongings were anywhere to be seen. Surely Thunder Horse had no wife!

That thought caused a tingling in Jessie's belly that was new to her. How deliciously sweet it was!

"Here is a blanket to warm you, too," Thunder Horse said as she sat down. He placed a lovely blanket of fine blue wool, heavily and tastefully adorned with silk ribbons of various colors, around her shoulders.

She gazed up at him and almost said thank you again, but instead smiled when she saw him smiling at her as if he knew what she was about to do.

He knew how grateful she was for his change of heart.

Yet how could she ever really convey her gratitude? If he had not come for her, her entire future would be in doubt, as well as that of her unborn child.

Now perhaps she had a chance. If Thunder Horse allowed her to stay until she had her future mapped out for herself, she might be able to figure out a way to make a living for her and her child without having to return to Kansas.

Deep inside her heart she wished to stay with Thunder Horse, forever and ever. She had feelings for him that she had never felt before for any man, but she doubted he would allow it. His kindness would go only so far. She was white. She had seen a look of contempt in some of his people's eyes and knew that to them she was one of the enemy, no different from the whites who had taken so much from them.

She would take this one day at a time and just be thankful she was no longer alone, frightened, and helpless. She would enjoy being with him for as long as she could remain.

Her thoughts were interrupted when Lone Wing entered the tepee, followed by a tall, gangly, elderly man wearing a robe of what she thought might be bear's fur. His copper face was framed by long gray hair.

Jessie was relieved when she looked into his eyes and saw no contempt, but instead the same kindness that she found in Thunder Horse's gaze.

She looked at the huge buckskin bag he set down beside himself as he knelt before her. "I am Hawk Dreamer," he said in a deep voice, smiling. "I am the Fox band's shaman. Lone Wing tells me that your hands need medicine. Let me see them. I will choose which medicine is best."

Jessie removed her gloves, laid them across her lap, then held her hands out for Hawk Dreamer.

When he touched her during his examination, his hands were gentle. She smiled at Thunder Horse, who had sat down beside her, with Lone Wing on his right side, his eyes wide and anxious as he looked past his uncle at her.

At first, when she heard that a shaman would be doctoring her hands, she had been apprehensive, for she had heard about Indian medicine men. She had been told that many worked with black magic.

But thus far, the shaman had done nothing that seemed wrong. He was just a kind and gentle man who was trying to help her.

He let go of her hands and reached inside his bag. He took out two vials and set them on the floor beside her.

He gave Jessie a reassuring smile, then scooped out a white, creamy substance, which he gently rubbed into her fingers. Surprisingly, the pain faded more with each gentle rub.

When Hawk Dreamer drew his hands away from Jessie's and returned the vials to the bag, she gazed in wonder at Thunder Horse.

He smiled and nodded at her, then looked at Hawk Dreamer, who had stood and was already walking toward the entrance flap. No words were exchanged between the chief and the shaman, for it was obvious to Jessie that words were not needed between these two. There seemed a connection between them that spoke of friendship, trust, and love.

Lone Wing came and knelt down beside Jessie as she gazed in wonder at her fingers and hands, which were still shiny from the cream.

"Do they feel better?" Lone Wing asked, his eyes wide as he looked into Jessie's.

"Much," Jessie said, smiling at Lone Wing. "But I think I should still wear the gloves, don't you?"

She purposely brought him into the decision, for he seemed genuinely interested in her welfare.

"Do they make your hands feel better?" Lone Wing asked, his eyes studying the gloves as she slid them onto her hands.

"Usually," she murmured.

"Then I would wear them if I were you," Lone Wing said, smiling broadly as she looked at him.

"Lone Wing, go to my *ahte's* lodge," Thunder Horse said, bending down on a knee beside his nephew. "If my *ahte* is awake, tell him I will come to his lodge soon and with me will be a friend. But do not alert him yet as to who. Especially do not tell him that my friend is a white woman."

Lone Wing nodded, gave Jessie another winsome smile, then leaped to his feet and ran from the tepee.

But Jessie wasn't smiling now. She had heard what Thunder Horse had said to Lone Wing.

She was going to be taken to Thunder Horse's father's lodge and be introduced to him. If his father didn't approve of her being in their camp, would Thunder Horse have no choice but to send her away?

Yet . . . Thunder Horse was the chief. He surely had the final word in his village.

She felt reassured as Thunder Horse took her by the hand and helped her to her feet. He took the blanket from her shoulders and laid it aside, then placed his hands at her waist and brought her closer to him. Their eyes met.

"My father is gravely ill," he said thickly. "If not for his failing health, and his relationship with the white chief in Washington, all of my people would even now be housed on the reservation."

He went on to explain the situation to her, how his father would be buried among the other departed chiefs in the sacred cave, and then how the rest of his people would go on to the reservation, where the others awaited them.

Hearing that he would be moving from this area when his father died, Jessie realized how fortunate she was to have made Thunder Horse's acquaintance before he left. How alone she would have felt without him.

Strange how she now felt as though she would never be alone again, even though she knew he would ultimately say that she couldn't stay with him forever. Once his father died, his people would begin their solemn journey to the reservation.

"You can stay with me and my people at our village as long as you wish," Thunder Horse said, stunning

Jessie, for it was as though he had read her mind!

"If you like, you can even go with us to the reservation in the Dakotas when the time comes," Thunder Horse said, searching her eyes. "It is a place totally separate from the white community. No one will interfere if you wish to stay there. And the reservation is far from Tombstone—so far that Reginald Vineyard will never know that you have gone there with me and my people. You will be safe from him there."

He searched her eyes, then said, "Will you go with me and my people to the reservation? I would not like to leave you behind, not knowing what might happen to you without my protection."

She was stunned that he had actually asked her to go with him, that he cared enough to see himself as her protector. With his hands still at her waist and their bodies only a few inches apart, Jessie was overwhelmed by her feelings for him. For a moment she was at a loss for words.

Then, afraid she was misinterpreting his feelings toward her, she cleared her throat uneasily and eased herself from his hands.

"Perhaps I should return to Kansas City," she murmured, even knowing as she said it that she had no money to travel anywhere.

And again she thought of Jade and Lee-Lee. Whatever she decided to do for herself, she wished she could include the two Chinese women.

But for now, she must do what was best for her child, to secure him or her a decent future.

Wondering what he might have said to make her draw away from his hands and turn down his suggestion to join him and his people, Thunder Horse said nothing for a moment. Instead, he gazed deeply into Jessie's eyes, trying to understand the meaning behind her words.

Then he said, "Is there a man in this place called Kansas City awaiting your arrival, someone who will see to your welfare?"

Feeling more certain by the minute that he truly did care for her, and was honestly worried about her welfare, Jessie lowered her eyes. She was wishing that she hadn't even mentioned Kansas City, for she wanted nothing more than to stay with Thunder Horse.

"No, no man is waiting for me there," she murmured. "The man I was married to in Kansas City is . . . dead."

"You were married?" Thunder Horse said, placing a gentle hand under her chin and lifting it so that her eyes met his. "The man . . . is dead?"

"Yes. He was killed in a most horrible way," she said, her voice breaking. Then she explained at length about how her husband had died and why she had come to Tombstone to live with her only remaining relative, her cousin.

She shuddered. "That name Tombstone alone should have warned me what I would find there," she said. "Meanness . . . greed . . . and . . ."

"And?" he said, again searching her eyes.

She told him about Jade and Lee-Lee and the danger

they were in, and from whom . . . the same man she had fled.

The mention of Lee-Lee made Thunder Horse's eyes widen. "I already know about the one called Lee-Lee," he said. "Lone Wing has seen and talked with her and knows that she is a prisoner of Reginald Vineyard, just as you would have been if you had stayed with him."

"Lee-Lee's mother, Jade, works for my cousin. She fears him dreadfully," Jessie said, shuddering. "I hated leaving Jade behind, but I didn't know if I would really be able to escape my cousin."

"Chieftain uncle, your father is awake and awaits your arrival," Lone Wing said as he held the entrance flap aside.

"*Pila-maye*, thank you, Lone Wing," Thunder Horse said, stepping away from Jessie and going to the entrance flap. "You can go and tell my sister that we will soon arrive."

Lone Wing gave Jessie a smile, nodded at Thunder Horse, then was gone again.

"He is a good nephew," Thunder Horse said, smiling at Jessie as he held aside the flap for her. "*Hiya-wo*, come. My *ahte* awaits our arrival."

Jessie could not help being a little afraid of meeting the ailing, elderly man. If he didn't approve of her, would he say so? Or would he keep his thoughts to himself?

She left the tepee with Thunder Horse and tried to avoid eye contact with the Sioux men and women as they stopped what they were doing to stare at her. If they knew she was going to stay among them, she wondered what they might do or say.

For the moment, that was not her concern. She must concentrate on meeting Thunder Horse's father.

"You mentioned a sister to Lone Wing," Jessie said as she gazed up at Thunder Horse.

"She is Lone Wing's mother. She sits with my father most times," he said tightly. "When she is not there, she prepares food for my father, herself, Lone Wing, and me."

"She sounds like a wonderful, caring person," Jessie replied, her heart pounding when she saw how close they were to a large tepee that sat among other smaller ones. She knew it had to be his father's lodge.

"Like you, she is a widow, and yes, she is a wonderful, caring person," Thunder Horse said as he stopped just outside the large tepee. "This is my father's lodge. Come inside with me."

She swallowed hard, then went with him.

A warm fire burned in the lodge's firepit. On the far side lay an elderly man on pelts and blankets, his gray hair surrounding his head on the pelts like a halo. At this moment his eyes were closed, his hands lying folded on his stomach, which was covered by a blanket.

Then she became aware of the beautiful Indian woman who sat on one side of the elderly man. When she caught sight of Jessie, she broke into a smile.

Introductions were made, and just as Jessie sat down on the other side of the fire, opposite Sweet Willow, the elderly Indian's eyes slowly opened.

He gazed at her for a long time, then looked over at Thunder Horse, who now sat down beside Jessie.

Jessie was only scarcely aware that Lone Wing had entered the tepee and now stood behind her and Thunder Horse.

"Why is she here?" White Horse asked as he frowned at Thunder Horse.

Thunder Horse looked over his shoulder at Lone Wing and questioned him with his eyes.

Lone Wing shrugged slightly, as if to say that he had told White Horse about Thunder Horse bringing a visitor, but it seemed that once again the elderly man's memory had failed him.

"*Ahte*, this is Jessie," Thunder Horse murmured, then explained why she was in their village.

"My *micinksi*, my son, the presence of whites in our village can only mean trouble, especially if that white person is a *mitawin*," White Horse said gruffly. "My son, send . . . her . . . away!"

Thunder Horse had never disobeyed his father and hated to now, when he was so ill and near death, but he could not agree with him.

He most certainly could not . . . would not . . . send Jessie away.

She was alone in the world, and something made him recall those times she had stood with her hands across her belly, as women do when they unconsciously protect the child inside their womb.

Thunder Horse looked over his shoulder at Lone Wing again. "Lone Wing, take Jessie outside," he said firmly.

Lone Wing reached a hand out for Jessie, which she took. She rose to her feet and gave Thunder Horse one last look, then left the tepee to stand just outside the entranceway while Thunder Horse talked with his father.

She was afraid now, afraid that Thunder Horse might not have any choice but to do as his father told him. Then where would she go?

Thunder Horse spoke gently to his father as Sweet Willow sat and bathed White Horse's brow. Thunder Horse explained how alone Jessie was and that he would not allow trouble to come to their village. He had enough sentries posted to protect their people.

He also explained that he believed she was with child. Who could send a pregnant woman away to fend for herself?

And if that man Reginald found her, Thunder Horse even feared for her life.

His father, whose heart was kind, and who was a *wicasa-iyotanyapi*, a man of honor, sighed deeply. "She can stay," he said, his voice drawn. "Though I would prefer that she go on her way, for she truly has no place among the Sioux."

He smiled at Thunder Horse. "But, *ho*, she can stay if that is what you want, my son," he said softly.

Thunder Horse reached out, bent over his father, and hugged him. "*Pila-maye*, thank you, for your understanding," he said softly. He thought about what his father had said about Jessie having no place among their Sioux people.

Thunder Horse knew just how wrong that was, for he had feelings for her that he was finding hard to fight. He would never forget how it felt to hold her in his arms . . . the sweetness of it.

He smiled at his sister, then rose and went outside, where Jessie still stood with Lone Wing.

When she looked up at him, with a question in her eyes, he smiled and reassured her quickly about the outcome of that short meeting with his father.

"It is alright for you to stay," he said, smiling. "I will have a place prepared for you. In the meantime, you can join me and my nephew in my lodge. It is time for Lone Wing's lessons today."

"Lessons?" Jessie said, raising an eyebrow. "Will . . . will I be in the way?"

"Never," Thunder Horse and Lone Wing said almost in the same breath.

She smiled from one to the other, then walked proudly with them back to Thunder Horse's lodge. On the way, she noticed that the people no longer stopped or stared at her.

She could only conclude that they had seen her enter White Horse's lodge and leave it smiling, which had to mean that Thunder Horse's father had welcomed her into their village.

She went inside Thunder Horse's tepee with him and Lone Wing and sat down on a blanket with them, amazed at how Lone Wing's behavior became more serious and adult as he and Thunder Horse discussed his lessons.

Lone Wing suddenly turned to Jessie. "I am studying to be our people's Historian," he blurted out, then explained what that meant.

She hung on his every word, amazed that he knew so much about his people's history. She was fascinated by their customs and was beginning to want to be a part of them.

Yes, she sorely wanted to stay with these people, with Thunder Horse and Lone Wing forever.

She gazed at Thunder Horse and remembered his invitation to stay with him. Soon she would tell him that she truly wanted to . . . that she would!

But . . . then what about her child? Would he still want Jessie . . . if . . . he knew about the child?

Chapter Seventeen

Learning everything she could about Thunder Horse, his people, and his family, Jessie sat across the fire from Lone Wing, impressed by how devoted he was not only to his uncle, but also to his lessons.

Lone Wing's mother had brought them food, all of which had been eaten. Jessie was feeling comfortably full as she and Lone Wing listened to his uncle telling a myth. Lone Wing would learn it and repeat the myth back to his uncle in a few days.

This was one of many ways he was preparing to become his people's Historian. When the "Old One" who was presently their Historian passed on to the other world or was no longer able to think clearly enough to record things, Lone Wing would take his place. Lone Wing had been chosen, not because he was their chief's nephew, but because he had aspired to be the Historian from the time he was old enough to realize the importance of this role.

He had proven his worth to his people already, yet

he continued to expand upon his knowledge so that he would be the best Historian his people had ever known!

"Listen well, nephew, to the myth that I am about to tell you," Thunder Horse said. "You know that even at your young age you could assume the task of preserving and transmitting the legends of our ancestors and our race."

Thunder Horse was very aware that Jessie was sitting across the fire from him, and that she was watching him closely.

He had looked up at her from time to time, returning her smile when she smiled at him, then had gone back to his nephew's lesson. This was the time of day when Lone Wing came to him for instruction. It would not change because someone new sat in Thunder Horse's lodge.

He knew that Jessie was interested in what he did and said, for she was attentive to all of it. That was good, for if he had any control over her decision at all, she would never return to her world. She would become part of his.

"Jessie, even at Lone Wing's young age, he could become our Historian," Thunder Horse said, wanting to make certain that she understood why his nephew's lessons were so important. "Almost every evening in my people's lodges where there are children, a myth or a true story of some great deed, is narrated by parents or grandparents. The children listen with parted lips and glistening eyes, for they all want to be able to tell the same tales to their own children in the future."

He smiled at Lone Wing and placed a gentle hand on his shoulder. "But only one of those braves has been singled out to know *all* of those myths and stories," he said proudly. "My nephew is a keen listener and has a good memory. The stories and myths are easily mastered by him. The teachings that began when he was old enough to realize their importance enlightened his mind and stimulated his ambition. His conception of his own future became a vivid and irresistible force. Whatever there was for my nephew to learn, he would learn."

"I hope I'm not a distraction," Jessie said, looking slowly from Thunder Horse to Lone Wing. "Will I be?"

"No, never," Thunder Horse said quickly. "You, too, will learn from the myth that I will tell today. You do want to learn, do you not?"

Jessie's eyes widened. "Oh, yes, I do, so very much," she said softly. "I want to know everything that I can about you and your people, since . . . I . . . will be living here among you."

Thunder Horse's heart skipped a beat, for he could not help hoping, from the way she said she would be living among his people, that she wanted to be there forever!

Or did she mean that she needed to understand his people to make it easier for her during the time she would be there . . . until she found somewhere else to go, or someone to care for her?

He looked quickly away from her and tried to focus on the lessons instead of thinking too much about Jessie.

"There once was a young brave who was called by the name Proud Boy," Thunder Horse began, forcing his eyes to see only his nephew, not the woman. "He wandered along many trails. One day, when he came to a lonesome place beside a river, he sat for a long time and listened and heard things."

"What kind of things?" Lone Wing asked, not for the sake of interruption, but in order to understand today's myth fully.

"All things," Thunder Horse said, slowly nodding.

"Tell me more," Lone Wing urged, leaning forward, his eyes wide as he became totally involved in the story.

"There was a meadow place where an old doe lived with two spotted fawns," Thunder Horse continued. "On this day the young brave saw the doe, but not the fawns. He knew they must be hidden somewhere in the long grass in the meadow. The afternoon was warm. Mosquitoes bothered him a great deal, but he knew that the fawns would not move from their beds until their mother came to them. So he waited."

Thunder Horse paused, slid a slow gaze at Jessie, whom he found as taken by the story as was Lone Wing, then turned his eyes back to his nephew and continued. "A rabbit bobbed across the trail not far from Proud Boy," he said. "When it entered the bushes, it turned suddenly and almost ran into Proud Boy's foot. Something had scared the rabbit. Proud Boy's eyes searched the bushes. He wanted to see what might have frightened the rabbit, because it might be something that he also should run from. His eyes widened when he thought he saw a man's nose."

Thunder Horse smiled at Lone Wolf and Jessie. "But Proud Boy knew that sometimes shadows and sunshine play tricks in the forest," he said. "He looked steadily at the nose and waited. Then he thought he saw an eye, but it did not wink. It did not move, but stared straight ahead."

He chuckled when he saw Lone Wolf get up on his knees, his eyes wide and filled with wonder. "But Proud Boy knew that if it was a man's eye, it had to blink sometime," he said. "Suddenly there were more mosquitoes than ever. But Proud Boy did not dare brush them off for fear that the eye would blink and he would not see it."

He paused, then continued. "A breeze suddenly moved the leaves on the bushes," he said. "A braid of hair was then revealed to Proud Boy. And he thought that the eye might have blinked! Proud Boy spoke to the unknown one, but the unknown one did not speak back. Thinking that he was imagining all of this, Proud Boy rose to leave, but a voice spoke to him from behind the bushes. The voice said that he was one of the Echo People. He told Proud Boy that Echo People always hide behind rocks and bushes, that they speak every language and make every note the large birds make."

"Echo People?" Lone Wing asked. "I have heard of them. They are everywhere."

"*Ho*, nephew, wherever there are voices or birdsong

or coyote calls, there are Echo People," Thunder Horse said, nodding. "But this day, Proud Boy did not actually see or hear one of the Echo People."

"Then who was it that hid behind the bushes?" Lone Wing asked, his eyes widening even more.

"Proud Boy's imagination conjured him up," Thunder Horse said, laughing softly.

"But the Echo Person spoke to him," Lone Wing said, settling back down again on the blankets.

"Nephew, Proud Boy did not have only a vivid imagination, but he also sometimes talked to himself," Thunder Horse said, then reached a hand over and patted Lone Wing's bare shoulder. "Think about that when you walk to your lodge. And, Lone Wing, *hakadah*, look closely at everything *you* see and hear. Notice which side of the tree has the lighter-colored bark, and which side has the most regular branches. Now answer me this, nephew: How do you know there are fish in yonder lake?"

"Because they jump out of the water for flies at midday," Lone Wing said, pushing himself up to stand beside his uncle, who smiled proudly down at him.

"*Ho*, that is so," Thunder Horse said. "Go now. Think about your lessons today. Soon you can repeat the story, but put your own twist to it, nephew. Make it interesting and fun."

"I will," Lone Wing said. He smiled at Jessie. "I will see you again soon."

"Yes, soon," Jessie murmured. She said nothing else until the youth was out of the tepee; then she smiled at Thunder Horse. "That was all so very interesting."

"I did not get as serious as usual in my lessons today because I wanted to make your time listening to them more relaxed," Thunder Horse said, shoving a log into the flames of the fire.

"I did enjoy it," Jessie said, nodding. "And Lone Wing is such an astute student."

"He is already well enough prepared to become our Historian should fate require it before he grows into full maturity," he said thickly. "One never knows what tomorrow may bring, especially in these days when so much has been taken from my people."

"And I am blood kin to one of those who took so much from you and your people," Jessie murmured, lowering her eyes.

She looked quickly up at Thunder Horse again, her heart skipping a beat when she found that he had come around the fire and was now sitting beside her on the pallet of blankets.

She felt a blush heat her cheeks. He was so close she could reach out and touch him, and she was so tempted to do it.

She loved touching his smooth copper skin. She loved everything about him.

"*Ho*, Reginald Vineyard is one of those who took much from my band of people," Thunder Horse said, nodding. He gazed into the flames of the fire. "But he is paying for it. Every night he pays."

"What do you mean?" Jessie asked, suddenly picturing Reginald crying out as he ran down the corridor after having a frightful nightmare.

"Your cousin is visited by the spirits of my people's

sacred cave," Thunder Horse said, slowly turning his eyes back to Jessie. "Does he not experience the dreams that whites call nightmares?"

"Yes, he has nightmares," Jessie said breathlessly, her heart pounding in her chest. "How would you know that?"

"Because that was what was necessary to make him realize the evil he did by entering my people's sacred burial cave and disturbing the dead. He took white gold from the walls where the stories of my people were drawn long ago," Thunder Horse said thickly.

"The cave where he found the silver was—"

"A sacred burial place for the chiefs of my people," Thunder Horse said, interrupting her. "It is the cave where my own father will be placed when he finds peace in death."

"Then it *is* a curse that causes Reginald's nightmares," Jessie said, now recalling Jade telling her something about an Indian's curse.

"Let me tell you everything," Thunder Horse said, reaching over and taking her hands in his.

"Yes, please tell me," she murmured.

She swallowed hard as his eyes searched hers. Then he began the tale that explained Reginald's nightmares.

"The curse is having the effect you wished it would have on Reginald," Jessie said once Thunder Horse came to the end of the tale.

"And you?" Thunder Horse asked, gazing deeply into her eyes. "How do you feel about it?"

"I hate to say it, because of what Reginald once was

to me, but he has become an evil man, deserving of what you have chosen to do to torment him," Jessie replied.

"Tomorrow a hunt is planned," Thunder Horse said, suddenly changing the subject. "I do not want to leave you here at the village without me. Will you join me on the hunt?"

"I thought it was taboo for women to join in the hunt," Jessie murmured.

"Not if the chief requests her company," Thunder Horse said, placing his arms around her waist and drawing her closer to him. "And I am requesting it of you. Will you come?"

"Won't I be in the way?" she asked, feeling his breath hot against her lips.

"Do you truly think I would ever see you as someone 'in the way,' as you call it?" he asked, then brought his lips down upon hers in a fiery kiss.

With an effort, Jessie forced herself back to reality. She was not yet ready to give herself to him completely, especially since she had the child to consider. She eased from his arms.

She gazed into his eyes. "It . . . is . . . too soon," she murmured.

"I understand," he said. "It is enough for me just to have you with me, where you are safe."

"Yes, I feel very, very safe," Jessie said as she snuggled against him when he placed an arm around her waist and drew her close to him. "Never have I felt as safe as I do when I am with you."

"You have brought more into my world than you can

know," Thunder Horse said thickly. He left it at that, for he did not want to reveal everything he felt for her just yet.

He knew now that he had plenty of time to do that, for he could tell that she was not planning to go anywhere. It was the way she had said, "It is too soon," that told him there would be something more, later.

He had learned the art of waiting long ago. He smiled when he thought of how he felt when he had to wait for something special . . . waiting always enhanced the pleasure!

Chapter Eighteen

As the sun came through the dining-room window, casting light on the empty chair where Jessie normally sat, Reginald frowned and drummed his fingers against the tabletop.

When Jade came into the room carrying a platter piled high with bacon, flapjacks, and fried eggs, Reginald gave her a quick questioning frown.

He slammed a fist on the table just as she set the platter down, causing it to bounce. Some of the eggs slipped from the platter, their yolks breaking and running like orange tears across the white linen tablecloth.

"Where is she?" Reginald shouted, then suddenly began wheezing. "Jade, where is Jessie? She knows she's supposed to take breakfast with me."

Jade clasped her hands before her, wringing them as she glanced fearfully at Reginald. "I don't know where she is, sir," she said, her voice breaking.

"Are you telling me you haven't seen her?" Reginald demanded, his eyes narrowing angrily. "You normally help her dress in the morning. You brush her hair. So, where is she?"

Jade lowered her eyes, swallowed hard, then dared to look into Reginald's angry eyes again. Through the thick lenses of his spectacles his angry eyes seemed ten times larger than normal this morning.

"Nay I have not seen her," she murmured, still clasping and unclasping her hands.

"Stop that nonsense with your hands!" Reginald shouted. He coughed into his palm. "Stand still. Answer my questions. Do you hear? Tell me where Jessie is."

"As I said, sir, I have not seen her this morning," Jade gulped out, her heart pounding like a sledgehammer. "When I went to her room to awaken her, she . . . she . . . was gone."

"She was gone?" Reginald said, jumping from his chair so quickly it tumbled to the floor behind him. "Are you saying she's gone from my house?"

"Seems so, sir," Jade said, swallowing hard as she hid her hands inside her apron pockets.

Reginald threw his white linen napkin on the table, then swirled around and stamped from the room. Wheezing almost uncontrollably, he hurried to Jessie's bedroom.

He stared at the bed.

Either Jessie had made it upon first arising, which he doubted, or she had not slept in it at all.

His eyes slid slowly over to a window that was open. As he stuck his head out of it, he shouted Jessie's name at the top of his lungs.

Realizing now that she had run away, he paled. But then another possibility occured to him.

Yes!

No doubt she had risen at dawn and was even now out riding the lovely horse he had given her. He felt stupid for having gotten so alarmed just because Jessie wasn't at the breakfast table. Yet . . . it did appear that she had not slept at the house. And why was the window open?

The nights were cool, so she wouldn't have slept with it open.

His mind aswirl with questions, he hurried from the room and went out to the corral, where he found the horse he had given Jessie gone as well. Yes, she was horseback riding and would surely return soon to have breakfast with him.

It was foolish of him to think otherwise. She had no one to go to should she decide to leave his home. And she had no money to pay for her passage back to Kansas City.

Yes, she was horseback riding and he would wait for her on the porch. He would scold her and tell her never to do this again. He needed to know where she was at all times. She was not familiar with this land and she could get lost and be attacked again by outlaws, or . . . Indians.

His heart went cold to think that someone might do harm to his cousin. Although she had tried his patience recently, and he had not been all that kind to her at times, he did love her and wanted nothing to happen to her.

And . . . she was with child. She had to think about her baby. She would do nothing to endanger it.

He stood and stared into the distance, watching for any signs of someone approaching on horseback. Surely she would return soon.

But as the sun rose higher in the sky, and then began making its descent, and still there was no sign of Jessie, Reginald's anger began to swell within him.

He was feeling duped. He no longer believed she was only out horseback riding. She had left him for good.

"But where could she have gone?" he said, scratching his brow.

His jaw tight, he hurried to Jade, who was preparing food for their evening meal.

He took her by an arm and swung her around to face him. "You know all about it, don't you?" he said, wheezing hard as he waited for her reply.

"All about what, sir?" Jade asked, feeling weak. She was afraid that he was about to try to force answers from her, but no matter what he did, she wouldn't betray Jessie.

Jessie was the lucky one. She had escaped this madman. Now if only Jessie could find a way to include Jade and Lee-Lee in her plan!

"You knew about her plan to leave, didn't you?" Reginald said, his hand squeezing Jade's fleshy arm.

"Nay sir, I did not," Jade said, her voice small because the fear inside her was so great.

"Are you saying that you had no idea she was planning to leave me?" Reginald shouted, releasing her arm.

"Nay I did not," Jade said, flinching when he raised

his hand as though he was going to hit her. She breathed a sigh of relief when he dropped it back down to his side.

"Oh, well, she's not worth bothering over anyway," Reginald said. He turned and glared out the kitchen window toward the corral where his prized horses grazed on thick grass.

"Are you saying she's gone . . . forever?" Jade dared to ask, trying to pretend innocence.

"More than likely," Reginald said, shrugging as he walked away from Jade and left the kitchen.

He went to Jessie's room and opened the chifferobe, where the clothes he had recently purchased for her were hanging.

Angrily he yanked one from a wooden hanger and pitched it to the floor. He continued doing so until everything he had bought was piled in the center of the room.

He went to the corridor and shouted Jade's name.

She hurried to him, her eyes fearful as she gazed at him. "Yes, sir?" she said. "You called me?"

"Take all these clothes and burn them," Reginald shouted, gesturing toward the lovely creations. "I don't want anything in my house to remind me of her. Do you hear?"

"But . . . what if she returns?" Jade asked, playing her role to the hilt.

"If she does, I'll buy her some more," Reginald said, shrugging. "Go. Take them. Get them out of my sight, and yourself as well. You sicken me, Jade. Sicken me!"

Jade cowered beneath his glare, then gathered the clothes into her arms and ran from the room.

When she reached the kitchen stove, she began shoving one dress at a time into the flames, then stood back while tears rolled down her cheeks. How she felt Jessie's absence now! She feared she might never see her again. If only she could believe that Jessie would remember her and Lee-Lee, living with Reginald a few more days would be worth it.

But if Jessie didn't come back to help her, Jade had her own ideas as to how she would escape and rescue her daughter. Jessie's success had given her the nerve to try.

She heard Reginald stamping down the corridor toward his room, then flinched when he slammed his door. Afterward, the house was silent.

Reginald sank down in his rocking chair before the fireplace in his bedroom and began slowly rocking back and forth as he tried to figure out what he would tell his friends about Jessie's sudden strange disappearance. Although he had decided to forget her, and was even hoping the coyotes would remove all traces of her from this land, he had others to think about.

He had been stupid to allow Jessie to interfere in his life, yet she could have added so much to his parties. She was so pretty and all. But soon she wouldn't be pretty. She'd be fat with child.

The one thing that now concerned him about her disappearance was how he could explain her absence to those he so badly wanted to impress. It was crucial that he keep people's attention away from what he did besides attending church and giving parties.

If any of the decent townsfolk heard about his cribs, he would be ignored or treated like trash for the rest of his life. And he couldn't bear that thought. He enjoyed the kind of attention the upstanding citizens of Tombstone gave him.

"What can I tell them?" Reginald asked himself, wheezing.

He would have to make up some sort of story. He would say that Jessie had been called back to Kansas City because of a friend's death.

Yes, that would work. That story would save face for him.

"But if I ever come face to face with you again, you'll pay, Jessie," Reginald grumbled, suddenly wheezing so hard he could hardly catch his breath. "Damn it, you'll pay!"

As Reginald's hate for Jessie swelled inside his heart, Jade was crying from fear of what might happen to Jessie. She prayed Jessie had found a safe haven.

If only she could gain the courage to try her own plan of escape.

Soon.

Ai, she would, and soon!

"Lee-Lee, please have the strength to live another day," she whispered as she gazed out a window toward the town where the cribs so brazenly displayed her daughter's beauty. "Do not be one of those who commit suicide because of hopelessness!"

Chapter Nineteen

It was early evening. The meadow hummed with crickets. Cottonwoods shimmered along a creek that ran glassy-smooth through bear grass and camas.

The hunt was now over, and Jessie sat beside the huge outdoor fire where the overnight camp had been set up.

To her surprise, when Thunder Horse had led her back to the camp after the hunt, she had found many women from his village there, awaiting the arrival of the hunters.

They had come during the hunt and prepared the meat racks, which were ready now for the fresh meat. A fine bed of coals had also been prepared to cook the meat.

Fat ribs of deer were now roasting over these coals, and the dripping fat was popping and snapping, sending up a tantalizing aroma.

Jessie's attention was drawn to the sight of more

warriors and their packhorses entering the camp. The meat was folded inside skins on the packhorses, with the large bones tied on top to be broken later for the sweet marrow.

She turned and watched for Thunder Horse's return. He had left a short while ago to go to the top of a hill, where he would leave a gift of gratitude—the finest cut of meat taken today. This offering was made to their brother, the deer, because so many of the deer's relations had died to feed the Sioux, who would one day also die and feed the grasses the deer fed from.

That had touched Jessie's heart, to learn that the Indians never took anything without giving back. Oh, if only all white people could be as grateful for what they had received from heaven above. Instead, it seemed that many of her own people were greedy and never seemed to have enough.

Reginald was the worst of that kind. She felt so grateful that she was no longer a part of his life. She dearly hoped that he would not find her and try to ruin her life again. She had found a home among these Sioux people, thanks to the generosity of one man: Thunder Horse.

She had never met anyone as kind and giving.

Although her parents, and also her husband, had always thought of others before themselves, Thunder Horse was even more generous.

She thought back to this morning, when Jessie had awakened in Thunder Horse's lodge, where she had slept snugly wrapped in blankets across the fire from him. She had found him kneeling beside her, watching her sleep.

He had bent low and kissed her, yet he did nothing more than that. Then she had noticed what he had draped across his arms: the clothing of a Sioux warrior.

When he had explained to her that she must wear these garments in order to disguise herself in case Reginald Vineyard was out searching for her, she had willingly dressed in the fringed breeches, shirt, and moccasins.

She had sat in front of him as he braided her hair into one long braid down her back; then she had turned and smiled as he placed a beaded headband around her head.

She had departed for the hunt mounted on one of his horses. The beautiful white steed she had brought from Reginald's corral remained safely hidden in case her cousin came to the village.

Thanks to Thunder Horse's precautions, she had felt quite safe as she witnessed the hunt. She had been impressed by the skills of the hunters and the clever way they had brought down the deer.

As they had left the village, Thunder Horse had explained that there was a place the Sioux called the Deer Run. It was to this place that the Deer Dreamer, with his mysterious powers and medicine, sent the deer for the Sioux people. There the hunters could easily kill all the deer that were needed for meat and skins.

She had discovered that the Deer Run was an unwooded space on the bank of a river. This bank was high and steep, and at its foot the river ran dark and deep. No deer would dare leap from this bank.

She had sat back on her horse and watched as the warriors cut a path through the woods up to the clearing on the riverbank. On the forest side of the clearing, the woods were thick, and the limbs and boughs were interlaced to form an unbreakable fence that the deer could not penetrate. This had left but one entrance to the deer enclosure.

The warriors then rode in a great circle until they found a herd of deer. Steadily and slowly, they directed the deer toward the path that led to the enclosure.

Soon the deer were within the enclosure. The warriors had a great hunt, taking back to camp much meat, and many skins to be tanned for garments.

And as soon as all the warriors came in with their loads of meat, there would be a feast. Tomorrow they would return home so that the women could smoke the meat and tan the hides. No one would be without food or clothing during the long, cold months of winter.

Thinking about the winter ahead made Jessie think of something . . . someone . . . else. She placed a gentle hand on her stomach. She knew that when Thunder Horse learned about her child, it would not change how he felt about her. She and her unborn baby would have a safe, warm shelter this winter.

Yes, she knew that Thunder Horse, whose heart was filled with love and caring, would not turn away from her because she carried another man's child. The child was born of a rare sort of love. She and Steven had cared deeply for one another, but theirs had not been a passionate love, only one that was comfortable and respectful.

When she was with Thunder Horse, passions she'd never known could exist were awakened inside her. She felt a wondrous thrill to imagine how it would be the first time they made love. It would be something she would cherish forever and ever. . . .

She had become so lost in thought, she hadn't heard Thunder Horse come up behind her. He sat down beside her on the thick pallet of blankets a short distance from the fire.

"It is done," he said, reaching over and sliding a stray lock of her hair back from her brow. "I have thanked the deer for all they have given us today."

"It seemed to be a good hunt," Jessie said as she scooted closer to Thunder Horse. She noticed that he was fresh and clean from a bath in the river.

"My warriors are skilled hunters. They can smell a deer before the deer smells them," he said. "Every boy hunts from his fourth or fifth year of life, first chasing rabbits with a bow and wooden arrow, and later with larger bows and arrows that are strong enough to kill a deer or an antelope. He learns to creep upwind, slowly, with no more stirring than a bull snake easing up on a gopher in the grass. Those young boys grow up into the finest of hunters, men of patience, guile, and speed."

"Do you hunt often?" Jessie asked, wondering how often Thunder Horse would be gone from home after they were married.

Yes! She did believe they would be married! Although such a union was taboo among whites, she could not imagine life now without Thunder Horse.

"There is more than one fall hunt," Thunder Horse patiently explained as he stared into the leaping flames of the fire, his stomach reacting to the smell of the meat cooking over the coals.

"There is first the deer hunt, and then the hunt for buffalo to provide the heavily furred robes that keep us warm against the blizzard winds. The buffalo also give us beds and winter lodge floors and linings, in addition to the fat meat and the tallow for cooking," he said. "Fall also brings ducks and geese to hunt. Then during even the longest winter there are rabbits to be snared and trapped."

He stopped to nod a quiet hello to other warriors who had come from their baths in the river and were settling down around the fire, anticipating the food that would soon be offered by their wives.

Then he smiled at Jessie and continued describing the hunt. "After the midsummer hunt, the jerky hardens fast and sweet in a few hours of hot wind, and hides are easily cleared of their thin summer fur for lodge skins, saddlebags, shield and regalia cases," he said. "When we hunt the buffalo, young cows are selected. The skins are lighter and thinner, softer and easier to tan and handle; the meat is better, too, more tender and fat-veined."

He was interrupted when a maiden brought a large wooden platter of food, which he would share with Jessie.

Jessie gazed at it, not recognizing anything on it.

Yet knowing that she must not be rude, nor appear to doubt what was being offered her by the Sioux, she eagerly took a piece of meat and ate it as everyone else sat down to enjoy the fruits of their long day's labor.

Jessie gazed around her, noticing how happy everyone was, the women now sitting with their husbands, eating and laughing.

She noticed that no children were there. When she asked why, Thunder Horse told her that they were home with the elders, as were the warriors who had been assigned to remain in the village to protect the old as well as the young.

She noticed that Sweet Willow wasn't among the women and knew that she would be caring for White Horse in Thunder Horse's absence.

She knew that Thunder Horse's mind drifted often to his father; White Horse seemed to worsen now more each day. Thunder Horse had told her that the day was coming soon now when his father would be put to rest among the other great chiefs of their Fox clan.

"I have prepared a place for us to sleep separate from this camp," Thunder Horse said softly into Jessie's ear, causing her to turn and gaze into his dark eyes.

"Will you come with me?" he asked. "Will you sleep with me?"

"Do you mean . . . sleep separate as we have slept in your tepee at the village?" Jessie asked softly. Yet already she guessed the answer to her question from the look in his eyes, a look of love and need, which matched what she felt within her own heart for him.

"No, not separate," Thunder Horse said, shoving the empty platter aside. "I wish for you to share my blankets alongside me tonight. I prepared a special place for us after giving thanks for the hunt to my brother deer."

"You already prepared it?" Jessie asked, her eyes wide, her pulse racing.

She was feeling a sensation between her thighs that she had never felt before. It was a pressure of sorts, yet felt strangely delicious.

She had been told by friends how it felt to sleep with a man when one was deeply in love. The feelings that were being awakened inside her were surely what they had been talking about.

Her heart pounded. Her knees were strangely weak.

She wasn't sure if she could walk, even if she tried to go with him to this place he had made just for them—a lovers' lair!

When she had made love with her husband, she had never felt like this. She had just wanted to give him satisfaction because of his kindness toward her, his willingness to take her in when she had no one else to go to.

She had never shared the excitement she knew he felt. His pleasure had been evident in his hard breathing and the pounding of his heart as he thrust himself inside her.

And then at the end! He had seemed to enter another world as he groaned and moaned with pleasure.

She had wanted to feel the same things he felt, but she just didn't. She was a woman doing her womanly duty, that was all.

Now she was a woman who truly anticipated being

fulfilled in the most wondrous ways by the most wondrous man of all!

"*Ho*, I have prepared a place for us to spend the night together," he said hoarsely, his eyes searching hers. "The fire is built. The blankets are spread. Will you come with me?"

Her pulse racing, everything within her crying out for these upcoming moments with the man she would always love, she nodded. She took his hand as he offered it to her.

"Come then," he said huskily, rising to his feet and drawing Jessie up with him.

She didn't look around to see if anyone was paying heed to what their chief was doing. Feeling as though she were walking on clouds, she left the camp with him.

They walked only a short distance before she saw a small campfire up ahead, where a cozy nest had been made of blankets against an upcropping of rock. A slight bluff reached out just above them, providing a roof of sorts.

Suddenly Thunder Horse stopped and turned to Jessie. He swept her up into his arms and carried her onward to the camp. He kissed her as he leaned low and placed her atop the blankets.

"*Techila*—in my language that means, 'I love you,' " he whispered against her lips. "I have wanted you from the moment I first saw you. I want you for my *mitawin*, for always."

"I want you as much," Jessie murmured, overwhelmed by the emotions exploding within her.

As he kissed her he slowly removed her clothes until she lay splendidly nude beneath him. He quickly tore off his own clothes so that nothing remained between them.

He stretched out above her, his arms around her, nestling her close. Then he drew back a little, so his eyes could gaze into hers. He kissed her again, this time even more passionately, his hands going over her body, touching and awakening her every pleasure point.

She sighed and melted beneath his caresses, and soon learned that the man was not the only one who should receive something wonderful from lovemaking.

Thunder Horse was tender. His mouth was sensuous, not only as he kissed her lips, but also as he pressed them to her throat.

She clung to him as the very nearness of him shot desire through her. And when he came into her, filling her with his magnificence, his heat so thrilling inside her, delicious shivers of desire raced across her flesh.

As he enfolded her within his solid strength, she spread herself more open to him. He came to her, thrusting deeply, each thrust sending a message to her heart that he loved her without question.

Sheer happiness bubbled deep within her as he leaned low and kissed one breast and then the other, then sucked a nipple between his teeth, gently chewing.

She ran her fingers through his thick black hair, then down his solid, muscular back until she reached his buttocks. She spread her fingers across his tightness, pressing him even more closely to her as he stoked the fires within that had never burned until tonight.

Thunder Horse's passions, which had lain smoldering just below the surface, burst out tonight. They exploded within him as he felt the curl of heat growing, his world melting away in a passion he'd never known could exist between a man and a woman.

Her groans of pleasure fired his passion even more as he continued to stroke within her. His eyes were glazed, drugged with rapture, as he paused long enough to look down at her.

"We were meant to be together," he said huskily, a hand at her hair, brushing it back from her face. "I have waited a long time for you. Now I can never let you go."

"I'm not going anywhere," Jessie breathed out, sucking in a breath of rapture when he again kissed her. His body thrust deep, taking her to a plateau of feelings that soon exploded into a million sparks of light. She clung to him as he reached that same place, then rolled away from her and lay on his back, breathing hard.

"I still feel you inside me," Jessie said, laughing softly, for she did still throb where the feelings she had never experienced before had spread like fire.

"And I still feel as though I am," Thunder Horse said. He gazed at her as she closed her eyes, still smiling into the darkness of night. "My woman, you are everything to me. Stay with me. Bear me a son."

The mention of children brought her eyes open

quickly. She became aware that he was stroking her belly, oh, so gently.

It . . . was . . . as though . . . he already knew a child grew within her.

She reached for his hand and held it still on her stomach. "I am with child already," she said, and wondered why that confession didn't cause him to withdraw his hand in surprise, or worse yet . . . in disgust.

"I already knew," he said, smiling into her eyes as their gazes met and held in the fire's glow.

"You . . . did?" she gasped. "How could you?"

"I was not certain, but I believed that you were," Thunder Horse said, sitting up beside her. He stroked her belly with his hand gently, almost meditatingly.

"How could you?" she asked, aware of his gentleness and his acceptance of her baby.

"Many times when you were not aware of it, you have rested your hand on your belly as women with child often do," he said softly. "I saw this with my sister. She was oh, so protective of her baby before he was born. All women who want to have a child are."

"And it doesn't matter to you that I am carrying another man's baby inside my belly? I do love you with all my heart and want to marry you," she blurted out, her eyes searching his.

"Everything about you I love," he said thickly, slowly smiling. "Even the child that will be born of your other love."

"I loved my husband, yet not with passion," she confessed. "It was a gentle love. He . . . my husband . . . took me in and married me when my parents were killed. He wanted children so badly. But he didn't even know that I was with child before he died. I only realized it myself on the journey from Kansas to Arizona."

"I shall love the child as though it was born of our union," Thunder Horse said. "It will be my child. I shall raise it and protect it. I shall teach it everything the young braves of my people learn. We shall hunt together."

Jessie was almost in tears, she was so happy and grateful to have found such a love as Thunder Horse's. She sat up and flung herself into his arms. "I love you so," she sobbed. "Thank you for loving me."

He held her for a while longer; then they lay back down and loved again, this time slowly, leisurely, yet still with a passion they could only find together.

Chapter Twenty

Reginald rolled and tossed on his bed, fitfully throwing his blanket from side to side as another nightmare held him in its grip. This one was worse than any he had had before.

In his dream he was in the sacred cave.

The paintings of Indians along the cave's walls began turning into living beings, jumping from the walls, yet they weren't full Indians at all. They were bones that suddenly came together into hideous skeletons.

Howling and shrieking, they began running after Reginald, the click-clack-clack of the bones like something straight from hell.

There were skeletal remains of eagles flying around his head, squawking and clawing at him.

He awakened in a sweat. Panting, with sweat rolling from his brow, his eyes wide, he sat up and looked wildly around him.

He was in his room, where the moon's glow shone through his windows onto his bed.

Trembling, he closed his eyes as he recalled this newest nightmare. It had all seemed so real—the bones, the skeletons, the birds, all running after him, grabbing, clawing.

"I can't take any more of this," he cried, leaping from the bed. He yanked off his nightgown and hurried into his clothes and shoes, then put on his eyeglasses and ran from the room, only to find Jade standing there, her eyes wide with wonder.

"What are you gawking at?" he shouted, doubling a fist and knocking her to the floor. "Mind your own business, do you hear?"

He didn't stop to get a firearm. He had only one thing on his mind—to go to the Indian village and plead his case there. He went out to the stable, hitched a horse to his buggy, and headed out for the Indian village.

Surely the Sioux would listen to reason.

He would promise to do anything if they would only make the nightmares stop. If they didn't, he would surely go insane.

He rode onward until he reached the outskirts of the village and was suddenly stopped by a sentry.

"What are you doing here?" the sentry asked, raising his rifle as he gazed angrily and with suspicion at Reginald.

"Please let me speak with your chief," Reginald pleaded. "It is of the utmost importance."

"It is late," the sentry growled out.

"I know it is, but I must speak with Chief Thunder Horse tonight," Reginald said, losing his patience.

"That is impossible," the sentry said flatly. "My chief and many others of our warriors are gone. They are on the hunt. So turn around. Go back to your home."

"I'll talk with anyone who'll listen, then," Reginald begged. "I must. Please allow me to enter your village and have council with whomever is left in charge during your chief's absence."

"I am that man," the sentry said, his eyes gleaming. "And it is my decision to turn you away. Go. You are not welcome here now; nor will you ever be by any of our people."

"Please listen," Reginald pleaded. "I beg your forgiveness for going to your sacred cave and taking what I shouldn't have. I'll return it all if it means that these nightmares will stop."

"It is not meant for them to stop, ever," the sentry said bluntly. He pointed away from the village. "I will tell you one last time: go. Do not ever come again to disturb my people."

"You are wrong," Reginald said, near tears. "If your chief learns that you turned me away after I promised so much, you will be severely punished."

The sentry just laughed and turned away.

Reginald stared blankly at him, then wheeled his horse and buggy around and headed back in the direction of his home, a beaten man.

He felt so helpless. He hated to think he had been bested by a mere savage.

"What can I do?" he cried into the dark heavens.

Never in his life had he felt so helpless . . . so afraid.

And where was Jessie?

He truly believed that she could have helped him fight this terrible fear. If only he had been more decent to her when she had wanted to live with him.

Now he had not lost only his Sara, but also Jessie.

Life was becoming pointless, even though he had enough money to make him comfortable forever. But what had that wealth gained him but nightmares?

All of the wealth in the world wasn't worth what he was living through every night.

"Damn you to hell, Thunder Horse, for cursing me with these nightmares!" he screamed, causing birds that had been roosting for the night overhead to scatter and flutter above him.

And then he heard something else that made his insides turn cold with fear. It was a strange moaning that came with sudden gusts of wind.

Was it the moans of those dead chiefs he had disturbed in the sacred cave?

He flicked his reins and urged the horse faster, glad when he saw lamplight up ahead. It was his house, where he would be safe, providing he didn't allow himself to go to sleep.

Only then did he realize the full horror of what he had done when he had taken that damnable silver from that damnable cave! He would never really be safe anywhere.

He leaped with alarm when at his left side he saw the flash of something white. To his astonishment, he realized that it was a white wolf running alongside the gravel road that led to his house.

He gasped and drew rein when the wolf veered right and ran directly in front of the horse, causing it to stop and rear and snort and shake its head in obvious fear.

And then the wolf went on its way, a part of the night and its mysteries.

After getting his horse settled down, as well as his heart, Reginald drove the buggy to his house, his shoulders slumped, his head hanging.

"Where is it all to end?" he whispered, then began wheezing uncontrollably. He choked and gagged, then gasped in a breath of air.

When he saw Jade on the porch, seemingly watching for his return, he got a sudden soft feeling for the woman. She was the only one who had stuck with him through thick and thin.

After he left the horse and buggy in the stable, he went up the steps to the porch, gave Jade a nod of greeting.

But he could not bring himself to say anything kind to her, for he could not allow himself to get soft where the help was concerned.

"Get inside the house," he grumbled, then walked past her and hurried to the privacy of his room.

He listened until he heard Jade go to her room, and then there was silence in the house.

He stared at the bed, and then at his closed door, then hurried out into the corridor and knocked on Jade's door.

"Jade, prepare me some warm milk and be sure to

put quite a bit of sleeping potion in it," he said. "I need my rest."

Jade came from her room in her robe and slippers and edged past him, then hurried to the kitchen.

After warming the milk, she eyed the white powder that she had been told to put in his milk. Tonight might be a good night to give him all that he had and be done with him.

But she was too afraid to try. She poured in the right amount, took the milk to him, then went back to her room.

Hugging herself, she stood at the window, contemplating her next move. Somehow, she must get away from this place.

"Soon," she whispered. "Lee-Lee, I will come for you soon. I promise. . . ."

Chapter Twenty-one

Except for their concerns about Thunder Horse's ailing father, happiness and contentment reigned in the village of the Fox clan.

It was the day after the hunt and all were home now . . . except for Thunder Horse; who had come home to check on his father, but seeing there was no change for the worse, had left again.

He had told Jessie that he had one more thing to do before joining those who were already celebrating the successful hunt. The women were preparing a feast around several outdoor fires. Some stood over huge kettles of soup, stirring them with their big horn spoons.

Rib roasts were piled high on wooden platters lined with arrowhead leaves and watercress. There were huge wooden bowls of cooked wild mushrooms, cane shoots, and Indian turnips.

For dessert, there was a choice of wild fruits: June berries, chokeberries, plums, and grapes. They would be eaten fresh now, but what was left after today would be dried and stored for winter.

The air was alive with music and laughter. The ailing retired chief had given everyone his blessing to enjoy the day. He said that the warriors had labored hard and deserved some time of merriment; he wished them to know that his heart was with them.

Jessie could not help feeling somewhat out of place without Thunder Horse there. His sister Sweet Willow was sitting with White Horse, while Lone Wing was with the children, enjoying his own day of freedom from his studies.

Jessie stood back and watched the camaraderie of these people. Some sang along with the solemn beating of drums. She had learned that these drums were made by stretching parchment made of deerskin over the ends of powder kegs. Each was beaten in a slow, steady cadence with a single stick.

The sound that came from these drums was portentous, whereas the lighter portable drums, made by putting parchment on hoops five or six inches deep, and fifteen inches in diameter, had a much more pleasant sound. They played along with flutes made of sumac, and rattles made of gourd shells into which had been put the round teeth of white bass.

Several dancers, both men and women, began to move around the central fire in time with the throbbing of the music.

Everywhere feathers fluttered in the air from elaborate dance costumes. Some of the men carried painted quivers on their backs, and held lances decorated with strips of otter skin. There were also fans and banners waving in the air.

As the drums throbbed, the singers moved forward and backward, while the dancers circled, their shadows bobbing and skipping.

Then pretty little girls joined the dancers. They were dressed in soft deerskin dresses, moccasins, and leggings as white as snow.

Their long, black, shiny braids were tied with ornaments made from dyed porcupine quills strung on dyed deerskin strings. At the end of their hair strings were tassels of bright-colored feathers, which swayed as the girls danced in time with the music.

Soon many dancers and singers disbanded to complete the final preparations of the food. The children now occupied themselves with various games.

Although first the hunt, and now the partying, had gotten in the way of Lone Wing's lessons, he had told Jessie that he had not forgotten the myth he was supposed to memorize. As he played games today, inside his head he was repeating the myth, so he would be ready to tell it, when Thunder Horse asked him.

Jessie sat down on a blanket just outside Thunder Horse's tepee, still waiting for his arrival. Her curiosity about why he had left grew within her. Surely she would soon know why he was the only warrior, besides the sentries guarding the village, who was not there to join the fun.

Of course, she knew it must be something important that had taken him away, so she patiently waited as she tried hard not to feel so alone.

The only person who did not ignore her was Lone Wing, who frequently took time from his games to look over at her and smile.

After a while she realized that his occasional smiles were not only to make her feel less alone, but also to seek her approval of how he was doing in the games.

This meant a lot to Jessie. She was feeling a strong bond between herself and Lone Wing and she truly cared for the young man.

She watched the boys get ready to play what was called a mud and willow fight game. The moment it began, Jessie stiffened, for she saw that it could be a dangerous sport.

The boys had formed two lines facing each other. A lump of soft clay was stuck on the end of a springy willow wand and thrown at the boys on the other side. Simultaneously, those on that side threw apples from sticks as they shouted, "I, the brave, today do kill the only fierce enemy!"

Scarcely were those words uttered for the first time than Lone Wing let out a shriek of pain as one of the clumps of clay hit his head.

All activity stopped and everyone went quiet as Lone Wing crumpled to the ground. Blood was oozing from an open wound.

The boys hurriedly circled around Lone Wing, staring down at him. But one boy backed away from them after retrieving the lump of clay that he had thrown at Lone Wing.

Jessie saw him tear the lump of clay and remove a sharp rock from it. He quickly discarded the rock, then nonchalantly dropped the lump back down to the ground and joined the boys again, a look of mischief in his coal-black eyes.

Jessie gasped. The boy had purposely wanted to hurt Lone Wing. She wondered why. Surely it was because Lone Wing was so special and was treated with respect by both children and adults.

Jealousy.

Yes, that was the answer. She wanted to go right away and scold the boy and make it known that he had purposely hurt the chief's nephew.

But she didn't. She knew that it was not her place to do such a thing.

So she did the next-best thing. She hurried to Lone Wing and knelt down beside him just as the shaman reached him with his bag of medicines.

Jessie reached for Lone Wing's hand and held it as the shaman doctored the boy's wound, but she could tell by Lone Wing's expression that she shouldn't be there. The way she was holding his hand was surely embarrassing him.

Understanding his look, Jessie slipped her hand from his and stood up. She backed away slowly.

Lone Wing didn't want to look like a child when he was trying so hard to prove that he was a man. She hoped her gesture of caring hadn't diminished in the eyes of those he so badly wanted to impress.

Fortunately, something else quickly drew everyone's attention.

Jessie turned and gasped when she saw Thunder Horse walking into the village, bent over by his burden—a large deer that he carried over his shoulders. His fringed buckskin shirt was sprinkled with blood and his eyes were filled with pride as the warriors began following him, shouting in unison, *"Woo-coo-hoo!"* at the top of their lungs.

Jessie stood quietly by as the man she loved with all her heart stopped at his father's tepee and threw the deer down at the entrance.

And then all went quiet as Thunder Horse turned to the people, his eyes brimming with emotion, and said, "My father has his own deer today!"

Thunderous applause filled the air, and tears came to Jessie's eyes, for all understood his reason for bringing this deer: It would be the old chief's last participation in the deer hunt.

Jessie stifled a sob behind her hand as Thunder Horse went inside his father's lodge, stayed a moment, then came out again and gave instructions to two of his warriors, who nodded and took the deer away for preparation.

Thunder Horse went to Jessie. His hands were too bloody to touch her, but his eyes said it all . . . that he adored her.

"I will go and bathe in the river, then return to join the celebration," he told her.

"What you just did was so beautiful," she said, smiling into his eyes. "I hope to one day have a son who is as respectful to his father as you are to yours."

"We will together teach *our* son the way it all should be done," Thunder Horse said, emphasizing "our" to let her know that any son of hers would also be his, whether or not that son might have been fathered by another man.

"Yes, our son," she murmured, then watched him quickly strip to his breechclout, run to the river, and dive in.

He was soon back with her, dressed in clean clothes, ready to take part in the fun and merriment.

"Your father?" Jessie asked as she sat with Thunder Horse beside the large fire, where everyone was now sitting.

Some of the women were preparing to carry the food to the people in large platters. Jessie noticed one of the women stopping and looking heavenward, saying, "Great Mystery, do thou partake of this venison and still be gracious," just as she tossed a piece of the choicest cooked game into the flames.

"My father is much weaker," Thunder Horse said thickly.

"I'm sorry," Jessie murmured.

She nodded and smiled a thank-you to two women who brought Jessie and Thunder Horse a platter of food.

"It is the natural way of things," Thunder Horse said. "Life is given and life is taken away."

Lone Wing came and plopped down on Thunder Horse's left side. His eyes were bright. He started to say something, but Thunder Horse reached a hand to Lone Wing's injury.

"And what caused this?" Thunder Horse asked, gazing into his nephew's eyes. Lone Wing lowered his gaze in embarrassment. Thunder Horse placed a hand beneath the boy's chin and lifted it.

"Were you injured during the games?" Thunder Horse asked.

Lone Wing nodded as his face flushed again in embarrassment. "I was careless," he said softly.

"No, not tru—" Jessie began to say, for she had seen how it had happened. It was another young brave's meanness that was to blame for the cut.

Please don't, Lone Wing's eyes seemed to beg. Jessie stopped in mid sentence. She realized that she had a lot to learn about a young brave's pride.

"But, Thunder Horse, I am ready to repeat the myth to you if you are ready to hear it," Lone Wing said excitedly. He grinned. "And I have added some different twists and turns to it, as you suggested."

Thunder Horse gave Jessie a curious gaze, for he had noticed the looks between her and Lone Wing. He would not delve further into what had happened, for he sensed that his nephew's pride lay in the balance.

He looked quickly at Lone Wing. "I am ready to hear it," Thunder Horse said, lowering his hand. "Tell it to me and Jessie."

To Jessie's surprise, Lone Wing repeated the tale word for word. And then she noticed a difference . . . he had added his own ending to the myth.

"You do yourself proud," Thunder Horse said, patting Lone Wing's bare shoulder. "You left nothing out, and the expression on your face added to the description of the tale."

He smiled amusedly. "And the ending?" he said, nodding. "It was one even I could not have come up with. It was good, nephew. It was more than that; it was excellent."

"I am so proud," Lone Wing said, beaming.

"As you should be," Thunder Horse said, reaching over and giving the youth a hug.

"I am going to go and tell my friends that I did it," Lone Wing said, leaping to his feet. He was soon encircled by all his friends except the one who had secretly attacked him.

The guilty boy eventually joined the others and forced a smile. He looked slowly over his shoulder at Jessie, and she realized that he knew she had seen what he had done today.

She gave him a knowing look, then turned away from him and smiled into Thunder Horse's eyes.

"Lone Wing is such a special boy," she said, then joined Thunder Horse in sampling the delicious food.

"He will be a powerful, yet beloved, Historian," Thunder Horse said.

After everyone was done eating, the dancing and singing resumed until the setting sun splashed orange hues along the horizon.

"I would like to walk," Thunder Horse said, standing and reaching out a hand for Jessie. "Let us walk, talk, and enjoy the wonders of the sunset."

Jessie took his hand and went down to the river with him, where they slowly walked along the bank.

"This is such a lovely place," she murmured. "I imagine you hate having to leave it."

"A part of it will remain here with me always,"

Thunder Horse said as he patted his chest over his heart. "Inside my heart I will carry many happy memories of the time spent here."

He smiled at her. "But I can be happy elsewhere," he added. "You see, Jessie, we Sioux love pure water, pure air, and clean land on which to place our tepees. We will find another place to set up our lodges and be as happy as before, even if that place is one assigned to us by the United States government."

He sighed, then said, "This was all ours until the white pony soldiers came and took most of the land. But the one man who did the most damage was Reginald Vineyard. He took white gold from the sacred resting place of my Fox band's past chiefs."

"I'm so sorry," Jessie murmured.

"He is the sorry one now," Thunder Horse said. "My people's shaman went and asked the spirits of the cave to haunt Reginald forever and ever. That is vengeance enough. Now I wish only to stay here long enough to fulfill my promise to my father—that he will be placed in the sacred cave, after which the cave will be sealed forever."

Jessie again remembered those ghastly screams and sobs of fear that came from Reginald when he was having his nightmares. She now understood why those nightmares had tormented him so. She could not help feeling a little unnerved over the power the Sioux actually had to put curses on people.

"I'm so glad that the government gave you permission to stay until you were able to fulfill your promise to your father," she murmured. "It could have been so different."

"It has been a struggle to stay, for the white soldier chief, whom you call the president, at first said we could not stay. He said we had sold our land to him and it was not ours anymore," Thunder Horse said glumly. "But we had not sold it to him. Land is not owned by any one person. It has always been the land of our people. We took money for the use of the land. When the Sioux sold an acre, we thought of it as a temporary arrangement. We believed that when payment ceased, the land was to return to the tribe."

He paused, then said, "To us, the land, the earth, is revered as our mother. Nothing can ever be done to diminish this land, nor to make it less for all those whose moccasins walked upon it, and for all those whose tracks are still to come. The White Soldier Chief listened, and in the end allowed us to stay, but for only as long as my father lives. We must leave immediately after my father is placed in the cave. In the meantime, we were warned not to cause trouble with whites."

"Even my cousin," Jessie said sadly.

"Yes, even your cousin," Thunder Horse agreed. "But the form of revenge we have chosen is something he cannot prove even if he should try to explain what is causing his nightmares." He smiled. "Should he tell, people would see him as a man whose mind has become warped, and they would laugh at him."

He stopped and drew her into his arms. "Enough talk of such things," he said. "My woman, all day I have thought of you. Even when I was stalking the deer to bring home to my father, I was thinking of you and wanting you."

"I have thought of you all day, too," Jessie murmured, sighing with passion as he swept her closer, his dark eyes searching hers. "I love you so."

His lips came down upon hers in a heated kiss. His hands between them molded her breasts.

She leaned into his hands, everything within her melting as he now placed a thigh between her legs and pressed it up and against her throbbing center.

"I need you so," he whispered huskily against her lips.

"As . . . I . . . need you," she said, almost swooning when he reached a hand up inside her skirt, caressing her where she already felt tender from want of him.

Suddenly he swept her up into his arms and ran with her along the riverbank. He stopped when they were far enough from the village to have intimate moments together beneath the starry heavens.

Thunder Horse laid Jessie where the grass was thick and green. He quickly disrobed her, then stood and let her watch him remove his clothes until he stood nude over her, his eyes branding her as he slowly swept them over her.

Although it was dark, there was enough light from the moon to reveal the need visible on the face of each.

Thunder Horse's own ferocious hunger for her was like nothing he had ever felt before. He knelt down over her, a knee spreading her legs apart so that he could rest his throbbing manhood against her where she awaited his entry.

She twined her arms around his neck and smiled into his eyes as she felt pleasure beginning to spread through her. His fingers stroked her womanhood, and she was soon aflame with burning need.

This time there was no hesitation, only pure pleasure, especially when he thrust himself deep within her and began his rhythmic strokes.

Her entire being throbbed with quickening desire as she clung to him. His lips were on hers, kissing her wildly as their bodies strained together hungrily.

Feeling her tightening around his manhood as he reached even further within her, Thunder Horse felt electrified by a bolt of pure lightning. Her tightness, her yielding to his needs, made him groan against her lips.

And then he slid his mouth downward until he found one of her rosy nipples.

She sucked in a wild breath of wonder when he licked the nipple, then nipped at it with his teeth.

She clung.

She moaned.

She tossed her head as the pleasure mounted within her.

And then he again gave her a fierce, feverish kiss, as his hands moved between them to curve over her breasts.

Curls of heat tightened inside Jessie's belly. She was shocked at the intensity of her feelings.

She was overcome by sweet agony, then sucked in a deep breath as she felt the pleasure spreading. It burst inside her like millions of sparks of light as the climax came fiercely, yet wonderfully, throughout her.

Thunder Horse felt his own excitement building

within him just as he knew it had begun within her. He clung to her and thrust over and over again inside her, then groaned and gave himself over to the pure ecstasy of the moment. He felt as if lightning were flashing off and on again within his brain.

And then he felt as if he were floating above himself while he savored these moments of bliss with the woman he would love forever.

They lay there, clinging, kissing, and straining against each other, and once again he felt himself ready to enter her.

He sculpted himself to her moist body. He pressed endlessly deeper within her.

They both drew in deep, ragged breaths, as again, so soon, the wonders of their togetherness brought them total ecstasy and release.

Truly exhausted, and breathing hard, Thunder Horse rolled away from Jessie and stretched out on the grass beside her.

"The long wait today as I hungered for you was worth it," he said huskily. He reached for one of her hands and held it, smiling at her. "My woman, I want you to be my wife. I want you forever."

"As I want you," she murmured, finding it hard to believe that this was actually happening to her. Not so long ago, she had felt totally alone in the world.

She had not looked forward to living with Reginald. She had wanted her own life, her own man. She had wanted a father for her child.

And now she had it all.

Yes, it was like a dream, yet so very beautiful and real.

"We will marry as soon as it is possible," he said, turning to face her as his hand ran slowly across her body, causing her flesh to quiver when he touched a vulnerable place.

"I will be ready whenever you say the time is right," Jessie said, gazing in wonder at him when he suddenly stopped his hand over her belly, now slowly and gently stroking her there.

"A child," he said, smiling at her. "A child grows within."

"Yes," she whispered. "I . . . I . . . wish it were yours."

"It is," he said, then moved over her again. Their lips come together in a sweet, slow kiss.

Then he laughed throatily as he sat up. "Twice tonight is enough," he said, reaching for her clothes and pressing them into her arms.

"For me, too," she giggled, already sliding the dress over her head.

Before he pulled his buckskin breeches on, she reached for that part of him that still was a mystery to her. She wondered how it could be smaller one minute, and so much larger the next, rejoiced at how it could send her to heaven and back.

She slowly moved her hand on him, then gave him a questioning look when he twined his fingers in her hair and slowly guided her face down toward him.

"Just one touch with your tongue is all I ask of you," he said huskily. "Then we will return to the others."

"Truly . . . you want me to . . . ?" she said reluctantly.

"It is not wrong when two people love," he said, his eyes imploring her. "Just one flick . . ."

Stunned that there could be caresses such as this between a man and woman, she hesitated. Yet knowing that it meant so much to him, she cast aside all of her apprehensions and slowly placed her tongue on him. He threw his head back and moaned with guttural pleasure.

Then he straightened himself and took her hand away.

"I never knew. . . ." she said, her eyes wide.

"Lift your skirt," he said, his eyes gazing intently into hers.

"My . . . skirt . . . ?" she said, swallowing hard.

"Yes. Let me do it for you," he said, sliding the skirt of her dress up past her thighs.

"Lie down," he said, his eyes twinkling into hers.

"But I thought you—"

"Just a flick of the tongue, as you did to me," he said, smiling warmly at her.

"No, not there," she said, gasping and blushing.

"Yes, but as I said, only a mere touch. Later, when you realize the pleasure to be had from such a caress, we will go further," he said.

Recalling the intense pleasure that only one touch of her tongue had seemed to cause him, she could not say no to such a temptation.

She nodded, then closed her eyes and waited. She sucked in a breath of pure pleasure when he stroked her womanhood with his tongue, not once, but several times. Her head was swimming with the bliss it created in her.

It was so wondrous, she felt herself quickly go over the edge into a joy that surprised her.

He raised his head and smiled at her.

"I never . . ." she said, again blushing as he drew her skirt down to cover her.

"Yes, you did," he said, laughing throatily.

They finished dressing, then walked hand in hand toward the village. Jessie was reeling from all she had shared with him tonight. This was something she would have thought so wicked, yet it had been joyful, blissful.

She giggled as she cast him a half glance.

He smiled, for he knew what had caused the giggle.

"We shall do it again," he assured her.

Again she blushed and looked quickly away from him. She knew now that, when a man truly loved a woman, there were many more adventures than she would have ever dreamed of.

Chapter Twenty-two

Jade stood wringing her hands as she watched Reginald ride away in his buggy. She had heard him talking to himself only moments ago as he paced back and forth in his study. She had happened along in the corridor just in time to hear him say that he was afraid for night to fall, afraid to go to bed. He said that he would go talk with the Sioux again, to see if they would listen to reason.

Jade had another fresh bruise on her face, for Reginald had slapped her again, much harder than the other times. She couldn't help thinking of her Lee-Lee being abused by Reginald in the same way, to say nothing of the many men who frequented the crib where her daughter was imprisoned.

"*Tcha!* I have had enough!" she cried, having lost sight of Reginald as he made a turn in the road.

Ai, she had to be brave enough to leave today. Jessie had left and hadn't been found. So surely Jade could be as fortunate. She just couldn't wait any longer, hoping that Jessie might find a way to help her and Lee-Lee escape the madman's clutches.

Nay. She would have to help herself, as well as her daughter.

"But will Jessie be discovered today when Reginald arrives at the Sioux village?" she said to herself as she hurried to the kitchen and started packing food in a lunch basket, as she always did when she went to visit Lee-Lee.

Today this basket of food would be an excuse to get Jade inside the crib again. But this time Lee-Lee would be leaving with her, not staying behind at the mercy of Tombstone's unruly, filthy-minded men.

Jade already knew where she would take her daughter. She smiled as she thought of the safest place of all, a place where Reginald would never dare search for them. Jade and her daughter would be safe there until Jade thought of somewhere they could go to seek a new life away from this town that had meant nothing but heartache for Jade and Lee-Lee.

Breathing hard, her heart pounding with fear, she placed bread, cheese, a jar of jam, and other tasty morsels in the wicker basket, as well as matches and bottles of water, which would be necessary in their new temporary home.

By the time the food was all eaten, surely she would have devised a plan that would keep her and Lee-Lee safe. She must find a way to leave these parts and find a home where people treated Chinese women with a measure of respect.

She knew that she and Lee-Lee would have to work as servants in the homes of wealthy people. That was the only thing either of them could do in America.

If they were back home in China, ah, how different it would be. Her daughter would be chosen as someone's wife and given a good life, and Lee-Lee would have brought her mother into the household.

"Nay, that is never to be," Jade sighed as she covered the food with a red-checkered cloth.

She carried the basket out to the wagon in the stable, then hurried back inside and gathered clothes and blankets and took them out to the wagon, too.

She covered the satchel of clothes and blankets with one larger blanket and set the basket of food on the seat.

After hitching the horse to the wagon, Jade took a long look at the house where she had lived for the past year. Had the man who had employed her been a decent sort, she would have been comfortable living there for many years . . . if she could have brought Lee-Lee there to live with her.

Having dressed today in something besides her usual black servant dress, Jade already felt free. She smiled as she slapped the reins and rode away from this house of evil.

When she drove into Tombstone she headed directly for the crib.

It was still too early for her daughter to be displayed in the window. The men who paid for her services came later in the day, and at night, when her daughter stood in the window illuminated by candlelight.

She would never forget the first time she had been sent into town late for supplies. She had seen her daughter standing in the window, scarcely clothed, a look of despair and shame in her beautiful black eyes, lipstick smeared on her pretty lips, and rouge bright red on her round cheeks.

It had been at that moment she knew she had to find a way to free her daughter from such degradation. But it had taken the courage a white woman showed her to finally decide to better her daughter's life, as well as her own.

Ai, Jessie had instilled in Jade her own courage. Jade hoped they would meet again someday.

But first she had to free her daughter from the crib and then get her to safety inside the burial cave that terrified Reginald Vineyard more than any other place.

She and Lee-Lee would have to risk facing whatever dwelt there besides the bodies of long-dead Sioux chiefs. Anything was better than bowing down to the wishes of a deranged man.

As she drove through the streets of Tombstone, Jade held her chin high and tried to pretend that this was just another trip to buy supplies. Her heart thumping in her chest, her fingers quivering, Jade made a sharp turn left down a small alley between two cribs and stopped when she came to Lee-Lee's.

She sat a moment as she got the courage to continue with her plan. Then she approached the man who always guarded the cribs, handing him a note she had written herself, forging Reginald Vineyard's signature.

The note said that the guard was needed out at the ranch.

Mumbling a few curse words, the man gave Jade a hard look, then spat into the dust. "Looks like the boss needs me elsewhere," he said.

Still muttering to himself, he strode off toward the livery stable to retrieve his horse.

Jade tried to control her nervous breathing and the shaking of her hands as she grabbed the wicker basket from the wagon.

She tried to look ordinary as she went to Lee-Lee's door and knocked on it.

She was, oh, so relieved when Lee-Lee opened it and let her inside.

But the moment Jade saw Lee-Lee, she went cold inside. Like Jade, Lee-Lee had a bruise on her cheek, as well as a blackened eye.

"Daughter, oh, daughter, who did this to you?" Jade cried as she placed the basket of food on the floor.

Lee-Lee hurriedly closed the door, then flung herself into her mother's arms. "It was just one of those men who ask things of me that I do not want to do," she cried, clinging. "Oh, Mother, I cannot live like this any longer. I choose death over this terrible life. Please, oh, please understand."

Hearing her daughter actually say that she was going to take her life, Jade was so glad that she had come today to set her free.

Had she not, it might have been too late for her beautiful, sweet daughter!

"Do not speak of such a thing," Jade said, stepping back from Lee-Lee. She placed gentle hands on her daughter's tiny, frail shoulders. "We are leaving today, Lee-Lee. Get dressed in something more than a robe. But first, wrap some of your more decent clothes in a blanket. As you dress, I will take your clothes to the wagon."

"Mother, what are you saying?" Lee-Lee asked, her eyes wide as she wiped tears from them.

"I am saying that while Reginald is at the Indian village begging forgiveness, I will take you away to a new life," Jade said, stroking her daughter's pale cheek. She could see the imprint of a man's hand there.

"But where . . . how?" Lee-Lee asked, too stunned to move.

"We are going where Reginald Vineyard would not dare go," Jade said tightly. "It will be a perfect place to hide from him, Lee-Lee. Perfect."

"But where?" Lee-Lee implored. "No place is safe from him, especially once he finds us both gone."

"We are going to the cave that Reginald has nightmares about every night," Jade said, smiling in satisfaction at Lee-Lee. "It is a perfect hiding place because Reginald would never dare go there. To him it is cursed. The Indian spirits that dwell within haunt him."

Lee-Lee took a quick step away from her mother. Fear entered her eyes. "Mother, if we go there, will not the Indian spirits also frighten us?"

"Nay because, sweet daughter, we have done nothing to harm them, or the Sioux people whose departed chiefs are buried there," Jade said, stepping up to Lee-

Lee and again pulling her into her arms. She hugged her tightly. "Daughter, it is the only place we can go where we will be safe from Reginald Vineyard's evil."

Lee-Lee clung for a moment, then stepped away from her mother. "And . . . then . . . what, Mother?" she asked, her eyes searching Jade's.

"We will wait for a while, then go to the Indian village," Jade said softly. "They are a kind band of Indians, and that's where Jessie has gone."

"Jessie?" Lee-Lee asked, raising an eyebrow. "Who is Jessie?"

"I will tell you all about her once we reach the cave," Jade said, eyeing the basket of food that she had brought.

She grabbed it up and nodded at Lee-Lee. "Get the clothes you want to take with you," she said. "Hurry, Lee-Lee. The longer we are here, the more likely someone will come and see what I am up to."

Lee-Lee nodded and rolled some of her clothes in a towel as Jade took the food back to the wagon and quickly covered it with a blanket.

She had only taken it in the first place to provide an excuse for her visit in case someone spied her.

When no one had come down the alley, or from the other cribs, she felt safe enough to return the food to the wagon; it was what she and her daughter would exist on for the next couple of weeks.

They would have to wait at least that long to venture out again. After that period of time, Reginald would no longer be looking for her or Lee-Lee.

Jade hurried back inside the crib. She grabbed the

rolled-up clothes, then gave Lee-Lee a quick glance. She saw that her daughter was dressed and ready. She nodded at her.

"Come on, daughter, but hurry," she said. "And when we reach the wagon, Lee-Lee, hide beneath the blankets. That is the only way I can take you from Tombstone without someone seeing you."

After Lee-Lee was safely hidden in the back of the wagon, Jade climbed aboard and drove away from the cribs. As she traveled down the main street, she was glad that there were no men loitering on the boardwalk or gambling in the saloons. The town had a peaceful air about it, even decent.

But soon that would all change. Soon men would be drinking and gambling and choosing pretty women to give them pleasure.

Jade smiled, for today no one could choose Lee-Lee.

She rode onward, traveled far from the town and into a forest of trees, only stopping when they were far from where any passersby could see the wagon.

"Lee-Lee," Jade said, climbing down from the wagon. "It is safe now for you to leave the wagon. We're close enough to the cave to walk the rest of the way."

"Mother, how do you know?" Lee-Lee asked, throwing aside the blanket and climbing out of the wagon.

"I have seen the cave before," Jade said, rolling up the blanket that had covered Lee-Lee, then handing it to her. "It suddenly came to me that the cave could be a perfect hideaway," Jade said, taking the basket of supplies from the wagon.

Lee-Lee grabbed her clothes and as many blankets as she could carry.

"How far, Mother?" Lee-Lee asked as Jade started walking away from the wagon with Lee-Lee close beside her. She looked over her shoulder at the horse and wagon, then questioned her mother with her eyes. "And what about the horse? Will it be alright?"

Jade stopped abruptly. She looked over her shoulder at the horse, then set her supplies down and hurried back to the animal. She quickly released it from the wagon, then patted its rump and watched it run away, glad to see it ran in the opposite direction from Reginald's house. She hoped it would find its way to the Indian village, where it could be fed and have a good home.

She hurried back to Lee-Lee and resumed their walk toward the cave. "I think the horse will be alright now," she murmured. "As for the wagon? I only hope that Reginald doesn't happen along and find it, but I doubt that he will. It's way too close to the cave that haunts him.

"And we do not have much farther to go, Lee-Lee, to get to the cave," she said, glancing down at the basket of supplies. She had made certain there was enough food, water, and even matches to last them for the two weeks she planned to be in the cave.

And Lee-Lee was carrying the blankets.

Ai, it did seem that she had planned everything well enough. She was beginning to believe she would pull off their escape.

But she could see that Lee-Lee was very uneasy. She

could see fear in her daughter's eyes, in the way she kept looking over her shoulder as though expecting to get caught.

"Daughter, we are safe," Jade said reassuringly.

"I am so afraid of Reginald, and I am also afraid of . . . of . . . the cave and . . . what might be in there," Lee-Lee murmured.

"Sweet daughter, you have to learn never to be afraid again, of *any*thing," Jade said. "It is a cruel, complicated world, but we will make a new beginning. You shall see. Only goodness lies ahead for us both." She swallowed hard. "I should not have waited so long to do this."

Lee-Lee gave Jade a faint, quivering smile.

Chapter Twenty-three

Panting and wheezing, and mopping his brow with his handkerchief, Reginald walked onward. He had left his horse and buggy a mile back. He was trying a different tactic today. He was trying to elude all the sentries so that he could get into the village.

He was determined to get the young chief's attention. Surely Thunder Horse would take pity on him once he heard about the horrible nights that Reginald was having.

Surely the Sioux chief would have mercy. He had had enough nightmares already to last him a lifetime.

Reginald had watched carefully as he walked, keeping an eye out for sentries who would surely stop him. Thus far he had managed to stay hidden among the trees.

He wheezed and coughed into his handkerchief, hoping that he could stifle the sounds as he drew near the village. Only moments ago he had caught a glimpse of tepees, and even now he smelled the smoke from the lodge fires, so he knew that he had almost succeeded with his plan.

But he was ungodly tired. He wasn't used to walking this far. His legs were feeling rubbery and weak.

He wasn't certain he could make it back to his horse and buggy. Again he hoped the savages would have some mercy and take him back to the buggy on horseback instead of making him walk all the way.

His lungs ached as if they were on fire from the effort it took to place one foot and then the other forward.

Again he wiped the sweat that was pouring from his brow. His hair was wet with perspiration, dripping onto his expensive suit jacket.

"You damn savages," he whispered as he doubled a hand at his side in anger and humiliation. No one had ever seen him as disheveled as he must look now.

But he had only a short way to go before he would finally step into the village. He had succeeded in tricking them into receiving him.

Now if only they would let him talk. If only they would listen to reason.

He even had his pockets filled with coins. Money spoke volumes to poor people. And he saw the Sioux as poor. How else could anyone see a people who lived in tepees and who cooked over open fires inside small lodges?

Yes, coins might be the answer today where words had not worked. And today he would surely be able to talk to the chief.

Panting, and wiping more sweat from his face, hoping to look as presentable as possible, he stepped up to the very edge of the village. He was stunned that even now no one noticed him there.

He stopped and gazed slowly around him. The women were busy preparing meat. The children were laughing and playing games. The elders were sitting around an outside fire, smoking their long pipes and talking.

And then something else caught his eye, someone who made his heart skip a beat. It was Jessie! She had just stepped inside a tepee not far from where he stood, and she was dressed as a squaw, her hair hanging down her back in one long braid.

Stunned at the sight of her, for he had never thought in a thousand years to look for her in an Indian village, Reginald could not stop a sudden bout of terribly loud wheezing. He began coughing so hard, he felt as though he might strangle.

He grabbed at his throat, the handkerchief falling to the ground at his feet.

Finally he got some control of his coughing. He bent and started to retrieve his handkerchief from the ground. Just as he did, he saw moccasins step up before him and knew that his coughing had caught someone's attention.

Almost afraid to straighten his back and see who was there, Reginald breathed hard and stayed bent for a moment longer, just staring at the moccasins.

But when a hand fell upon his shoulder and a voice spoke, telling him to stand up, he knew that he had no choice but to look upon the face of whoever had discovered him standing there.

Breathing hard, his heart thumping wildly, Reginald straightened his back and found himself gazing up into the dark, stern eyes of none other than the young chief.

"Chief Thunder Horse," he said, hating the trembling in his voice. He was very aware of the heaviness of that large, copper hand on his shoulder.

"What are you doing here?" Thunder Horse asked, his voice stern, his anger obvious. "And where is your horse?"

"I . . . I . . . left my horse and buggy back yonder," Reginald breathed out, pointing.

"Why?" Thunder Horse asked, his eyes narrowing angrily. "And again, what are you doing here? You know that you are not welcome on our land."

"It doesn't belong to you anymore and you know it," Reginald said quickly, then wished he had not spoken.

But he didn't like hearing the savage claim something that was not his. It was only out of the kindness of the president that these savages were still in this area on land that belonged to the United States. Personally, he could not wait to see the last of this pack of wild, flea-covered savages.

He wanted to scream out that his cousin had no place among such savages, to demand to know why she was there in the first place. Had she been abducted?

Oh, surely she hadn't come here of her own volition.

Would she have truly chosen this sort of life over what he had offered her?

He cursed himself silently over having forbidden her to play the piano, for it seemed his reaction to her playing had precipitated her departure.

But he couldn't mention Jessie to this savage, for to do so would be to tip his hand . . . to reveal that he was trying to find a way to claim her again as his!

Thunder Horse found it unbelievable that this tiny, sweating man could stand before him and speak so coldly about whom this land did or did not belong to. Thunder Horse wanted this man out of his village. He couldn't stand the smell of him, or the sight!

"You still have not said why you are here, or why you chose to walk instead of ride into my village," Thunder Horse said dryly.

"I walked because I wanted to get into the village instead of being stopped as I was last night when I tried to come and talk with you," Reginald gulped out. "If I came in my buggy, it would have made too much noise. I felt that once I got inside your village, I would be able to get a few moments of your time to plead my case."

"And that is?" Thunder Horse asked, stunned to learn that this man had came last night to try to speak with him and no one had told him about it.

He was also surprised that this man had been able to elude his sentries. He had sneaked through the forest, where the trees were thick and the shadows dark. Thunder Horse had to correct this weakness in his defenses by making certain his sentries were placed among the trees, too.

"Thunder Horse, may I go to your lodge with you, where I can sit down while we discuss my situation?" Reginald asked, his eyes pleading through the thick lenses of his glasses.

Just the thought of this man being in his private lodge, where Jessie even now sat waiting for Thunder Horse's return, made him shiver with disgust. Jessie had heard the wheezing and coughing before anyone else. She had been aware at once that Reginald was somewhere close by.

"Say what you have come to say and then return to your home and never come here again," Thunder Horse said tightly. "You know that you are not welcome here, or else you would not have sneaked around like a frightened skunk to request time with this chief who sees you as evil and worthless."

"Alright, then, I'll say it and leave," Reginald replied. "Thunder Horse, I have come to beg for mercy. Please stop the nightmares. I . . . I . . . haven't gotten any decent sleep since they began. You know that you have the power to stop them. Please, oh, please, I beg of you."

He shoved his hands into his front suit jacket pockets and pulled out many shiny gold coins. He thrust them toward Thunder Horse. "Here, take these, and there are many more in my pockets," Reginald said, wheezing almost uncontrollably.

"Lord, Thunder Horse, what else can I do to make you understand the severity of the situation?" Reginald said, a sob lodging in his throat. "Please, oh, Lord, please, take the coins. They can buy you a lot of supplies. Hand me a bag. I'll fill it with these and all the others I have in my pockets. I . . . just . . . need a decent night's sleep."

Thunder Horse's jaw tightened. He gazed at the coins, and then raised his eyes and glared at Reginald.

"No, no payment," he said. He gestured with his hand toward the forest. "Return to your horse and buggy, for you see, little man, there will never be any forgiveness from my people. Your life is what you made it to be; now live it."

"Forever?" Reginald choked out, unaware that the coins were spilling from his hands as he dropped them to his sides. "I will be forced to have . . . these . . . nightmares forever?"

"Forever," Thunder Horse said firmly. "You disturbed the peace of our sacred cave forever. Leave. Do not return."

Reginald was struck dumb by Thunder Horse's refusal to have mercy. He stared up into the chief's dark eyes.

And then a rage filled him that he had never felt before. He leaned into Thunder Horse's face. "You will pay for this," he growled out. "I will find a way. I'll go to the authorities and tell them what you're doing to me. They will come and force you and your people to go to the reservation now, not later."

"You know what will happen if you do this," Thunder Horse said, a slow smile quivering across his lips.

"What . . . will . . . happen?" Reginald gulped out.

"They will think you mad," Thunder Horse said, now openly smiling down at Reginald. "So do as you must and then live . . . and die . . . with the result."

Reginald took a slow step away from Thunder

Horse, then turned and began running as fast as his weak legs would take him. Yet his heart was filled with an almost uncontrollable hatred.

Jessie.

Yes, Jessie.

He would get back at Thunder Horse through Jessie.

He would kill two birds with one stone.

He would take Jessie away from the Indians and he would at the same time make her pay for what she had done to him.

No woman double-crossed him and lived to tell of it, not even a cousin.

Thunder Horse watched Reginald until he couldn't see him any longer, then gazed down at the coins. He stepped up to them and with a heel, he ground what he could into the ground. It was the hunger for such coins that had sent Reginald Vineyard into the sacred cave to take silver from it.

Thunder Horse wanted nothing that came from such greed.

"Thunder Horse, I am sorry that I didn't tell you Reginald Vineyard came here last night while you were gone," one of his warriors said from behind him, drawing Thunder Horse quickly around. "He did not make it into our village. I stopped him and sent him away."

"He will not come again," Thunder Horse growled, then walked past the warrior and hurried into his lodge, where Jessie stood over the fire, visibly trembling.

She turned quickly when she heard him enter.

She hurried to him and flung herself into his arms.

"He is gone and will not return," Thunder Horse said, holding her close.

"What if he saw me?" Jessie said, leaning away so that she could look into his eyes.

"It would not matter if he did, for he knows better than to bring trouble into my village for any reason," Thunder Horse said. He framed her beautiful face between his hands. "My woman, you are safe. Nothing will ever come of this meeting, even if he did see you."

"He is an unpredictable man," Jessie said, still bewildered that he had turned into such an evil man after being a decent person in his youth.

Of course the children poked fun at him then, because of his bad eyesight and small stature, but she had thought he had ignored those humiliations and had made a good life for himself as an adult.

She knew now that she'd been terribly wrong. He had made a true mess of his life.

"He might be unpredictable, but he is also a coward who tries to seem otherwise," Thunder Horse said. "He will never get a chance to harm you. I won't allow it."

Feeling truly safe, and loving Thunder Horse so much, Jessie eased back into his arms. "I know that you will keep me safe," she murmured. "I shall not worry another minute about what happened here today, not even if he, by chance, got a glimpse of me."

Yet inside her, where her fear of this cousin of hers was centered, she knew that no one could watch her one hundred percent of the time for the rest of her life, not even this strong and wonderful Indian chief!

She would just have to be cautious in everything she

did from now on. She would have to be certain to watch all around her whenever Thunder Horse wasn't near.

She clung to Thunder Horse, reveling in the safety she felt while she was in his arms.

Chapter Twenty-four

A fire burned softly in the cave where Jade and Lee-Lee sat beside it. On every side they were surrounded by solid rock, except overhead, where the cave gave way in places to open sky, and smoke from the fire filtered slowly through the spaces.

"What if someone sees the smoke created by our fire?" Lee-Lee asked, watching the slow streamers float up. "Mother, what if Reginald Vineyard sees it?"

"The smoke is not enough to draw anyone's attention," Jade reassured her. "By the time it escapes through the cracks, it is quickly dissipated into the air. I planned all this, Lee-Lee, after I found the cave and came inside to see if it could be used for our temporary hideaway."

She laughed softly. "And you do not have to worry about Reginald seeing it," she said. "He would never come close to this cave again. He fears the spirits of the cave too much."

"Mother, you are more daring than I ever knew,"

Lee-Lee said, giggling as she reached a soft hand out to her mother and twined their fingers together. "Oh, Mother, had I been forced to stay another night in that . . . that . . . horrid place, I surely would have killed myself."

Jade gently squeezed Lee-Lee's hand. "Do not ever talk that way again," she said. "You are free, and soon we shall find a new life where we can feel like humans again. Reginald Vineyard treated us as though we were slaves and tried to take our spirit from us, but as you see, he did not succeed."

"Spirits," Lee-Lee said, visibly shivering as she looked slowly around her. On the cave walls were paintings that had been drawn by the Sioux many years ago; they were fading and sometimes even crumbling from the wall, leaving images that were hardly discernible. "Are . . . we truly . . . safe from the spirits . . . of this cave?"

"Do you feel them around you?" Jade asked, following the path of her daughter's eyes, also seeing the faint drawings.

"Nay," Lee-Lee said, turning her eyes back to her mother.

"They are here, but they will not bother us," Jade said firmly. "We are good people. They know it. They only torment the bad."

"Reginald Vineyard is very, very bad," Lee-Lee said tightly. "I am so glad they are causing him distress as he tries to sleep. Mother, I would have loved seeing him running down the corridor, screaming and afraid, as you saw him. That would have almost made my long stay in his crib worthwhile."

"Nothing could make what you were forced to do worthwhile," Jade said, smoothing her daughter's long black hair back from her face. "Oh, daughter, what you had to do is too horrible to think about, yet . . . you . . . were made to do it."

Lee-Lee humbly lowered her eyes. "*Ai*, Mother, it was like living in the pits of hell," she said, swallowing hard. She looked quickly up again. "It is true, nothing would make that worthwhile. I . . . was . . . only—"

Jade placed a gentle hand on her daughter's lips. "I know," she said. "You do not need to explain anything to me. I am your mother. I know everything about you, even your deepest thoughts."

Lee-Lee wiped tears from her eyes. "You are such a good mother," she said softly. "But I loved Father, too, and, oh, Mother, I miss my brother Tak Ming so much."

"*Ai*, as do I miss them both," Jade said, then reached for another piece of the cheese she had brought from Reginald's kitchen. Then she took a slice of bread that she had sliced only moments ago from the loaf she'd made late the night before in anticipation of her escape.

She placed the cheese on the bread and handed it to Lee-Lee. "Daughter, eat this," she softly encouraged. "You have wasted away to almost nothing while in that *puh-kao*, that bad place."

"While I was there, I did not wish to eat," Lee-Lee said, taking the bread and cheese. She eagerly ate as her mother took an apple from the food basket and bit into it.

Jade again gazed at the drawings on the wall. "I find the drawings in this cave mystical," she murmured. "They are not frightening at all to me."

"*Ai*, they are becoming less frightening to me, too," Lee-Lee said. "But, Mother, when can we leave? It is damp and dark in here. I feel chilled through and through."

Jade laid the apple aside and went to pick up some of the firewood that she and Lee-Lee had gathered when they first arrived.

She took several small branches to the fire and placed them amid the flames.

She sat down again beside her daughter, then lifted a blanket and placed it around Lee-Lee's frail shoulders. "We must stay here at least a week," she said, her voice drawn. "We must wait for Reginald to give up on finding us. *Ai*, perhaps a week will do. Then we will go to the Indian village that Jessie was trying to find."

"What if they do not like it that we stayed in their sacred cave?" Lee-Lee asked, wrapping the blanket more closely around herself.

"Did you not say that the nephew of the chief is kind and understanding?" Jade asked.

Just then something on the far wall caught her eye as the flames of the fire cast a brighter glow around her. Her eyes widened, for she thought she was seeing streaks of silver.

She knew that silver was what had made Reginald rich. Surely he had come and taken it from this cave.

That could be the reason behind the Sioux curse that caused him such horrible nightmares!

She looked quickly away, for she did not want to have the same temptation that Reginald had had. She wanted nothing to do with the silver, although she knew that it could possibly pay her and Lee-Lee's passage back to China.

But it could also give them a lifetime of miserable nightmares.

Nay. She would not look at the silver ever again. Let it stay with the spirits!

"Lone Wing is sweet and kind, and he told me that his uncle was a very compassionate man," Lee-Lee said.

"Then you see, Lee-Lee, that when we go and ask for help, it will be given to us," Jade said.

"Especially if Lone Wing is there when we arrive," Lee-Lee said, suddenly getting stars in her eyes. "He is a handsome brave."

"*Tcha!* He is younger than you, Lee-Lee, so do not dream of things that can never be," Jade said tightly.

"He is not that much younger," Lee-Lee quickly corrected. "And does age truly matter that much when you fall in love?"

"Love?" Jade said, her voice filled with shock. "Remember your age. You are older than that young man. It was not written in the stars for you to be with him in the way you are imagining."

Lee-Lee smiled softly, lowered her eyes humbly, then ate the last of her bread and cheese. She knew, down deep in her heart, that there was something good between her and Lone Wing. If they should marry when they both got somewhat older, she knew the stars would smile down on their union. They had a special bond already. Nothing would tear it asunder.

"Mother, I miss Tak Ming so much," Lee-Lee then said, tears in her eyes. "My big brother would have favored Lone Wing as my future husband. There is much about Lone Wing that reminds me of Tak Ming."

"Tak Ming is gone from us forever. It only hurts to talk of him, Lee-Lee," Jade said, swallowing hard.

She was transported back in time, to the ship that she and her children had been forced to board. The long journey from China to America had been hard. Tak Ming had not survived the grueling work the Americans had forced him to do.

But she and Lee-Lee had survived . . . and they would continue to survive, for she would not allow anything to stand in the way of their freedom or happiness.

"I hope these days in the cave pass quickly by," Lee-Lee said, stretching out on a blanket close to the fire. "I am so weary, Mother, of this life we have been forced to live. And now? The cave? It is horrible."

"It is by fate that I found this cave; by hiding here we will survive," Jade said. She reached out and stroked her daughter's face. "This is our destiny, Lee-Lee. Be happy that we are here, not sad."

"*Ai*, I shall try," Lee-Lee said, then closed her eyes and fell into a restful sleep, the first since she had arrived in America.

Jade watched her daughter sleep and prayed that she could make things better for her. It did seem that it all depended on one man, and that man was Chief Thunder Horse.

His studies completed for the day, Lone Wing made his way swiftly toward Tombstone.

As always, he was on foot, having left his pony some distance away. He felt he would be less noticeable if he were traveling by foot as he came into the horrible town. He always ran fast until he came to the cribs, then darted quickly into the alley where he had first met Lee-Lee at the door of her assigned crib.

It was the hour of the day when he knew she would not be on display in the front window.

It was the time when she rested or prepared herself for the dreadful nighttime hours when she was forced to spend time with the filthy men who came filled with spirit water, their grubby hands and mouths ready to touch his Lee-Lee's beautiful, frail body.

He so badly wanted to find a way to help her escape. And he had to do it before he and his people started on the long journey to the reservation.

He could not even think of how it would be to leave Lee-Lee behind. No. He could not leave her behind. He had to convince his uncle to help effect her escape.

But there were two things foremost on his uncle's mind now: his ailing father, and the woman.

He was now so close to the door of Lee-Lee's assigned crib, he could almost see her standing there, smiling a sweet welcome to him. Lone Wing broke into a faster run and stopped at the door of the crib.

He looked cautiously from side to side. There was

no sign of the man who guarded the crib, so he knew it was safe to knock on the door.

He would ask her if he could come inside this time, for while he'd been standing in the alley talking to her, there had been a chance they both would be caught. He did not want to think what might happen to them if they were caught together. He knew that the white men who frequented the cribs would get much pleasure in humiliating him, would possibly even go so far as to kill him.

He knocked on the door and clasped his hands behind his back as he waited. When the door swung open, he took a quick step backward, for it wasn't Lee-Lee standing there.

It was another woman.

He could tell that she was much older. She had a hardness about her that made him cringe.

And when she reached a hand out for him, smiling, he knew that she wanted him to go inside the crib for all the wrong reasons.

"My, oh, my, don't they come young in this town?" Marla Bates said, raking her violet eyes slowly over Lone Wing. "And Indian. I think it would be interesting to have an Indian boy in bed with me." She beckoned with a hand. "Come on. Don't be bashful. You knocked on my door. Surely you have coins to pay for my time with you."

"No, I do not," Lone Wing said, blushing. He looked quickly past her. "Where . . . is . . . Lee-Lee?"

Marla shrugged. "No one knows," she said. "She just up and disappeared. But aren't I pretty enough for you? Much older, yet I'm good—"

Lone Wing didn't stay to hear anything else. He swung around and ran from the alley, not stopping until he reached his pony.

Panting, he slumped to the ground, his head hanging. "Where is she?" he whispered, near tears.

He could only conclude that Reginald Vineyard had done something horrible to her.

What if he'd found out about her being visited by a young Indian brave? Would he have killed her for that reason alone?

Could something else have happened to her? The lady had said she'd disappeared.

A sick feeling swept through him as he mounted his pony. He sank his heels into its flanks, riding hard until he finally reached his village.

He could not get to his uncle's lodge quickly enough, even though he knew he would be scolded for going into Tombstone again to see the lovely woman.

"Thunder Horse!" he cried outside Thunder Horse's tepee. "Chieftain uncle?"

Thunder Horse opened his entrance flap and gazed down at his nephew. "What is it?" he asked, holding the flap aside so that Lone Wing could enter.

Lone Wing stepped past him. He stopped and looked from Jessie to Thunder Horse as she came to stand beside his uncle.

Then Lone Wing gazed intently into his uncle's eyes. "She is gone," he said, his voice breaking.

"Who is gone?" Thunder Horse asked.

Lone Wing lowered his eyes as he drew up the courage to tell his uncle he had ignored Thunder Horse's warning.

"Lee-Lee," he blurted out. "I went to see her again. She is gone. The woman who is now in her crib said that Lee-Lee had disappeared."

Panic entered Jessie's heart, for she could only imagine the worst—that Reginald had done something to Jade's daughter.

And then . . . what . . . of Jade?

"Thunder Horse, I'm afraid for not only Lee-Lee, but also—" Jessie said, but stopped when Sweet Willow ran into the tepee.

"You must come quickly," she said, gazing into Thunder Horse's eyes through streaming tears. "Our father. He . . . is . . . dying."

Thunder Horse gasped, then brushed past Sweet Willow and Lone Wing and left the tepee.

"How long . . . ?" Jessie murmured, already feeling Thunder Horse's pain inside her own heart. She knew the anguish of losing someone you loved. She had lost everyone she loved, her whole family. Reginald was her only living relative, and he was no longer anything to her.

She would never claim him again as her cousin!

"Soon," Sweet Willow said, taking Lone Wing into her arms and hugging him as he began sobbing.

They forgot everything and everyone but their imminent loss. Even sweet and beautiful Lee-Lee. . . .

Chapter Twenty-five

Enraged that the Sioux seemed to have the upper hand, and that Jessie had hidden from him in their village, Reginald had made a rash decision. He needed help, and he knew just the man to provide it: an outlaw friend of his.

Reginald was approaching his hideout even now in his horse and buggy. He was driving through winding trees, where there was just barely enough room for the conveyance to pass.

He had seen a lookout, watching for intruders, and was glad that the man had recognized him and let him pass. If he was a stranger, he knew that he wouldn't still be alive.

Bulldog Jones couldn't afford to get careless.

He had lived many a year without being caught. He wasn't about to let it happen now.

Sweat poured from Reginald's brow, his fingers trembled with fear, even though Bulldog Jones knew him. They had become friends several years ago when they had been traveling the same road and Bulldog Jones had seen a snake coiled up in the path of Reginald's horse, ready to strike. He had thrown a knife at the snake, cutting its head off in an instant.

Reginald had been speechless when he saw what had happened. Bulldog Jones had come up to Reginald, holding his hand out for a handshake, and that had been the beginning of a strange sort of friendship that even today puzzled Reginald.

In time, Bulldog Jones had learned how rich Reginald was, but he had never attempted to steal from him. Bulldog Jones could brag of having his own riches. In fact, these days he rarely attacked innocent people who happened along in their wagons on the trail.

Reginald went for visits at Bulldog Jones's established hideout, where the outlaw still kept many men to protect him and his riches.

Reginald wasn't sure whether Bulldog Jones would agree to help him; since the outlaw hardly ever ventured forth from his hideout nowadays. Reginald hoped that the man would be restless and itching to do something exciting, like kill a few savages.

He smiled as he slapped his reins and rode onward, now able to see smoke spiraling lazily from the outlaw's stone chimney. He also saw many horses in a corral at the back of the log cabin.

Although rich, the outlaw lived simply. He had once said to Reginald that all he needed was a roof over his head, a warm fire to sit by in his rocking chair, and an occasional pretty lady whom his men brought to him for one or two nights' stay.

Of course, they were blindfolded so they couldn't lead the authorities back to the hideout. The ladies of the night had also been threatened with their lives if they told anyone that they had been with the famous outlaw.

Yes, Reginald was fortunate to have been rescued that day by this man, not only because Bulldog Jones had probably saved his life, but also because of who he was. He was the very outlaw who killed Jessie's father, who had been his associate before Jessie's father hung up his guns and became a family man.

Reginald had recently learned that Bulldog Jones was the very same outlaw who had recently robbed the stagecoach Jessie had been on, not knowing that she was the daughter of Two Guns Pete. He had heard the story in town from some of the outlaw's men.

"Well, now, won't Bulldog Jones be pleased to know just where the daughter of his most hated enemy is hiding?" Reginald snickered to himself.

Yes, Reginald knew just what to say to the outlaw to bring him out of retirement and to send him after the daughter of his longtime enemy Two Guns Pete!

Reginald rode up to the house and drew rein as several men appeared out of nowhere, their rifles poised and ready to fire if Reginald made a wrong move.

Reginald swallowed hard as he looked slowly from man to man, praying that Bulldog Jones would step from the cabin soon. Otherwise, he was afraid these men might shoot him down in cold blood. He was so scared, he thought he might wet his pants.

"Guns down, gents," a gravelly voice said, drawing Reginald's eyes quickly to the tall, lanky outlaw, whose coppery red hair hung down to his shoulders. "Don't you recognize Preach, our friend?"

Bulldog Jones came down the steps and took the horse's reins, wrapping them around a hitching rail. "Come on inside, Preach," he said, nodding toward the door. "Have a cup of java with your old buddy."

Relieved, and wheezing, Reginald stepped from the buggy.

His shoulders slightly hunched, he shuffled along, watching the men over his shoulder sheepishly, until he came to the steps and hurried up them.

"You look like you've been cornered by a polecat, Preach," Bulldog Jones said, opening the door for Reginald.

"I feel like I have," Reginald said, reaching a hand to his brow and swiping beads of sweat from it as he stepped past Bulldog Jones into the cabin.

"They meant you no harm," Bulldog Jones said, motioning with a hand toward two rockers that sat before a roaring fire in the huge stone fireplace at the far end of the room. "Come and sit with me. Tell me what's on your mind."

Reginald nodded and sat down while Bulldog Jones poured two cups of coffee and brought one to Reginald.

"Want some spirits in yours?" Bulldog Jones said, nodding toward a bottle of whiskey on the table between the rocking chairs. "Do you think that'd calm you down a mite?"

"I'm fine," Reginald said. Yet his hand was trembling so much, it splashed coffee over the side of the cup and onto his brand new breeches. He knew it would leave a stain, but Jade would be able to get it out. She was good at such things.

Bulldog Jones settled himself into the cushion of the chair next to Reginald and began slowly rocking. "Tell me what brings you here today, Preach," he said, eyeing Reginald with dark brown eyes. "It's an uncommon thing . . . you coming here like this."

"Yes, I know," Reginald said, nodding. "And I know you'd rather I didn't unless you've requested my company. But I had to come. I'm in trouble; bad trouble."

"What sort?" Bulldog Jones said, lifting an eyebrow. He took a slow sip of coffee, then placed the cup on the table next to him. "What can I do for you? You did come here to ask for my help, didn't you?"

"I hate for you to think that's the only reason I'd come," Reginald said, again wiping sweat from his brow. "We're friends. I appreciate your friendship. And I know friends shouldn't take advantage of each other. But, damn it, Bulldog, I'm in a lot of trouble. And because of it, I'm not able to sleep. I'm tired. So damn tired."

"What on earth could get in the way of your sleep?" Bulldog Jones wondered. "Spit it out, Preach. Tell me everything. If there's something I can do to help you, you know I'll do it."

"Well, it's this way," Reginald said, then told him all about how he had come to be cursed by the Sioux. Up until now he had not told anyone where he had found the silver.

But now it was different.

And if Bulldog Jones wanted to go and take silver from that damnable cave, let him. He was welcome to it, if he wanted to start having the same nightmares that Reginald was now having.

That made him smile.

"And are you saying that your cousin Jessie is at the Indian village?" Bulldog Jones said, leaning forward, his eyes squinting. "And you want me to do away with the Injuns and make sure the offspring of my old rival is dead?"

"Exactly," Reginald said, suddenly overwhelmed by an attack of wheezing. He tried to suck in a deep breath, only to wheeze even more violently.

"I think you need that whiskey," Bulldog Jones said, rising quickly and pouring a shot into a small glass, then handing it to Reginald.

Reginald swallowed it in fast gulps, and sighed with relief when the whiskey momentarily checked his wheezing and coughing.

"Thanks," he said, handing the empty glass back to Bulldog Jones. "Well, what's your answer? Will you help me? I'll part with many of my coins if you'll do this job for me."

"Yep, it'd be my pleasure," Bulldog Jones said, his eyes gleaming. "I've gotten blisters on my butt from sitting too long in this rocking chair. It'll be good to be back on my horse wreaking havoc."

"Thank you, oh, thank you," Reginald said, his heart pounding at the thought that this outlaw was actually going to help him in his time of crisis. "When can you do it?"

"Soon," Bulldog Jones said, going to stare from a window. "I'm eager to get my hands on my ol' buddy's daughter. And I hate Injuns; all sorts. They don't have a place among us civil folk."

"That's true," Reginald said, rising from his chair. "In a few days I'll bring you a bag of money for what you're going to do to help me. Name your price. It'll be in the bag."

"You know me well enough to know the price I need for this job," Bulldog Jones said, turning on a heel and smiling greedily at Reginald. "Preach, I'll send word when I want you to come with the money."

Then he stared from the window again. "And a cave is where you got it, huh?" he said, drumming his fingers on the windowsill. "I'll wait awhile and then give that cave a visit."

"You'd best leave no Sioux behind if you plan on going to that damnable cave," Reginald said, walking toward the door. "If you had the sort of nightmares they've cursed me with, you'd think twice before going to that cave. I'll give you enough coins so that you may change your mind about going there."

"There's never enough coins for my pockets," Bulldog Jones said, walking out of the cabin with Reginald. "Seems my pockets have holes in them."

Reginald laughed, then boarded his wagon and nodded a farewell to the outlaw. He was escorted from the property by several men, glad when they finally stopped and rode back toward the hideout.

Feeling smug now, and anxious for Bulldog Jones to do his work, Reginald hurried home.

He gazed down at the damnable coffee stain. "Jade," he whispered. "I've got to find Jade."

He hurried into the house, only to find silence there.

He went to the kitchen, expecting Jade to be standing over the stove preparing food for the evening meal. He frowned when he found no signs of her there, or of food being prepared.

He turned on a heel and stomped from the kitchen, shrieking Jade's name. But no matter where he looked, he couldn't find her.

He stormed into her bedroom. His face blanched when he saw that all of her belongings were missing, as were the blankets from her bed.

"She's gone," he said, a sick feeling gripping him in the pit of his stomach. "That damnable wench has left me!"

He ran out to the stable and saw that the wagon she used to travel into town was also gone.

"Lee-Lee," he said, his eyes widening. "Lord, Lee-Lee!"

Realizing that Jade had done far more than go into town to visit her daughter and take her the usual basket of provisions, Reginald was afraid to go and check on Lee-Lee. He suspected that Jade had finally worked up the courage to help her daughter escape. Surely both were long gone from the area by now.

"She'd better not have dared," he growled, boarding his buggy again and slapping the reins on the back of his horse. "I'll hunt her down. I'll scalp her and leave her for the vultures. The Indians will be blamed. No one'll ever think I'd do such a thing."

He rode hard until he pulled up in the alley between the cribs.

He hurried to the door that led into Lee-Lee's assigned crib and yanked it open.

He stopped dead when he found another woman in bed with a man.

"Where is she?" he shouted, going to the bed to stand over the two naked people. "Where is Lee-Lee?"

The man grabbed his pants and jerked them on, then fled through the door, while the woman named Marla recoiled on the bed, her eyes filled with fear.

"She's gone," Marla muttered. "So I took her crib. It's better'n mine, so clean and all. I didn't think you'd mind." She gave a sly smile. "Didn't you give her permission to leave?"

"You know the answer to that," Reginald shouted, flailing his hands in the air. "She was mine. Mine!"

"I'm sorry," Marla gulped out, visibly shivering. She yanked a blanket around her shoulders. "You're not going to hurt me over somethin' she did, are you? Or over . . . me . . . taking her crib?"

"No, you aren't at fault," Reginald said, kneading his chin as he tried to figure out what to do next. He nodded toward Marla. "Sorry for intruding. I'll give you what the gentleman would've paid you."

He reached inside his front right pocket and jerked

out several coins, then dropped them on the bed. "Again, sorry," he said. "You're one of my best. You deserve the best crib."

"Thank you," Marla said, quickly gathering the coins into a pile on the bed. "I'll never disappoint you."

Reginald nodded and left the crib.

He stood outside and looked up one side of the alley and down the other, then hung his head. He couldn't go and ask for help from the sheriff. None of the decent townsfolk knew of his connection to the cribs. He couldn't let them know now.

He had to accept his losses.

Then he went pale at the thought of the man who had just run from the crib. Should he start spreading the word about who had interrupted his time with Marla, and why, all hell would break loose. Reginald would be washed up in this town.

He boarded his buggy and headed back toward his home. He knew he would have to wait and see if there were any consequences of his actions today at the crib. If there were, he'd handle them at that time.

For now he wanted the comforts of his home. Its peace and serenity.

"Where could Jade and Lee-Lee have gone?" he wondered as he approached his ranch.

He frowned as he thought more about what he had done today at Bulldog Jones's hideout. He had made a bargain with the devil, but he would do anything to get back at the Sioux. He knew he could count on the outlaw to do what he had promised.

Reginald just hoped that Bulldog Jones didn't wait

too long to act, for Reginald didn't think he could take many more sleepless nights.

He turned down the lane that led to his ranch, his thoughts on Jade and Lee-Lee again. How would they stay alive without him and his help?

The thought of them not making it made him laugh wickedly, for they deserved such a fate for having duped him.

Chapter Twenty-six

Filled with deep sadness, and already missing his beloved *ahte*, who had sunk into a deep sleep, Thunder Horse sat at his father's side.

The shaman had already left, having performed all the rituals that he could for his dying chief. Thunder Horse sat alone, filled with memories that would now have to sustain him the rest of his life.

His father had been so good to him. He had taught Thunder Horse to be brave and courageous in the eye of danger.

He had given him the strength and insight to be a great chief. His *ahte* had been one of the greatest and most beloved of the Sioux tribe.

And now his father, that once powerful chief of the Fox band, was living his last moments of life.

It just did not seem real that this was happening, although Thunder Horse knew it was inevitable that he would soon say a final good-bye to his *ahte*. He had already lost his beloved *ina* to death. The loss of his mother had been hard to accept at the time. Just as hard as it was now to await his *ahte's* dying breath.

But Thunder Horse had to remind himself that he still had the love and support of his people, as well as his sister Sweet Willow and nephew Lone Wing, and now, ah, his beloved, sweet Jessie.

Soon he would take Jessie as his wife and fill that gap in his heart that had waited for such a woman as Jessie to fill it with her love and devotion.

Ho, soon he would marry this woman and would have children born of their love. He had much to look forward to, those moments he would share with his family, always with the presence of his *ina* and *ahte* inside his mind and heart.

Suddenly he heard a low gasp.

He saw his father's eyes take on a strange sort of peaceful look as he took his last breath of life. It was not the usual stare of death, but instead a look of peace.

"*Ahte*, oh, *Ahte*, how I will miss you," Thunder Horse cried, fighting back tears, for he knew that he must face his people soon with the horrible news that they had lost the man who had been their leader for so many years.

He anticipated the heartache of his people even before telling them, for he knew how much they all had loved Chief White Horse.

Gently he reached out and closed his father's eyes, then embraced him one last time.

After he made the announcement that all were expecting, yet dreading, he would prepare his father's body for burial.

He had a promise to fulfill, one that his father had made to the White Chief in Washington. As soon as Chief White Horse was dead and interred in the sacred cave of the Fox band of Sioux, the band would move on, to where the rest of their band awaited them.

A reservation.

Oh, how Thunder Horse hated that word and what it stood for and meant to his people. It meant the loss of their freedom to live as their band had lived from the beginning of time.

They would no longer be free to do as they wished when they wished, for they would be on land assigned them by white eyes, not their own land.

But the White Chief in Washington had promised Thunder Horse's father that their life on the reservation would not be so very different from how they lived today.

They would be free to hunt when they desired. They would have a vast stretch of land on which to hunt, and where they could plant seeds that would grow food for their people.

He had already arranged that seeds were set aside for the long journey. After a while, once they had settled in the Dakotas, their gardens would be filled with food, just as they were here in this village.

Ho, if the White Chief in Washington had not spoken with a forked tongue, the reservation would not be like moving to the pits of hell.

Thunder Horse took one final moment with his father, inhaling his familiar smell and feeling the familiar skin of his cheek as he laid his face against his father's. He then stood proudly tall over the fallen hero, taking strength from his father one last time before doing a deed that broke his heart.

"*Ahte*, I will follow your teachings until I am an old man who will leave the leadership and my own teachings to a son of mine," Thunder Horse said thickly. "I promise you that I will never be lax in my duty as chief to our people, nor in my duties to my children or wife."

It was as though he heard his father say, "I know that you do right in all things. Go in peace and with much love in your heart, my son, as you spread the news of my passing. Tell them that I am happy as my soul has departed to the land of ghosts, and that I already see your mother, my beloved wife, with hands stretched out for me. Go, my *micinksi*. Go."

Having truly felt as though he had heard the words of his father inside his head, Thunder Horse shook his head quickly, then turned and followed his father's last bidding.

After stepping outside, he found that all who lived in his village were there, awaiting the news. Word had spread quickly that their elderly chief was taking his last breaths of life.

Eyes looked anxiously back at Thunder Horse, among them his woman's. Jessie stood with his people as one of them already.

"My *ahte's* soul has departed to the land of ghosts,"

Thunder Horse announced. "He walks with those now who departed before him."

There was much wailing and crying as his people clung to each other.

Jessie went into Thunder Horse's arms. "I am so sorry," she murmured as Sweet Willow came, too, and stood at her brother's side, Lone Wing beside her.

"I have duties now that must be done quickly," Thunder Horse said, setting Jessie away from him by placing gentle hands on her shoulders. "His burial must be carried out swiftly, for the White Chief in Washington was promised that as soon as Father passed to the other side, what was left of our Fox band would go to join our fellows on the reservation."

"I know," Jessie said, tears burning at the corners of her eyes.

"Go to my lodge and wait for me," Thunder Horse said, searching her eyes. "What I must do must be done alone. Even my sister and nephew cannot join me as I prepare my father for burial. It is the duty of a son. I . . . am . . . that *micinski*, that son."

He quickly drew her into his arms and gave her one last embrace, then turned and went back inside the tepee where his father awaited him.

Jessie hugged Sweet Willow and Lone Wing, then went alone to Thunder Horse's tepee, where she began gathering things and packing blankets and clothes in parfleche bags for the long journey ahead. She did not want Thunder Horse to have to do this after burying his father. She was his woman and she would perform a wife's duties for the man she would soon marry.

The thought of marrying Thunder Horse made these moments less sad, for soon she would be the wife of a wonderful, caring, powerful Sioux chief.

"Sioux chief," she whispered, knowing that just a few weeks ago she would have been astonished to learn that one day she would be the wife of a powerful Sioux chief. That was not an ordinary thing—a white woman with an Indian, much less a chief.

But things had happened that made this so, and now she could not see how her life could ever be any other way than intertwined with Thunder Horse's forever.

"I will always be here for you," she whispered as she picked up one of his fringed shirts and held it tenderly to her bosom. "My love, oh, my love, I wish I could do something to help erase the pain of your loss, for I know how deep it goes. I have lost many I love, too."

As she remembered the loved ones who had died such untimely deaths, and in such horrible ways, Jessie's thoughts went to her one remaining relative.

Reginald Vineyard.

It did not seem right to have such a man as a relative. He had become a stranger to her in every way.

A shudder raced across her flesh as she thought about what Reginald might do in a desperate attempt to get rid of his nightmares. She was afraid of what he might do now that the Sioux had refused to lift the curse from him.

And, Lord, where was Lee-Lee? And how was Jade?

Would Reginald be cruel to Jade now that Lee-Lee had disappeared?

She felt as though she had let Jade down by not

helping her escape her cousin's madness. But doing so would have jeopardized her own bid for freedom.

With so many concerns weighing on her mind, Jessie put her head in her hands and cried while Thunder Horse knelt beside his father and prepared him for burial.

He gently and lovingly placed new embroidered moccasins on his father's feet, as well as a new robe, also with fancy embroidery work to match his moccasins, all of which Sweet Willow had prepared for her father's burial.

After taking one long last look at his father, Thunder Horse slowly wrapped him in a red death robe, for in the Sioux culture, red was the color of honor.

When all of this was done, and prayers had been said over his father, Thunder Horse stepped outside and beckoned eight of his heftiest warriors to come to him. When they did, he gave them instructions about how to carry their late chief's body to the sacred cave.

After they went into the tepee to await him, Thunder Horse announced to his people that the time had come. All but a few guards and the elderly, who must save their energies for the long trip ahead, would go to the cave for interment.

Jessie went to stand with Sweet Willow and Lone Wing as Thunder Horse stepped back inside his father's tepee. Before long he reappeared, helping to carry the body of his beloved father.

With moans and wailing filling the air, the slow procession started off toward the sacred cave.

Jessie felt chilled through and through although it

was a warm, bright day, with only a few soft, puffy white clouds floating overhead in the blue sky.

Birds sang their sweet songs in the trees and eagles soared peacefully overhead, following the procession as though they knew the powerful man who would soon be placed with the other fallen chiefs of the Fox band.

To Jessie, it all seemed magical, mystical. She had a strange feeling that something was about to happen.

She looked slowly around her, at the people whose faces were like masks of sadness, and then sought the warriors who seemed to be lagging behind for a purpose, their powerful bows in one hand, their quivers of arrows on their backs. Their eyes seemed ever searching, and that added to Jessie's apprehension.

She hugged herself with her arms, then walked onward, trying to banish such concerns from her mind and think only of Thunder Horse's sorrow. He was carrying more than one burden on those powerful broad shoulders today.

The procession seemed to take forever, but finally she saw the entrance to a cave up ahead. She stopped suddenly when Thunder Horse and the others abruptly came to a halt. She smelled the smoke of a campfire, and wondered where it came from, and who had built it.

She watched as Thunder Horse stepped away from the warriors who held his father's body. Her eyes widened when other warriors went to him and stood around him, talking and glancing toward the cave's entrance.

And then suddenly they went inside, their bowstrings notched with arrows. Everyone waited, looking questioning at each other.

Sweet Willow stepped closer to Jessie. "It appears that someone is inside the cave."

"The smoke," Jessie said. "Do you think it is from a campfire inside the cave?"

"I believe that's what my brother thinks," Sweet Willow said, nodding.

The color drained from Jessie's face, for she supposed that Reginald had decided to ignore all the Sioux's warnings and had returned to take more silver from the cave, regardless of the nightmares he had been experiencing. Wouldn't it be the best way for him to get back at Thunder Horse and his people?

Jessie raised her eyes heavenward and prayed that what she was thinking wasn't so.

Suddenly everything was quiet.

There was no birdsong in the trees any longer.

The eagles had flown away.

A strange sort of eerie thunder rumbled in the distance, where dark clouds had suddenly appeared and lightning could now be seen, sending its lurid streaks downward into the land. To Jessie, it was as if the gates of hell might be ready to open.

"Reggie, oh, Reggie, what have you done?" she whispered to herself. "May the good Lord be with you if you are the one who is found inside that cave."

Chapter Twenty-seven

Jessie's throat was tight and dry as she waited for Thunder Horse and his warriors to come out of the cave. She hated to think that Reginald would be daft enough to return there.

She grimaced when she heard Thunder Horse shouting from inside, asking if anyone was there.

"Your life will be spared," he called. "Just come out with your hands over your heads."

There was a moment of total silence, and then Jessie gasped and her eyes widened when she saw two warriors come out of the cave followed by Jade.

And surely the young woman behind her was Lee-Lee!

They were walking with Thunder Horse, their eyes filled with fear, their hands trembling as they held them up in the air.

Thunder Horse stepped around them as they all came into the sunshine. He gazed from one to the other.

It was apparent that they hadn't yet spoken their names to Thunder Horse, or he would have looked at Jessie and smiled. He knew how concerned she had been about them.

Since it was evident that Jade and Lee-Lee were too afraid to speak, Jessie ran to them and flung herself into Jade's arms, hugging her.

"Jade, you are alright," she cried. "How did you manage to break away from my cousin?"

She stepped away and gazed at Lee-Lee, then smiled slowly as she took one of the young woman's hands in hers. "And you must be Lee-Lee," she murmured.

Thunder Horse stepped up next to Jessie. "These are the women you were concerned about?" he asked, seeing now that the fear had left Jade's eyes, as well as Lee-Lee's.

He smiled at Jade. "You must be the one who is named Jade and the other is your daughter Lee-Lee," he said.

Suddenly someone else stepped up with excitement shining in his eyes. Lone Wing smiled at Lee-Lee and then up at Thunder Horse. "*Ho*, this is Lee-Lee," he said, grinning broadly.

He wanted to embrace her but knew that it would not be appropriate. "Lee-Lee, I am so happy that you are no longer in that crib, and that you are safe," he said, turning to her. "When I went to the crib today, you . . . were . . . gone. I feared what might have happened to you."

"Mother came for me," Lee-Lee said, her eyes shining as she gazed into Lone Wing's. "We came to live in the cave until we felt it was safe to come to you at your village. If we had come, would your uncle have welcomed us?"

Lone Wing cast Thunder Horse a quick glance, then turned back to Lee-Lee. "*Ho*, he would have, just as he will welcome you and your mother now," he said, nodding.

He turned and faced Thunder Horse again. "Can they come with us as we make our journey to our new home?" he asked, searching his uncle's eyes. "They would not be safe to stay in this area. Reginald would find them and . . . and . . . probably kill them."

Thunder Horse placed a gentle hand on Lone Wing's shoulder. "Nephew, *ho*, they are welcome among us for as long as they want to be with us," he said.

He felt other eyes on him.

Turning, he saw Jessie smiling brightly at him.

He returned her smile, then looked first at Jade and then at Lee-Lee. "It is good that you are no longer with Reginald Vineyard," he said kindly. "You will find much peace and love among my people."

Lee-Lee gave Lone Wing a quick, bashful glance, then nestled close to her mother, whose arm swept around her waist.

"I am sorry if we disturbed anything in the cave," Jade said. "But we knew that would be the one place Reginald would not look for us. I know how he fears the cave. I have witnessed the nightmares caused by his disturbing the spirits of the cave."

"You do not have to worry about nightmares, for all know that you went there for good reasons, not bad," Thunder Horse said, then turned to his people. "We will proceed with the burial. There is not enough time to have the usual ceremony. It is best that we get my father inside the cave and then leave as soon as possible for the reservation. When I make promises, I do not break them, ever."

He watched as his father's body was taken into the cave. Then he went to Jessie and embraced her and gazed down into her eyes. "I want to sit for a while with my father and then I will join you," he said sadly.

"I understand," she murmured, then hugged him. "I will be waiting for you."

She stepped away from him and went to stand with Lee-Lee and Jade. Lone Wing joined the others who now stood closer around their chief.

"My people, I need some time with my father," Thunder Horse said, then gazed at the warriors who had just came from the cave. He nodded at them. "Escort our people to the village, then return to the cave at sunset to help me roll into place the boulder that will make it difficult for anyone else to enter our sacred burial cave."

His warriors nodded, each embracing him in turn.

As they departed, Jessie felt uneasy about leaving Thunder Horse there alone. And she felt vulnerable without him.

She wondered if she would ever get over fearing what Reginald might do, especially now that he had lost not only her, but also Jade and Lee-Lee. She could not begin the journey to the Dakotas soon enough, for surely once they were gone, Reginald would forget them all.

It didn't seem to take as long to return to the village

as it had to go to the cave, but just as they reached the point where they could see ahead into the village, Jessie felt her knees buckle.

"No!" many voices cried as others saw what Jessie had seen.

Sobbing and wailing, many broke into a mad run toward the village. Jessie stopped with Jade and Lee-Lee, stunned speechless by what lay ahead.

Bodies lay strewn all over the ground. The defenseless elders of the tribe had been ruthlessly slaughtered. The proud warriors who had stayed behind to stand guard had also been ambushed.

Killed!

Whoever had attacked the village had done it in a silent way—with arrows, which led Jessie to believe that an enemy tribe had come and taken advantage of Thunder Horse's absence.

As Jessie stopped just inside the edge of the village, tears spilled from her eyes. Even the "Old One," their band Historian, was dead.

"There is one survivor!" Jessie heard the warrior named Two Stones cry out. "It is not one of us, but a white man!"

"White?" Jessie whispered, again staring at the many arrows lodged in the backs and bellies of the fallen.

This ghastly deed wasn't the work of an enemy tribe, but of white men? She shivered at the realization that Reginald must have had a role in this.

She knew he would not have been among the actual murderers, for he was too frail and cowardly to do something so daring.

She ran over to where warriors stood around the one survivor. Two Stones knelt beside him and held his head off the ground by a grip on his thick red hair.

"Who did this?" Two Stones asked through gritted teeth. "Who rode with you? Who . . . was . . . the leader?"

"I . . . am . . . part of an outlaw gang led by Bulldog Jones," the man gasped out, although his shirt was covered with blood from a chest wound; the arrow still protruded from it ominously.

When the man said the name of the man who'd killed her father, Jessie ran to the bushes and vomited. She couldn't believe that this man was still wreaking havoc and death everywhere he went . . . even killing those who were too old to defend themselves.

And why? Why would he do this?

Nothing had been taken from the tepees. Was it for the sheer pleasure of murdering that he'd led the attack? Jessie wondered.

Jade came and wiped Jessie's mouth clean of vomit with the tail end of her dress, then held her for a moment.

But Jessie could see over Jade's shoulder that the warriors were forcing more words from the outlaw before he died. When he said the name Reginald Vineyard, Jessie felt another urge to vomit, but swallowed it back. She hurried to stand over the man so she could hear what else he had to say.

"Reginald is going to pay Bulldog Jones many silver coins . . . to do this . . . for him," the man whispered.

Jessie flinched when Two Stones, who still held the man's hair in his fingers, yanked hard on it. He broke the arrow in half, leaving only a portion of it in the man's chest. Then, Two Stones placed his knee on the man's wound.

"Tell us where Bulldog Jones's hideout is," Two Stones demanded, pressing his knee down slightly. "Tell me now, or I will slowly draw my knife across your throat. Your pain will be intense and your death will come more slowly than you will want it to."

"Please . . . please move your knee," the man gasped out. "Then . . . then . . . I will tell you."

Two Stones moved his knee and let go of the man's hair. He leaned into the outlaw's face as the man gasped out directions to the hideout, then died.

Jessie was mortified at the extent to which Reginald would go to get vengeance on these people. How could he be so evil? Because of him, many innocent and lovely people had died today.

Her hatred for this man boiled like a hot fire in her belly. She most certainly wanted a role in his comeuppance, and she would have it!

She stood back and watched as the warriors divided up—half to stay and protect those who remained of their people as well as Lee-Lee and Jade, the other half to go and tell Thunder Horse what had happened.

Jessie would not take no for an answer when she mounted a horse and said she was going with them. As she rode out of the village with the warriors, she silently prayed that her decision to accompany them wouldn't make her lose her child.

If so, Reginald would also be responsible for that tragedy!

Chapter Twenty-eight

The air was sweet and still again, the lightning in the distance gone, as Jessie and the warriors rode up to the cave. The countryside was so peaceful, so beautiful, it was hard to believe that back at the village there was a horrifying scene of bloodshed and violent death.

How could Reginald have ordered this? Jessie wondered.

Had he thought he could get away with it? Surely he did, or he would not have asked the outlaws to do his dirty work for him.

Everyone drew rein before the cave.

Jessie's pulse raced as she dismounted with the warriors, then stood beside her steed as one warrior went inside the cave for Thunder Horse. She closed her eyes and gritted her teeth, guessing that even now he was being told what had happened to his people.

And she was right, for the air was suddenly filled

with a cry of terrible remorse and sorrow. And then there was silence.

Jessie wanted so badly to go to Thunder Horse, to be with him at this time of unbearable sorrow, but something told her that her place was to stay put, rather than to interfere.

Tears fell on her cheeks when Thunder Horse emerged from the cave beside the warrior, the rims of his eyes swollen and red from crying as he had sat beside his father's lifeless body, and again after hearing the news of his fallen people.

For a moment, Jessie's eyes met his.

She didn't know what to do. She wanted to go to him! She wanted to hold him, like a child who has lost someone dear.

But she knew that this wasn't the time for them to hold one another. That would come later.

When he gave her a slow, gentle, reassuring smile, one that told her he didn't hold any of this against her, even though her own blood kin had wreaked havoc again upon him and his people, she felt relieved.

She silently mouthed, "I'm sorry," to Thunder Horse.

He nodded to her to let her know that he understood. And then he stepped out into the midst of his warriors.

His hands were doubled into tight fists at his sides as he spoke in a voice that was unfamiliar to Jessie. It was a voice rough with anger and hate, as well as hurt and sorrow.

"My warriors, it is time to do more than cause Reginald Vineyard nightmares," Thunder Horse said thickly. "And then we have outlaws to find, those who massacred our people today."

"I know where the outlaws make their hideout," Two Stones spoke up, drawing Thunder Horse's eyes quickly to him. "I forced it out of the man who was left behind before he took his last breath."

"That is good," Thunder Horse said, nodding. He glanced toward the cave, then back at his warriors. "Two of you stay and protect my father. I have placed his body far back at a private place in the cave. We will come back later to roll the boulder in place."

Jessie's eyebrows rose in wonder. Why didn't he close up the cave entrance now instead of later? It would seem that it would be best to finalize the burial in that way, rather than risk someone else coming and possibly doing more harm.

But she said nothing, for she knew that Thunder Horse thought through the decisions he made very carefully. Surely he had thought of the possible consequences of not sealing up the cave before leaving.

Thunder Horse nodded to several of his warriors. "You . . . you . . . you . . ." he said. "Come with me."

Jessie's pulse raced as she waited for him to tell her what she should do. When he did look her way, she stepped up to him.

"May I go with you?" she asked. "Thunder Horse, please let me."

"That is not wise," he said firmly. He took both of her hands in his. "My woman, what I have planned must be done by me and my warriors. It is not best that you join us. You have already done more than you should. It is not good for your unborn child. Please stay. I will be back soon to roll the boulder across the opening of the cave."

She questioned him with her eyes, again wondering why he was delaying closing up the cave. But she knew that it was not her place to question his decisions about anything. And she was deeply touched by his concern about her baby.

"You understand why I do not wish you to come, do you not?" Thunder Horse asked, searching her eyes. "You must reserve your strength for the long journey ahead. Stay here with my warriors, and I will return soon."

She was still curious to know what his plans were, but again sensed it was not her place to ask him. She knew it was important to do as he asked since he had made the request in front of his warriors.

"Yes, I see why I shouldn't go with you," Jessie said. She flung herself into his arms and clung to him. "Thunder Horse, please be careful."

"I will be gone for only a short while," he said, holding her close. "But then I will have to leave again."

"Where are you going now?" she asked, her eyes now looking into his.

"To your cousin's house," he said.

She could hardly control the shiver that raced up and down her spine, for she knew that Reginald was soon to reap what he had sown. This time he would not suffer mere nightmares.

"And . . . then . . . ?" she murmured, swallowing hard. "Are . . . you . . . going to find the outlaws' hideout?"

He nodded. "I cannot leave anything to chance," he said thickly. "All who had a role in today's attack must die."

Again shivers raced up and down Jessie's spine.

She gave him a last hug, then stepped away from him.

A warrior brought Thunder Horse's horse to him. Another handed him the quiver of arrows they had brought from his lodge, and his huge, powerful bow.

Jessie looked at the deadly arrows and knew that today they would be savage arrows, used to avenge those who had died.

She didn't want to envision her cousin dying in such a way. Yet she knew he deserved whatever happened to him today.

As Thunder Horse and his warriors rode away at a hard gallop, Jessie replayed scenes of her past inside her mind . . . moments when she had enjoyed Reginald's company and loved him as a cousin.

It was hard to remember that time, though. More recent ugliness kept getting in the way.

She sat down on the ground, but the warriors who had been left behind to guard the cave stood stoic and silent, their eyes ever watchful as they scanned the land around them.

At loose ends in his empty house, Reginald had come out to check his horses, taking the time to brush his favorite steed. He stepped out of the stable, then stopped stock still.

The blood drained from his face when he found Thunder Horse standing there, blocking his way, an arrow notched on his bowstring.

"You! . . ." Reginald gasped, taking a step back from Thunder Horse.

Then several warriors came up from behind the stable on their steeds, their bowstrings also notched with arrows.

"What do you want with me?" Reginald cried, beginning to wheeze almost uncontrollably. "Get out of here, you . . . you savages. You are on private property."

"Property paid for by the silver that came from my people's sacred cave. I believe that makes it our land, not yours," Thunder Horse said, holding his bow and arrow steady, the arrow aimed for Reginald's belly. "Get a rope from your stable. Bring it out to me."

"Why?" Reginald asked, pale as a ghost as he stared slowly around at the many arrows aimed at him.

He gazed into Thunder Horse's eyes again. "What did I do?" he gulped out.

"You know the answer without my saying it," Thunder Horse replied, then nodded at Reginald. "You get the rope. Now!"

"What are you going to do with it?" Reginald asked, again wheezing hard. "Are you . . . going . . . to hang me?"

"No, nothing like that," Thunder Horse said, smiling slowly at Reginald. "I have something better in mind."

"You . . . do?" Reginald gulped out. "Oh, Lord. What?"

"Get . . . the . . . rope," Thunder Horse said, his patience growing thin. "Now, *wasichu*."

"What did you call me?" Reginald said, taking slow steps backward into the stable.

"White man," Thunder Horse said, again smiling slowly. He dismounted. "*Wasichu*, bring me the rope."

Reginald began sobbing. "I don't want to," he cried. "Please don't make me."

Thunder Horse nodded toward one of his warriors. "Get the rope for me," he said.

He looked back at Reginald as the warrior went inside the stable and came out with a rope.

"Tie it around this man's neck," Thunder Horse ordered.

"I thought you said you weren't going to hang me," Reginald cried, his eyes wide behind his thick-lensed glasses.

"I am not going to hang you," Thunder Horse said flatly.

Thunder Horse waited for the rope to be secured around Reginald's neck, then took it when the warrior brought it to him. Thunder Horse slung his bow over his right shoulder and placed his arrow back inside his quiver. Then he took the end of the rope and tied it to the back part of his saddle, leaving a good length of it stretched out between Reginald and the horse.

Reginald was clawing at the rope as Thunder Horse

mounted his steed. "It's choking me," he cried. "Please remove it."

"Soon," Thunder Horse said, slapping his reins against his steed and riding away from Reginald's stable with his warriors following behind, leaving a space where Reginald was forced to walk.

"Where are you taking me and why?" Reginald screamed, still trying to pull the rope from around his neck, but not succeeding.

"You will soon see," Thunder Horse said, moving slightly faster, so Reginald was forced to run behind him.

They rode onward and onward until the cave came into view where the two warriors still stood vigil. Jessie was standing and looking toward the sound of horses approaching.

"The cave!" Reginald cried. "Oh, Lord, please don't take me to that cave!"

Thunder Horse only smiled slyly over his shoulder at Reginald, then rode onward until they finally stopped directly in front of the cave's entrance.

Jessie's eyes were wide when she saw Reginald tied behind the horse, with blood seeping from a raw wound on his neck where the tight rope had rubbed while Reginald was forced to run behind Thunder Horse's steed.

When he saw her there, he gaped at her, then frowned. "You've turned into a savage squaw! How could you let savages do this to your very own blood kin?" he growled, crying out when Thunder Horse yanked hard on the rope to shut him up.

Thunder Horse dismounted, then went and stood beside Reginald. "You have been brought here for one final act of vengeance, and then you will never see me again," he said sternly.

"Thank the Lord," Reginald said as Thunder Horse untied the rope and yanked it away from Reginald.

Reginald wiped his sore neck. Then Thunder Horse's words sank in.

"What . . . final . . . act?" he gulped, his eyes pleading with Thunder Horse. "What are you going to do with me . . . and again . . . why? Why are you so angry?"

"One of the outlaws who attacked my people was killed," Thunder Horse said thickly. "The others left the fallen white man behind. He had enough breath in him to tell us who came and killed today, and by whose orders."

Thunder Horse leaned into Reginald's face. "You are the one who sent the outlaws into my village," he said tightly. "You even thought Jessie would be killed, too, didn't you? You hate her so much that you would want her dead!"

Jessie paled. She hadn't even thought about that . . . that Reginald had wanted her to die in the midst of the massacre!

"Oh, Reggie," she cried, covering her mouth with a hand.

"I told you never to call me Reggie again!" he shouted. "And, yes, I wanted you to die! You went against your own blood kin by taking sides with Injuns. You're no better than those savages, Jessie." He grimaced as his eyes moved over her. "You are even dressed like one."

He frowned at her again. "You make me want to vomit," he said, visibly shuddering. "My own flesh and blood."

Jessie didn't say anything. She didn't know what to say, for this man standing before her surely wasn't blood kin to her. He was nothing but a villain!

She slowly shook her head, then stepped farther away when Thunder Horse grabbed Reginald by the throat and forced him to the cave entrance.

"What . . . are . . . you doing?" Reginald shrieked, his eyes wild.

Thunder Horse purposely knocked Reginald's glasses off. "You will need those no longer," he said, grinding the heel of his moccasin into the glasses.

"No!" Reginald cried. "I can't see a thing now. Why? Why would you do that?"

"Where you are going you will not need eyes," Thunder Horse said flatly.

"What . . . do . . . you mean?" Reginald gulped out, squinting as he tried to see Thunder Horse's face.

"You will soon understand," Thunder Horse said.

"Please tell me what you're going to do," Reginald cried, tears pouring from his eyes. "I'm sorry for everything I did. Please forgive me. I promise never to cause you trouble again."

"It is too late for words, especially words that are empty and mean nothing," Thunder Horse said. He glared into Reginald's eyes. "In the world of the Sioux, it is said that whatever a man steals in this world, he will be compelled to carry into the next. In other words, you, who are a notorious thief in the eyes of the

Sioux, will have a heavy load to carry in the afterworld. Your load will be heavier than that of most criminals, for you are responsible for so many wrongful deeds against my people."

"Oh, Lord, no," Reginald said, then cried out in a strangled voice when Thunder Horse took him by the arm and pulled him into the cave.

"Here you will stay for eternity," Thunder Horse said, giving Reginald a shove and causing him to fall to his knees.

"Lord, no, you can't do this!" Reginald whimpered, scrambling to his feet.

He tried to leave the cave, but Thunder Horse hurriedly ordered his warriors to help him roll the huge boulder in place, stopping Reginald, but not his screams for mercy. His muffled cries could still be heard even after the cave entrance was completely blocked.

Jessie was shocked by what was happening, yet understood why Thunder Horse had chosen to avenge his people's deaths in such a way.

It would be the worst possible death for Reginald, to be entombed forever among the spirits of the Sioux whom he had wronged.

A strange sort of silence emanated from the other side of the boulder, then a sudden bloodcurdling cry . . . and again silence.

Jessie looked quickly at Thunder Horse.

He gazed into her eyes. "It is over, finally over," he said thickly. "Reginald Vineyard will never again work his evil against anyone."

He raised his face to the sky, and his voice seemed to reach beyond the clouds as he cried, "It is done!"

Jessie was still numb from what had happened. She didn't ask what had transpired inside the cave. She didn't want to know.

They all mounted their steeds and left the cave, Jessie riding beside Thunder Horse.

They returned to the village to mourn and prepare the dead for burial. The preparations had to be quick, with solemn, hurried ceremonies.

Lone Wing knew that he had duties to perform, those of his people's Historian. His first assignment was to record on buckskin what had happened today to those beloved people who would no longer hear the laughter of the young, who could no longer smoke their long-stemmed pipes as they sat around the fires of their people.

It was a bad day, one that no one would ever forget.

Later, after the burials, while final preparations were being made for the long journey ahead, Thunder Horse came to Jessie and embraced her. "I have one more thing to do before leaving for the Dakotas," he said tightly. "I must make the outlaws who murdered my people pay for their deed."

Although Jessie would like nothing more than to know that the man who'd killed her father and so many others was dead, she was afraid for Thunder Horse to go.

She was afraid that he wouldn't return!

"Please don't go," she said, her voice breaking as

she gazed into his eyes. "Let it alone. Reginald, the one who set everything in motion, is dead. Were it not for him, those who died today would not have died."

"It must be done," Thunder Horse said, his eyes narrowing. "I cannot let my people down again, or I will feel I am not worthy of being their chief."

Trying to understand, Jessie moved tenderly into Thunder Horse's embrace. "If I lost you, I would not want to live," she sobbed. "Please, oh, please come back to me . . . come back to your people."

"I have many reasons to come back, so I assure you that I will," Thunder Horse said. He stepped away from her and joined his warriors, who were streaking their faces and bare chests with black paint . . . black, the color used for warring!

Chapter Twenty-nine

Jessie was trying to be brave as she waited for Thunder Horse's return, but she couldn't help being terribly afraid for him. Bulldog Jones was one of the worst, most notorious outlaws in history.

Though her father had been linked with Bulldog Jones, he had convinced her that he had been a very different kind of outlaw. He had told her, after she'd heard about his past, that he had tried to use his skills with his gun to do good.

He had said that was why Bulldog Jones had eventually gunned him down. After his separation from her father, the notorious outlaw had realized that all along Two Guns Pete had been duping him. Though he had pretended to be vicious in front of Bulldog Jones, in truth he had helped the families who were affected by Bulldog Jones's reign of terror.

Of course, Jessie had not known if that tale was true or not. It was possible her father had made up the story of being a "good outlaw" in order to save face with her.

The fact remained that it was Bulldog Jones who'd killed her father and mother. She would never know for certain what had motivated him to kill her parents, or just what had transpired between him and her father.

And now, her beloved Thunder Horse, the man she wanted to live out her life with, was going up against the same red-whiskered villain who had claimed her parents' lives. She couldn't help being afraid that Bulldog Jones would get the best of Thunder Horse and his warriors.

"I can tell by the look in your eyes that you are afraid for my uncle," Lone Wing said as he came to sit next to her.

Jade and Lee-Lee were napping before the start of the long journey. Sweet Willow and many of Thunder Horse's people were also resting.

Everything was packed on horses and travois, awaiting Thunder Horse's return. As soon as he and the warriors arrived home, the journey would begin.

"Jessie?"

Lone Wing's voice brought her out of her reverie. "I'm sorry, Lone Wing," she murmured. "What did you say?"

"I came to reassure you about my uncle and those who ride with him today," he said softly, so as not to awaken those who slept. "No one can best him, not even the most notorious of outlaws."

"But Thunder Horse isn't a warring chief," Jessie said, swallowing hard.

"That is true," Lone Wing said. "But that does not mean he is not skilled enough to war against his enemies. He was taught those skills early in life."

He reached over and took one of her hands in his. "He will return soon, victorious over evil," he said softly. "And then we will leave for our new life in a new country."

"Do you dread living on a reservation?" Jessie asked, enjoying the warmth and comfort of his hand in hers.

"No one wishes to be penned in," Lone Wing said with the voice of a man. "But our people, the Sioux, have learned well the art of adapting. So shall we now."

"Now that you are your people's Historian, you have much to write, don't you?" Jessie said somberly.

"*Ho*, I do," Lone Wing said, turning his beautiful brown eyes toward the fresh graves in the distance, where the newly dead lay beneath the mounds of dirt and rocks. The rocks were used to keep animals from their loved ones.

He then turned his eyes back to Jessie. "I will be accurate in what I write," he said. "Long years from now, when the next generation of the Fox band is curious about these times, our people will know what occurred this day. I will wait until the end of our journey to the Dakotas, and then I will go and sit alone on a bluff. As I look down upon my people while they prepare their new lodges for a new life, I will begin, truly begin, my time as Historian. I will leave nothing out about what happened here today, or on the long days of our journey."

He swallowed hard, then gazed into Jessie's eyes

again. "I will record the names, too, of those who will die on the trail to our new assigned home," he said. "I hope those names are few."

"I'm so sorry that my own flesh and blood interfered so terribly in your people's lives," Jessie said, tears of regret stinging the corners of her eyes. "I wish it could have been different. I fear that too many of your people will be reminded of my cousin's evil when they look at me, for I am—was—his cousin."

She shivered as she thought about Reginald's horrible last screams. She had to believe that although it was pitch-black in the cave, he had been able to see something that had actually frightened him to death, for moments after that scream, there had been nothing but silence.

Yes, she truly believed he had died then, for surely what he had seen, or thought he had seen, had been far worse than anything that had appeared in his nightmares.

"You are never to concern yourself about my people's feelings for you," Lone Wing said softly. "They see the good in you, as do I, just like my chieftain uncle. They know you had no control over how your cousin behaved. Some people are born good . . . some bad. Your cousin was one of the worst of the bad."

"Thank you for reassuring me," Jessie said, reaching over and hugging him. "Lone Wing, you are so dear."

He returned the embrace; then as Jessie scooted back to where she had been sitting, he looked again at the graves.

His eyes lingered on one in particular. "I find it so hard to believe that the Old One, our people's Historian, is dead," he said, his voice breaking. "He was all that was good on this earth. How could anyone have killed him?"

"Those who came today and took the precious lives of your loved ones had no sense of what it is to be good," Jessie said.

She closed her eyes as she recalled her mother and father in their caskets on the day of their funerals. How needlessly they had died.

Her jaws tightened when she envisioned the look of victory on Bulldog Jones's ugly face, even though she had never actually seen it. She just knew that he must have felt the thrill of victory. She hoped today that look would be erased forever.

"I hope he dies slowly," she found herself saying aloud. She opened her eyes quickly, blushing when she saw Lone Wing gazing at her.

"I'm sorry," she murmured. "I . . . I . . . was thinking of the day Bulldog Jones left others dead . . . my mother and father." She hung her head. "I have to admit that I want him to feel the lingering pain of death, to know that he has killed his last victim."

"It is only natural that you would think that," Lone Wing said. He reached a comforting hand to her cheek. "I am fighting the same feelings. That man cannot die slowly and painfully enough to satisfy me."

Lee-Lee had awakened and she came to sit on Lone Wing's other side. "Lone Wing, I still cannot believe that I am with you, and that we have a long life ahead of us, together," she said, tears sparkling in her beautiful dark eyes.

She looked over at her mother, who still slept. "*Ai hao*, my mother is no longer an unfortunate," she murmured. "She is brave and free."

That word "free" made Jessie look quickly at Lone Wing. She wasn't sure if he felt truly free, now that his people would be living a life ruled by the United States Government.

How shamefully the government had treated the Indians. But nothing could be done now to change the past. No doubt it would be written down in history that the government had finally gotten the best of the "savages," taming them like some would tame wild horses.

"*Ho*, Lee-Lee, you are free, and you will stay with me and my people and be sheltered and loved by us all," Lone Wing said.

To him freedom was a feeling inside one's heart. He would never allow himself to feel anything less than free, even though the United States Government might try to dictate everything his Fox band would do.

"I only wish that Tak Ming were here to feel the same freedom and love that I feel," Lee-Lee said, a sob catching in her throat.

"Who is Tak Ming?" Jessie asked.

"My brother," Lee-Lee murmured, as Lone Wing wiped tears from her cheeks with his fingertips. "He died on the big ship that brought us from China." She lowered her eyes. "My brother was not a strong man. He died after only a few weeks out at sea."

Jessie's heart broke for the young and beautiful woman. She went over and held her in her embrace. "I can see how much you miss your brother," she said softly. "But it is good that you and your mother made the passage alive. And now, Lee-Lee, you and your mother will never have to feel like slaves again. You will be loved by the Sioux."

She didn't see Lee-Lee looking past her shoulder at Lone Wing. The look in her eyes was proof that she loved the young man who had befriended her.

"I already feel very loved," Lee-Lee said, smiling at Lone Wing through her tears.

"That is wonderful," Jessie said. Then her heart skipped a beat as she heard horses arriving in the distance. How she hoped they were bringing her loved one back to her.

She stood quickly and stepped away from Lee-Lee and Lone Wing. Her pulse raced when she saw the riders in the distance and realized they were the Sioux, not the outlaws. She was now sure that the Sioux had been victorious and the damnable outlaw and his gang would spill no more blood.

Her heart melted when she made out Thunder Horse in the lead, his chin held high and victorious.

The sound of the horses had awakened everyone who had been sleeping beside the fire. Quickly, they scrambled to their feet.

The women broke into victory songs as the warriors who had stayed behind to protect the village ran to meet Thunder Horse.

Thunder Horse waved to his warriors as they approached him, then rode past them toward his people, who were standing and singing for him. His eyes smiled into those of his people. Then he spotted Jessie standing there, tears filling her eyes as she smiled and waved at him.

Jessie broke into a run and met him halfway.

He dismounted and took her into his arms. "It is done," he said with deep feeling.

He stepped away from her and faced his people as the rest of his warriors came into the village and dismounted. He smiled all around him at his people as silence fell among them.

He raised a fist of victory into the air. "It is done, and not one of our warriors fell or was injured during battle!" he cried, the war paint still gleaming on his face and bare chest. "It is time now, my people, to move onward with our lives."

Jessie was choked up with a happiness she had never felt possible as she watched everyone take turns hugging Thunder Horse and the other warriors.

She was so proud of the man she adored. It was a miracle that no one had died, or even been injured.

"Will you come with me?" Thunder Horse asked as he came to Jessie, his eyes searching hers.

She wasn't sure where he was going, but she knew now that she would go anywhere with him, anytime.

She walked with him to the river. She held his hand as he led her down into the water, clothes and all. She stood with him as he washed the war paint from his face and body, then turned to her and embraced her, where they stood waist high in the water.

"We will now begin the rest of our lives," he said, his voice filled with emotion as he searched her eyes. "But we do not have time just yet for a wedding ceremony. It is imperative that we start on the long journey so we will not have to answer for what we did today."

"But you took the lives of outlaws," she protested. "No one could fault you for that. They have been wanted men for some time now. Posters of Bulldog Jones hang in all the jails, and even banks and post offices. You have done everyone a favor. How could anyone fault you?"

"My skin is red; the men whose lives my warriors and I took today were white," he said, his voice drawn. "That is where the difference lies. So you see, my love, we must put many miles between us and those who look for any excuse to take action against the red man."

"Oh, surely not. The fact remains that you *did* do everyone a favor," Jessie said. "Now there will be no more deaths or destruction left by that madman outlaw and his gang. There will be peace."

"*Ho*, I did a favor for the white people, but since they would enjoy finding a reason to arrest me and my warriors, this might be all they need to take a few more red men as captives in their iron-windowed jails," he said. He brushed a soft kiss across her lips. "We must leave. Now."

"Everyone is ready," Jessie murmured. She walked out of the river with Thunder Horse, water dripping from the long fringes of her dress.

"Change your clothes as I change mine and then we will be on our way," Thunder Horse said. He stopped and turned Jessie to face him. "My woman, the journey will be long. Will the child in your womb be able to endure it?"

"I am strong, so I am certain the child I am carrying is, too," Jessie said, placing a soft hand on her stomach.

He embraced her again. Then they took clothes from their travel bags and went to change behind a tall stand of bushes.

When they stepped out into the open again, everyone was lined up, the packhorses and travois at the rear.

Thunder Horse stepped forward. "Remember, my people, that a part of us all will always remain here," he cried. "But it is important that we create the same feelings for the land where we establish our new homes."

There were soft chants and grunts of approval, and then the procession began.

Jessie was on her horse beside Thunder Horse and his powerful steed.

Lone Wing was on his pony. Lee-Lee was sitting behind him on the pony, her arms twined lovingly around his waist.

Jade was walking with the women, her chin held high, her eyes filled with peace.

Jessie looked forward to her own new life, to living with the Fox band of Sioux as one happy family.

She laid a hand on her belly again. She had not been completely honest with Thunder Horse. She was not really certain her child would be able to endure this long journey, but she would fight hard to keep it safe.

Chapter Thirty

The journey had been long and sometimes gruelling, especially for those who were older. Many stops had to be made along the way for people to eat and rest.

Jessie had soon learned that water was carried in bags formed of the dried intestines of animals. She had found it interesting that when the Sioux expected to walk far, they put fine, dry grass in their moccasins to cushion their feet.

She, too, had walked some days when she had gotten tired of being on her horse. She had filled her moccasins with dried grass. To her surprise she had felt as though she were walking on clouds.

But she was riding again today, filled with an excitement she had not felt now for many days. Everyone now knew that they had only a short distance to travel before they finally reached their destination.

Two Stones and some other warriors had gone on ahead, scouting, and had returned only moments ago saying that by nightfall, fires would be built where their new lodges would soon be erected.

They would have no more long days and nights on the trail.

Two Stones had reported that, upon quick observation, the reservation they were assigned to was very different from those they had seen elsewhere. It would be a place where the next generation of Sioux could still know the thrill of the hunt. The land was filled with white-tail deer, and was beautiful.

Soon they could plant their seeds; there would be a bountiful harvest next autumn.

Two Stones had spoken to those members of their band already camped on the reservation. The most wonderful news of all was that during the time when the Fox band had been separated into halves, hardly anyone already at the reservation had died.

Those at the reservation had felt deep sorrow when they heard about the massacre of their elders by the outlaws, especially the Old One, their band Historian. Learning of the deaths had thrown them into mourning, yet at the same time, they were grateful to the Great Spirit that they would finally be reunited with their chief and everyone else who had survived the massacre.

They would finally be as one heartbeat again, sharing the same hopes and dreams.

Jessie looked around and saw the relief in everyone's eyes as they learned they were almost at the reservation.

She gazed at Jade. The older woman had stopped

walking long ago. She had made most of the journey on a travois that Jessie had helped prepare for her with Lone Wing and Thunder Horse.

Jessie had learned that a travois consisted of a set of rawhide strips, securely lashed to poles that were harnessed to the sides of a horse.

The free ends dragged on the ground, providing a stretcher of sorts for the happy passenger whose feet ached too much to take another step!

That had been Jade. Her feet had been swollen and bleeding, like many of the other women, who were now on travois, too. When they arrived at their new home, they would have plenty of time to recuperate. Their feet would heal.

Yes, many women were on the travois now, weariness etched on their faces.

There had been five births on the trail. Fortunately, all the babies had survived, as had their mothers.

The remembrance of those babies' first cries of life made Jessie place a hand on her own belly. Her pregnancy was very visible now. Thus far, the traumatic experiences she had gone through had not caused a miscarriage, nor had traveling on a horse for so many weeks.

But it was certain that Jessie would be one of the happiest and most relieved when she no longer had to be on a horse, hour after hour, day after day. She closed her eyes and envisioned herself sitting beside a lazy fire in her new home, with Thunder Horse sitting next to her. She would lean against him as they watched the fire together.

That was when their life together would truly begin. Up until now, they had had no time to enjoy each other.

At last, they would have the time to be married. They had not wanted to conduct the ceremony while on the trail. They both wanted it to be a special time . . . something they could remember, and look back upon, as the most precious day of their lives.

And they had wanted the ceremony to be shared by all of the Fox band, not just a few.

"Soon," she whispered to herself, looking over at Thunder Horse.

Sadness swept through her as she gazed at him. Although he was muscled and strong, she could see that the long days on the trail, and the loss of his *ahte* and so many other loved ones, had taken their toll on him. She could see weariness in the slight slump of his shoulders and traces of wrinkles at the corners of his eyes.

That made her heart ache, for these things that now marred his handsomeness proved the weight of responsibility that he carried on his shoulders. He had an entire band who depended on him to make all the right decisions.

Thus far, he had proved to be the leader they needed, for only two graves had been left along the trail. Those who had passed to the other side were people who had been already ill before they began the long journey to the Dakotas.

No matter how much they were prayed over by Hawk Dreamer, the Fox band's shaman, they had not been able to endure the gruelling trip. Weakened already by illness, they had succumbed to the cold, damp nights and the roughness of the journey on travois.

But the terrible trip was almost over now for everyone else. A new beginning awaited them all!

To Jessie, this land was almost jarring in its loveliness. So much about South Dakota was breathtaking. Even now as they rode beside a river, it seemed to lead into a fairyland of rainbow mesas and flaming buttes.

The banks of the river were thick with blackberry and wild rose bushes. Jessie had learned along the way that the berries growing in sunny places were the sweetest.

Western trillium bloomed pretty and white in the red duff of the pine needles. At Jessie's left side, climbing slopes of evergreens struggled over fallen timber.

Suddenly the damp air rang out with the song of a cedar waxwing, its beating wings thrumming as it was frightened by the approaching procession of people.

A female pileated woodpecker landed on a sunlit branch not far away, while a colorful male landed beside her.

"We are almost there," Thunder Horse said, smiling at Jessie. Then he gestured with a wave of a hand toward the distant mountains. "Mountains are important to the Sioux. They are mysterious and powerful. The 'Old Ones' said that we Sioux came up out of the earth through a hole in the ground at the base of a special mountain, one which is distant from our people now."

He paused, then said, "But look around you, Jessie. See the wonders of South Dakota, the tall, white bluffs and the stunted pines. Even the rough terrain, partly covered with buffalo grass, is welcomed by this chief. Finally my people will be together again as one group. It has been too long since we joined together around the night fire to listen to stories and to share our love for one another."

Jessie nodded and again looked around herself. All was peaceful and quiet.

Here and there were little meadows, looking fresh and green after being covered with snow all last winter. The leaves of the cottonwood and willow trees glistened with every little breeze.

"Yes, it does seem a paradise," Jessie said, smiling at Thunder Horse. "We will be happy here, Thunder Horse. All of us will be happy."

"Reservation life has been forced upon us, so we must make of it what we can," Thunder Horse said thickly. "And after seeing the land that has been assigned us, I see now how it will work for us."

He did not tell her that he still did not trust the word of the White Chief in Washington, even though Thunder Horse's father had been impressed by his kindness and the sincere, polite, and respectful way he had talked with him.

Thunder Horse's father had said that it seemed as though he was in council with another Sioux, having a friendly parley. He had left Washington with much hope for his people, although he had been told that he had no choice but to take his people onto the reservation.

Still, the White Chief had promised White Horse that life would remain the same for his people. They would still enjoy the hunt without the accompaniment of white soldiers.

"I will hope that my father was not tricked by a man who spoke with a forked tongue," Thunder Horse said wearily. "Jessie, if that were true, I am not certain what I would do. I would feel that my father had let my people down by being tricked by the White Chief. And perhaps I, too, let them down by listening to my father, who I always felt was astute enough to know when he was being lied to."

"It will be alright," Jessie said, edging her horse closer to his. She reached a gentle hand to his arm. "My beloved, you will see that things will work out. Please don't think anything negative at this time, or become doubtful of what lies ahead. Feeling positive is the only way this will work, darling. Please feel positive, for me . . . and for your people."

She slid her hand across his arm. "But most of all, Thunder Horse, feel positive for yourself," she murmured.

He nodded and smiled at her. "You are a wise woman," he said. "You should be a woman chief."

Jessie threw her head back in a soft laugh, then smiled again at him. "You have a way with words," she murmured. "A woman chief? Thunder Horse, you are the only chief I want in our family."

"Family," he said, covering her hand with his.

He gazed at her belly, which was as round as a ball with the child that grew in her womb.

Then he gazed intently into her eyes. "As soon as we see that my people—our people—are settled into their newly built lodges, we will have our marriage ceremony," he said. "It will be a time for celebration, my love. We will become as one, you and I."

He chuckled as he looked at her belly, then into her eyes. "You and I *and the child* will become as one," he corrected himself.

Then he gazed over at Lone Wing, who rode tall in his saddle with Lee-Lee still behind him on his horse. Now that Lone Wing was his people's Historian, he had been told that he had earned the right to ride a horse instead of a pony.

"One day there will also be a wedding between those two who are so in love," Thunder Horse said. "It will be a day of celebration when the band Historian takes a wife whom he obviously loves with all his heart."

"The age difference between them seems not to matter," Jessie said. "Although she is older, she is still a child compared to the adult that Lone Wing has become."

"*Ho*, Lone Wing has matured right before our very eyes after having so many responsibilities placed upon his shoulders when the Old One died," Thunder Horse said, smiling with pride for his nephew.

"I am anxious to see his first records of the Fox band's history," Jessie said.

"No one but he will see them until much later, when he hands his duties over to someone else," Thunder Horse explained. "He records, then puts his records away. The important thing is that he does his duty. It will be many years before the things he draws will be interpreted and acknowledged."

"I see," Jessie said. "I still have so much to learn about your customs . . . about your people's lives."

"You are now one with my people, so do not refer to them as 'your people,'" Thunder Horse said. "Although we have not spoken vows yet, you are already a part of the Fox band."

Thunder Horse looked over his shoulder into the distance, where far behind him was the only home he had ever known.

He then looked slowly around him again, at what was becoming his new home. "No people ever loved their country or enjoyed it more than we Sioux," he said, pride in his voice. "Oh, how we loved the beautiful streams by which we made our homes, and the trees that shaded our tepees. We loved the green stretches of plains with gardens here and there of golden sunflowers over which hovered and played myriads of yellow-winged birds."

He went silent as he gazed straight ahead.

"We will love this new land as much some day," he said, his voice breaking. "Memories will be born here that will sustain our young people as they grow into adults and have to say farewell to those who brought them into the world. *Ho*, I must think of the good to come, my woman, or a part of me would break into a million tears."

Those words touched Jessie so deeply, she had to fight back the tears. She heard such pride in her beloved's voice, and also such pain.

If the president could see the pain and suffering of these beautiful, innocent people, oh, surely he would regret what had been done in haste.

"We will be happy, and so will our people," she quickly said. "Happiness is born of trust, love . . . and hope. I see so much of all those in our people's eyes today."

"*Ho*, I see it, too, and hope it will build within them so that the days and weeks and years ahead will be good ones," Thunder Horse said.

He then broke into a broad smile when he saw many of his warriors who had come ahead and were already living on the reservation riding toward him.

"There is Wind Eagle!" Thunder Horse cried, eagerly waving a hand. "Do you see the warrior who rides ahead of the others? My woman, that is my friend Wind Eagle, whom I appointed chief in my absence."

Wind Eagle came up beside Thunder Horse, his dark eyes filled with pride and happiness. "My chief, it is so good to see you," he said, drawing rein as Thunder Horse and Jessie halted, as well.

Thunder Horse and Wind Eagle clasped hands, then gave each other a bear hug.

"Things are well at the reservation but will be even better now that you are here," Wind Eagle said. As he leaned away from Thunder Horse, he slid slow eyes over Jessie.

His gaze moved to her belly, lingered there for a moment. Then he questioned Thunder Horse silently with his dark eyes.

"My *mitawin*, my woman," Thunder Horse said as the other warriors on horseback circled around him, their eyes anxiously gazing at their chief, and then at Jessie.

"This is Jessie," Thunder Horse announced for all to hear. "She will soon speak vows with your chief."

Again the eyes went to Jessie's swollen belly.

"She is with child, but the child is not mine," Thunder Horse said, knowing that he would draw gasps from his loyal warriors. "She is a woman wronged in many ways. I took her in. She will be my wife, and the child she carries will be raised as my son, or daughter, whichever is born to her."

Jessie was worried by the strained silence among the warriors. Then she inhaled a breath of relief as, one by one, they came to her and took her hand, kissing it and smiling. At that moment, the other travelers joined them and there were greetings all around.

"Let us go home now," Thunder Horse said, sinking his heels into the flanks of his horse and riding off with Jessie at his side, his warriors and people close behind them.

"For a moment I—" Jessie began, but Thunder Horse interrupted her.

"All is good now," he said, nodding. "No one will question who you are again."

"But what about those waiting in the village who have not yet seen me?" Jessie said, swallowing hard.

"*Ho*, you are right to be wary, but I will see that you have no reason to worry ever again," Thunder Horse said.

He gestured toward Wind Eagle, drawing him up beside them. "Wind Eagle, ride ahead and explain about the arrival of my woman so that we will see no wonder in their eyes when we arrive there," he said. "She deserves better."

Wind Eagle nodded, clasped his hand with Thunder Horse's, then released it and rode away at a gallop.

"So you see, my *mitawin*, I have taken care of that," Thunder Horse said, riding again alongside Jessie.

"As you do everything," Jessie said, smiling up at him. "Thank you. I mean *pila-maye*."

"Hearing the Sioux words being spoken by you brings gladness to this chief's heart," Thunder Horse said.

When Jessie smiled broadly at him, he knew that once again he had chosen the right words to make his woman feel comfortable in her new role.

Tomorrow, after the lodges were erected, he would take the time to exchange vows with Jessie. She would wait no longer to become this chief's wife.

"Tomorrow, my *mitawin*," he said suddenly. "We will marry tomorrow."

Jessie felt a radiant glow within her. Finally! She had her own life and someone she truly loved to share it with.

Nothing could get in the way now.

Nothing, and especially not her cousin!

Chapter Thirty-one

Thunder Horse was dressed in a deerskin jacket, with bright-colored beads down the front. He also wore his long-fringed leggings as he prepared himself for the wedding that would take place today.

He slid his feet into his porcupine-quill-embroidered moccasins and folded his best robe about him.

Sweet Willow stood behind him and brushed his long, glossy hair with a brush made from the tail of a porcupine, then perfumed his hair with scented grass before arranging it in two braids with an otter skin woven into them. Since he was a powerful warrior and chief, Sweet Willow added an eagle feather to his hair, held there by a beaded headband.

Thunder Horse had risen early today and brushed the horse that was his gift to Jessie until it shone. Then he had woven wreaths of sweet grass around its neck and tied eagle feathers to its tail and mane.

"It is your day, and Jessie's," Sweet Willow said, stepping around in front of him. "My brother, you deserve this day and all the happiness that comes with it. You have brought your people on a long journey and helped them through much sorrow and sadness. Today is for laughter and loving. It is your day."

"My woman will be beautiful as she comes to me today as my bride," Thunder Horse said thickly. He stepped up to the entrance flap of his newly built tepee and gazed outside, over at Sweet Willow's lodge, where he knew Jessie was being helped by Jade and Lee-Lee to get ready for the short ceremony.

"The horse you chose for her is lovely," Sweet Willow said, clasping her hands together as she gazed at her brother's handsomeness.

"The husband-to-be always takes pride in the fine horse his bride will ride, especially in ceremonial parades," Thunder Horse said, gazing at the tethered horse that stood outside his lodge.

He silently admired the white-faced bay with its white hind legs. The horse was made even finer by the handsomely beaded saddle trappings that were also a gift to Jessie on this, her and Thunder Horse's special day.

"Do you think Jessie is ready for you to go to her?" Sweet Willow asked as she stepped to his side and looked past him at her own lodge a few feet away.

Smoke spiraled lazily from the smoke hole. Her son had lit the fire late last night, and it would not be allowed to go out until next year when the spring days arrived with the deliciousness of the sun's warmth.

"I will give her more time," Thunder Horse said, stepping back from the entranceway. He sat down before the fire, and Sweet Willow sat next to him. "This is a moment in my life I will savor, especially when I have troubles heavy on my mind. These moments with my woman will erase bad and add good to my memory. I will make Jessie happy. I will bring comfort to her heart when she bears her first child. And then the time will come when she bears me a son from our own union. And . . . then . . . a daughter."

Jessie's heart pounded as Lee-Lee and Jade fussed over her, helping to arrange the gown of whitened deerskin that was heavy with beads and long fringes.

Her belly pulled too tightly at the dress that Sweet Willow had secretly made for her before they left for the Dakotas.

Sweet Willow had not expected Jessie to be this big with child when she married Thunder Horse.

"I love the fringes and beads," Jessie murmured, but blushed when she saw the swell of her bosom where the dress fit too tightly across her breasts.

She saw too much cleavage, but Lee-Lee ingeniously corrected the problem by placing a cluster of white mountain flowers at her neckline. The blossoms not only hid her cleavage, but also gave off a sweet aroma that smelled like rich French perfume to Jessie.

"You are so clever," Jessie said, giggling. "Now I won't have to blush so much when I step before Thunder Horse's people to speak vows with my beloved."

She sighed with appreciation when she gazed down at her leggings, which were trimmed with quills of porcupine, as were her moccasins.

"I will complete you now," Jade murmured as she dusted the part in Jessie's hair with pulverized ocher ore, as well as the dried powder of a prairie dustball.

She used a small piece of doeskin to pat some vermilion on Jessie's cheeks.

"And now matching flowers in your hair," Jade said as she placed sprigs of white flowers above Jessie's ears.

"You smell like jasmine," Lee-Lee said, sighing.

"I cannot tell you how I feel," Jessie said, again giggling. "I just feel so . . . so . . . heavenly."

"And soon you will be married to a powerful, wonderful, and caring Sioux chief," Jade said, taking a brief peek through the entrance to see if Thunder Horse was on his way toward the tepee.

She gasped when she saw him step from his lodge. She placed her hands to her cheeks, sighing when she saw just how handsome he was, and how radiant his smile as he stepped up to the most beautiful horse Jade had ever seen.

"It is so beautiful," Jade said, looking over her shoulder at Jessie.

"What is so beautiful?" Jessie asked. She hurried to the entranceway and stepped up beside Jade. She looked outside and gasped. She felt herself melting when she saw Thunder Horse take the reins of a beautiful white-faced bay.

"I wonder if it is to be mine," she murmured, having heard that he would be presenting her with a special steed today.

"Surely it is," Lee-Lee said, coming and squeezing between Jade and Jessie. She, too, sighed with pleasure as she saw the horse and the handsome man now mounting it.

"I just know that Lone Wing will be as handsome as his uncle when he becomes a man," Lee-Lee said, blushing as she gazed over to where Lone Wing stood with others around the huge outdoor fire, awaiting the marriage ceremony.

Much food had been cooked this day, and now stood in large pots around the edge of the fire, staying warm until it was to be eaten.

The drums and other musical instruments of the Sioux awaited the moment when Thunder Horse would give the sign to begin the music. Dancers were clustered together in bright clothes, ready to dance and celebrate their chief's wedding.

It was all magical, and Lee-Lee wanted the same one day when she could marry Lone Wing.

Jessie continued watching Thunder Horse as he mounted the horse, holding the end of a lariat tied about the animal's neck. He guided the lovely horse altogether by the motions of his body.

"Why, the horse seems to be entering into the spirit of the occasion," Jessie said, admiring its graceful movements in perfect obedience to his master.

Thunder Horse had told her in advance that when he got close to where she was waiting, it was the custom to pull his robe over his head, leaving only a slit to look through.

That was what he was doing at this very moment. Then he stopped just outside Sweet Willow's lodge, directly in front of the entrance.

Jessie knew what she was supposed to do next. She had been taught about the ritual between a man and a woman just prior to speaking their vows.

If she wanted to hear what the man had to say, she would step outside and listen. If she didn't want to hear him, or marry him, she would stay inside the lodge until he turned and left.

Wanting him more than anything, she hurried outside.

Although she could only see a portion of his eyes, she saw how they widened when he saw her. She knew then that he approved of what she wore, even the flowers thrust between her breasts.

"I am so glad that you came to me," she said, knowing those were the words she was supposed to speak if she wanted him as her husband.

"I bring you the gift of a horse," Thunder Horse said, not dismounting until she said she accepted it as her own.

"I love it, and, yes, I want it," Jessie said. "I also love you and want you."

He flung aside the robe and dismounted.

Jessie sighed with appreciation when she saw his handsomely beaded outfit. She trembled as he approached her now, like one would approach any shy creature of the earth, gently, slowly, one step at a time. Indeed, her heart felt as shy as that of a young antelope trembling behind a cactus plant.

Then he took Jessie's hands and led her out of the lodge. Lone Wing came and took the lovely steed away and placed him among his uncle's other prized horses.

The drums began softly beating, and someone

played a flute in the distance. Several women started to sing softly as the shaman came and stood before Thunder Horse and Jessie. All the people of the Fox band stood around them, smiling and watching.

The drums and flute continued playing as the shaman, Hawk Dreamer, ministered to the two who were seeking his blessing today, as well as the blessing of the Great Spirit.

"You now speak words to each other that can come only from your hearts, for I have said all that I can to bless this union of my chief and his woman," Hawk Dreamer said, slowly stepping back and suddenly disappearing amid the crowd.

Thunder Horse held Jessie's hands as he gazed into her eyes. "Today I take you for my wife, to protect and love you forever and ever," he said with deep emotion, his eyes searching hers. "What is mine is now yours, for my shaman has not only blessed us, Jessie, he has married us. We are now as one with each other. Your heart is joined with mine. Our souls are as one until the day we part from this earth, and even then they will remain united, for nothing can ever separate us. Not even death. Jessie, from here on, I will care for you and the children you bear me. You will never be out of my mind. My *mitawin*, my wife, you are with me now for always."

Jessie was amazed that she was already married and had not even been aware of when Hawk Dreamer had joined them as man and wife.

But she was glad that the ceremony wasn't as complicated as she'd thought it might be.

She was Thunder Horse's wife!

She could hardly hold down her excitement, but knew that she must, for she had words to say to Thunder Horse, too, words to tell him of her love and commitment.

"My love, my chief, my husband, I will always be here for you, as your wife and the mother of your children," Jessie murmured as his hands gripped hers gently. "However you want me to be, I shall be. I want never to disappoint you. When I bear children, I will eagerly hand them over to you to hold and to love. My darling Thunder Horse, my husband, I love you now and forever and ever."

He drew her into his arms and kissed her gently at first, and then more ardently and passionately.

The singing began again, and the drums beat more loudly. Many other instruments added their voices to the music, sending the wonder of it heavenward.

And then Thunder Horse took Jessie by the hands and turned her so that they both faced all of his people, which now were definitely also hers. "My people, may I present to you my bride?" he cried.

Cheers and chants rose into the sky.

Dancers began dancing around the huge fire.

Thunder Horse grabbed Jessie into his arms and carried her at a half trot to their new lodge.

After the ties were secured to ensure their privacy, they stood and faced one another. Between two stones a fire burned with the coal-like glow of cottonwood bark. Across the stones lay a large buffalo bone, the meat cooking slowly.

Before Jessie and Thunder Horse had come into the lodge for their first night as man and wife, a woman had been there to turn the meat so that it would cook evenly and thoroughly.

It would be their first meal as man and wife, awaiting them after their lovemaking. They would crack the bone and before they ate the meat, each would suck out the tasty marrow.

"It is done," he said, his eyes dancing. "We are now husband and wife!"

"It is a day I shall never forget," Jessie murmured, flinging herself into his arms. "And I shall never disappoint you. Never."

Slowly he lifted the flowers from her hair, and then with his teeth he removed those from between her breasts.

He dropped those flowers to the rush mats on the floor, then slowly removed her dress so that he could devour every inch of her with his feasting eyes.

"You cannot say that I am much to look at now," Jessie said, smiling shyly at him.

He laughed softly. She knew that her body was terribly out of shape with the baby rounding her belly into a ball.

"No matter how your belly grows, you will always be beautiful to me," Thunder Horse said hoarsely. "A child growing within a woman's womb causes a radiance within the woman. I remember my sister when she was carrying Lone Wing inside her belly. She glowed. I recall how her husband could hardly take his eyes off her. Yet surely he did not love her as much as I love you, for I love you with every ounce of my being."

"As I love you," Jessie murmured, closing her eyes

in ecstasy as he kissed a slow path across her belly, and then downward, where she throbbed with need of him.

She threw her head back and sighed as he touched her with his tongue where she was already tingling and alive.

She wove her fingers through his thick hair and brought him closer to her. She felt as if she were floating on wings, as he brought her close to that realm of total rapture.

But wanting to be with him when she reached that treasured moment, she leaned back away from him.

He smiled at her, then removed his own clothes and soon lay over her. Their bodies moved together as though one, their lips meeting passionately in lingering kisses.

A flood of emotions overwhelmed Jessie as Thunder Horse, her husband, groaned against her parted lips while he moved slowly with acute deliberation within her. Gradually he moved faster with quicker, surer movements, each thrust almost sending Jessie over the edge into total bliss.

But she wanted it to last longer than this.

This was what she and Thunder Horse had waited for. The long journey now seemed far away. Finally they were together in their new lodge, married, she was so happy she felt she might burst from it.

Even now, she felt his hunger in the hard, seeking pressure of his lips. He held himself up and away from her, his eyes slowly moving over her.

"You awe me with your beauty," he said huskily. "My *mitawin*, my wife, I shall love you for eternity."

"As I shall always love you," Jessie said, hugging his words to her.

She sucked in a wild breath of joy as his steel arms enfolded her again and he pressed himself more deeply inside her. She was overwhelmed by a need she was familiar with, now that her husband had taught her the true meaning of what it was to be loved. The ecstasy spread and swelled within her until it almost blotted out all other sensations.

Yet she still clung to the moment, wanting it to last as long as possible before reaching the ultimate pleasure with her new husband.

Thunder Horse reveled in the touch of her soft flesh against his, as licking flames spread through him. He could not get enough of her tonight as his hands moved over her.

He then reached his hand between their bodies, where they had come together as man and woman had since the beginning of time. He moved slightly away from her so that he could caress her warm and secret place, feeling a tremor go through her body as he touched that most vulnerable spot of a woman.

He flicked it with his forefinger, rubbed it, then moved down where he could touch her with his lips and tongue. He could hear her suck in a breath of pleasure as he moved his tongue over her. His hands were on her breasts, kneading.

But when he heard her breath coming more quickly, he knew that he had readied her for the ultimate bliss and moved over her with his body again. He thrust his manhood inside her again and felt the euphoria that came with the final moments of ecstasy.

Then he could not hold back any longer. He clung to Jessie as his body exploded in spasms of desire. Simultaneously he felt her body jerking and quivering against his as she reached her own peak.

They clung for a moment, their breaths mingling as they kissed, and then Thunder Horse rolled away from her and lay on his back, gazing up through the smoke hole where the stars and the moon had taken the place of the sun in the heavens.

Outside, the celebration continued with much music and laughter, all of which was filled with hope for all their tomorrows.

"It will be a good life here in the Dakotas for my people," Thunder Horse said as Jessie sat up beside him. "It was good to find the lone buffalo today before our celebration. It means that a herd cannot be that far away."

Jessie said nothing to that, for she knew that most of the buffalo had been annihilated by the white man to starve the Indians.

It was as though God had placed this one buffalo near the village for their night of merriment. The largest portion of the animal now cooked slowly over the outdoor fire, the tantalizing aroma of its drippings filling the air.

"There should be many deer for your hunt," Jessie said reassuringly. "And for our children, too."

"This land that the government has put us on impresses me," Thunder Horse said, wrapping a blanket around them so that they sat beneath it together, their shoulders touching.

"Yes, it seems very nice," Jessie murmured, not wanting to think negative things at such a time as this.

But she could not help worrying that what they had would not be everlasting. She just didn't see the government being that generous when all along they had tried to make the red man disappear from the face of the earth.

"Our children will be happy here," Thunder Horse said as if he was trying to convince himself of what he was saying.

"We will make it so," Jessie said, then watched as he reached for a chunk of buffalo meat.

He gave it to Jessie. She took a bite, then handed it back to him. She was reminded of the weddings she had attended in Kansas City, where the bride and groom gave each other bites of the wedding cake. This meat was their cake!

"It is good," Thunder Horse said, chewing.

"Yes, it's good," Jessie said, not wanting him to realize just how much she disliked the taste.

She preferred deer meat. Perhaps it was just as well that deer would be the main meat found in these hunting grounds instead of buffalo.

He laughed softly. "It is not all that good," he said, his eyes twinkling as he gazed into hers.

Jessie laughed, too, as she tossed the greasy, tough piece of meat into the fire. "No, not really," she agreed.

He reached for her and gently laid her back down on the blankets.

Her body became liquid as his eyes touched her, and then his fingers caressed her breasts.

He covered her with his body again, his lips trembling as he touched hers in a gentle and lingering kiss and thrust himself deep within her again.

The night was new to them, and they clung and rocked and found ecstasy again . . . and . . . again. . . .

Chapter Thirty-two

The Moon of the Popping Trees—December

The years had flown by, it seemed. Jessie had had her first child, a son, whom they named Little Thunder, and then another, a daughter born of her love with Thunder Horse, whom they named Pretty Heart.

She was radiantly happy, and Lone Wing and Lee-Lee were making plans for their marriage now.

After eating their venison roast for supper, Jessie and Thunder Horse were sitting beside a slow-burning fire in their tepee, reminiscing about these past five years.

"It is not the ideal life here on the reservation, but we are making the best of it, as are all the other Sioux who have now been directed here to the Rosebud Reservation," Thunder Horse said. "We are all one big family on the reservation, looking out for the best interests of each other."

"It is good that the government didn't force your

people into performing pretend hunts for whites in order to get your meat," Jessie said. "*Ho*, the buffalo are long gone. But there are plenty of deer for our venison roasts."

"*Ho*, there have been many black-tailed and white-tailed deer and elk, even grizzlies," Thunder Horse said, nodding. "And there is plenty of stored food now that will last us the full winter."

Jessie got up and held the entrance flap aside. She peered out onto what looked like a winter wonderland, where the snow sparkled beneath a winter sun.

The branches of trees were snapping and cracking all around the tepee like pistol shots. Inside, the tepee was lit and warmed by the immense logs her husband had provided for the lodge fire.

"The children are wrapped warmly in their buffalo robes with the hair inside," Thunder Horse said, going and standing with Jessie as he, too, peered outside at the loveliness of the land.

"After the heavy thaw, a crust has formed on the snow, making it better for sledding, don't you think?" she asked, gazing at Thunder Horse.

"*Ho*, and I am certain that Lone Wing and Lee-Lee have become children again as they sled with our son and daughter," Thunder Horse said, closing the flap.

He took Jessie's hand and walked with her back to the fire, where they again sat, their shoulders touching. "Lone Wing used his skills to make a sled for our children," he said. "Hear them even now? Their laughter fills my heart with such joy."

"The first time I saw the sled I was amazed at what it

was made from," Jessie said, laughing softly. "Who would have guessed that you could make a sled from old buffalo ribs and hickory saplings? It is clever how the runners are bound with rawhide, the hair side down. The sled slips so smoothly over the icy crust."

"It is good that Lone Wing made use of the ancient buffalo bones he found before the first snowfall," Thunder Horse said. "It was he who saw them as a perfect sled."

"He is such a wonderful young man, so talented in so many ways," Jessie murmured.

"My pride in him is no less than if he were my own son," Thunder Horse said, smiling at her.

He reached a hand to the hem of Jessie's skirt. "We have privacy now, which is rare during the day. Do you think we should take advantage of it?" he asked, his eyes shining.

"You must have read my mind," Jessie said, turning to him.

She climbed on his lap, facing him, her legs straddling him.

In that way he made love with her, thrusting into her as he held her shoulders.

He watched her eyes become filled with rapture as he, too, felt the wonder of their joined bodies. He held his head back, groaning, when he heard her soft, repeated moans with each of his thrusts inside her.

"Let's make another child," Jessie murmured, sighing when she felt the euphoria building. "Another son, my husband. I want another son."

He placed his hands on her waist and slid her down

on her back on the warm blankets, then lifted her skirt. "A son . . . many sons . . ." he said huskily, then with one swift movement was inside her again.

He pressed his lips to her throat, his hands up inside her dress now, caressing her as he felt her open herself more fully to him.

His mouth covered hers in a passionate kiss.

With a moan of ecstasy she gave him back his kiss, clinging to him, her skin quivering with the desire that was spreading through her.

She was, oh, so acutely aware of his familiar body and his ways of making her head spin with joy.

Their bodies strained together.

His hand moved away from her as her body arched toward him, and then they found the ultimate of pleasure again. Afterward they lay quietly together, holding one another.

"It is always so good," Jessie murmured. "Will it always be this way? When we are older, will we still feel such intense pleasure as we do now?"

"Always, my *mitawin*," Thunder Horse said thickly. "Always."

Jessie smiled, for she knew that her future would be filled with the same wonderful moments she was experiencing now.

And she was glad that warring was a thing of the past for the Sioux people. No more savage arrows had to be loosed from the powerful bowstrings of the Sioux warriors!

For now, *ho*, it *was* the best of times for her and her family, and she couldn't be happier!

LETTER TO THE READER

Dear Reader,

I hope you enjoyed reading *Savage Arrow*. The next book in my *Savage* series, which I am writing exclusively for Leisure Books, is *Savage Beloved*, about the Wichita Indians. The book is filled with much passion, intrigue and adventure.

Those of you who are collecting my Indian romance novels, and want to hear more about the series and my entire backlist of books, can send for my latest newsletter, autographed bookmark, and fan club information by writing to:

Cassie Edwards
6709 North Country Club Road
Mattoon, IL 61938

For an assured response, please include a stamped, self-addressed, legal-sized envelope with your letter. And you can visit my website at www.cassieedwards.com.

Thank you for supporting my Indian series. I love researching and writing about our beloved Native Americans, our country's first people.

Always,
Cassie Edwards